FIRST COMES LOVE

SHANA JOHNSON BURTON

URBAN CHRISTIAN

www.urbanchristianonline.net

Urban Books
1199 Straight Path
West Babylon, NY 11704

First Comes Love copyright © 2008 Shana Johnson Burton

ISBN- 13: 978-1-60162-974-6
ISBN- 10: 1-60162-974-5

First Printing December 2008
Printed in the United States of America

10 9 8 7 6 5 4 3 2 1

This is a work of fiction. Any references or similarities to actual events, real people, living, or dead, or to real locales are intended to give the novel a sense of reality. Any similarity in other names, characters, places, and incidents is entirely coincidental.

Distributed by Kensington Publishing Corp.
Submit Wholesale Orders to:
Kensington Publishing Corp.
C/O Penguin Group (USA) Inc.
Attention: Order Processing
405 Murray Hill Parkway
East Rutherford, NJ 07073-2316
Phone: 1-800-526-0275
Fax: 1-800-227-9604

This book is dedicated to everyone who read, purchased, reviewed, supported, promoted, or told someone about Suddenly Single. Thank you for blessing me. It is also dedicated to my hero and mother, Myrtice Champion Johnson.

ACKNOWLEDGMENTS

As always, I have to acknowledge and thank God for everything He's blessed my family and me with and for all of the favor He's granted me on this journey. God is the reason for any success that I may have now and in the future.

I would like to thank my family for their support; especially my husband, Shelman, my mother, Myrtice C. Johnson, and my kids, Shannon and Shelman III. Thank you for always being in my corner. I love you all so much!

I want to thank all of the bookstores, magazines, and radio stations that gave me a voice and outlet to promote my work. A special thanks goes out to my cousin, Michelle Price, at Holy and Hip, Rhonda at Mocha Readers, the Richardsons at Cushcity, the Cheek family at Not Just a Bookstore, and Christa Rumph of Copy, Print, Design. I hope to repay your kindness someday.

I would like to thank my agent, Nancey Flowers, my editor, Joylynn Jossel, and everyone at Urban Christian for your patience and hard work on my behalf.

I especially want to thank my "play brothers" Demetrius Hollis, Scott Harris, Phillip Lockett, and my real brother, James "Jay" Johnson, for being the composite for the lead male character of this book; and my friend, Mike, for being the inspiration for the character, Creighton.

Thanks to my sisters, Deirdre Neeley, Theresa Tarver, Tralia Matthews, Aaliyah James, Kurtina Cordy, Shameka Hunter, Stephanie Smith, and Erika Davis, for coming to my signings and supporting me in everything that I do. I thank God for you every day.

Lastly, I want to thank everyone who has prayed for me and supported me as I've tried to get my writing career off the ground. I love you and happy reading!

FIRST COMES LOVE

Chapter 1

It wasn't the first time she'd woken up with a hangover. Truth be told, it wasn't even the first time that she'd woken up with a hangover while lying next to a half-naked man in a strange hotel room. Nevertheless, this time was different.

The feeling that enveloped London Harris now was more than the nauseating sensation that came along with praying that God would spare her any STDs, HIV, or KIDs from a man whose last name she couldn't remember. It was a gut-wrenching anguish born out of the knowledge that one bad decision had just changed her life forever.

London stared up at the ceiling, clad only in lacy lavender panties and his brick-red *Sean John* emblazoned t-shirt, looking into the cheap circa 1970 mirror hanging over the bed in their gaudy, pink Las Vegas hotel room. By the looks of it, this was the place where cotton-candy came to die. She gazed at her body as it reflected in the mirror, trying to ignore the faint smell of urine and baby powder that clung to the sheets. From that angle, she looked a little like an umbrella with her long, toffee-brown legs protruding from the oversized shirt. The bags darkening her saucy and temporarily bloodshot eyes—tell-tale signs of the night's debauchery—made her look much older than her twenty-eight years. Her thick, chestnut brown hair was pushed off of her forehead and crushed beneath the weight of her head on the pillow, exposing the small scar on her temple sustained from a car accident twenty-one years earlier that left her with nineteen stitches and two dead parents. Plum-colored lipstick was smeared across her full lips and onto her left cheek. Admittedly, she was a hot mess.

As much as it pained London to see herself this way, she didn't dare shift her eyes to the left or right. If she looked to the left of her, she would have to glimpse at the diamond ring secured around her finger, a ring that was purchased for another woman less than 24 hours ago. To her right slept the man whom the ring confirmed to be her husband, and straight ahead lay the repercussions for making the biggest mistake of her life.

The one thought that played over and over again in London's head was, *This is not happening. This cannot be happening.* She tried to pinpoint the exact moment when everything went wrong. She surmised that it was around two o'clock the day before, sitting in a booth at a sparsely-populated Dairy Queen in Atlanta, Georgia, with her best-friend-turned-husband, Bernard Phillips, as sunlight poured in through the window. If London had known that things would turn out the way they did, she would have ditched Bernard and the sundae and settled instead for watching reruns of *Girlfriends* with a glass of Chardonnay.

"Now I see why they say, 'If it sounds too good to be true, it probably is!'" declared London that day at Dairy Queen.

Looking on as she drove a plastic red spoon into a

mountain of vanilla ice cream topped with chocolate syrup, whipped cream, and cherries was a scene all too familiar to Bernard, who knew that it could only mean one thing: London had been dumped once again. He slid into the opposite side of the booth and piteously shook his head, turning the brim of his baseball cap to the side.

She noticed that the hat was the exact same cerulean blue as the basketball jersey covering his broad shoulders and butterscotch skin. Bernard was almost as meticulous about his wardrobe as she was, though his style was decidedly more Phat Farm than Fifth Avenue.

"Is this why you wanted me to meet you here? To listen to you murmur and complain like the children of Israel and eat your weight in ice cream?" he asked. "I thought you were supposed to be on your way to Las Vegas."

London flipped her hair off of her shoulders. "You're here because it's been a very emotional day for me. And, no, I'm not going away for a romantic weekend in Vegas because," she paused for the dramatic build up, "Creighton is married."

As collected as ever, Bernard shrugged his shoulders indifferently, then mumbled, "I figured that," and proceeded to check his cell phone. It was not the public outcry that she was expecting and, in fact, looking forward to.

"That's it?" spat London. "You're not livid? You're not outraged?"

"What do you want me to say, London? I told you from the jump that he was married, but as usual, you chose to listen to your hormones or your biological clock or whatever it is that you women listen to when you're in denial about being played."

"You've been wrong so many times, Bernard. How was I to know that this time would be different?" She shook her head. "You know, this just further proves what I've been saying all along about love and marriage. Love sucks; marriage does, too. Nobody is faithful anymore. It's depressing." London began mixing the chocolate syrup into her ice cream. "And when I think about all of the plans we made, the future that I thought we were building together," she whined. "None of it's going to happen now."

Bernard helped himself to one of her cherries. "Well, Lon, life goes on. Are the chicken fingers here any good? I'm getting kind of hungry."

London's eyes widened as she watched him scan the wall menu. "I can't believe you're acting like this! I just told you that the man that I'm in love with is married, and all you can say is, 'I told you so. How are the chicken fingers?' How could you be so insensitive?"

"*I'm insensitive?*" he repeated. "What about the clown who's been screwing you over for six months?"

She flung her napkin at him. "This is not about *Creighton*; this is about you and me. You're supposed to be my boy and have my back, not make me feel worse."

Bernard relented, flashing a cool smile. "You're right, I'm sorry. Go ahead and cry, scream, or anything else you need to do. I'm here for you. Just promise me that you're not about to become one of those scary, bitter, I-hate-men chicks."

London pouted and slouched down in her chair. "No? just one of those scary, bitter, I-hate-married-men-who-lie-about-being-married chicks."

"Come on, Lon, you had to have known he was married. The cell number, the out-of-town dates, and the lame excuses on holidays had *lockdown* written all over them."

"I know," she conceded. "But he was so nice, and we were so good together."

"I'm sure his wife says the same thing," Bernard mused.

She sighed. "Okay, I'll admit that I knew something was up, but I just figured he had an old girlfriend or a baby's mama stashed away somewhere. I never would've guessed he was married." She shook her head. "Why is it that I end up losing everybody that I love?"

Bernard pilfered London's spoon and lowered it into the sundae. "So, how did you find out? I know he wasn't man enough to tell you the truth himself."

"At work, of all places. You remember that hundred-year-old Tudor my realty company has been trying to unload for the past year? Well, we finally got a buyer. It turns out that the new owners are none other than Mr. and Mrs. Creighton Graham. They just closed on it today."

"That's messed up. The least he could've done is let you have the commission."

"A few thousand dollars wouldn't begin to cover all he owes me in time invested and lost in this relationship. When I confronted him about being married, the punk didn't even have the decency to deny it. He acted like it was no big deal."

Bernard dipped into her ice cream again. "What are you going to do about it?"

London hung her head. "Other than drown my sorrows in confectionary delights, nothing. What would be the point?"

Bernard passed her the spoon. "Revenge! Isn't that what all of that 'woman scorned' nonsense is about? At least, that's what my last girlfriend called it after she took a hammer to my truck."

London twirled the spoon around in her bowl. "I thought about calling and telling his wife what a cheating, lying rat he is, but hurting her to get back at him just seemed desperate and pathetic. Unfortunately, what I possess in evil intentions, I lack in creativity to orchestrate any real kind of revenge."

Bernard reclined in his seat. "That's why you shouldn't be so quick to up and fall in love with the first man who pays you some attention." He reached into his pocket.

"See, Vanessa and I are the real thing, and I'm planning on making it official tonight." He pushed a small, black velvet box across the table to London, awaiting her approval.

"Bern, is this—?"

He squirmed in his seat. "Open it. Tell me what you think."

London gasped when she saw the round and emerald-cut diamond eternity band tucked inside of the box. "Bernard, this is gorgeous! Can I try it on? This may be the closest I ever get to one."

He nodded and she slipped the ring on her finger. "I've got my speech all planned out. Been working on it since last week."

London rotated her hand to make the ring sparkle. "Well, let's hear it. You be you, and I'll pretend like I'm Vanessa."

"All right." Bernard cleared his throat and exhaled, obviously tense.

"Wow, if I didn't know better, I'd swear you were nervous."

"If I seem like it, it's because this speech has to be perfect. I only plan to recite it one other time for the rest of my life, and that's tonight with Vanessa." He seized London's right hand and stared into her eyes. "Vanessa?" London didn't respond, captivated by the ring. "You're supposed to be Vanessa, London."

"Oh, right!" She sat upright and raised her voice a few octaves to mimic Vanessa's. "Yes, baby?"

He gazed at her and smiled. "We've been together for about three years now, but I knew from our first date that I wanted to marry you."

London snapped out of character and interrupted him with, "Did you really? Because I thought that you were still messing with that white girl when you met Vanessa."

Bernard sneered and argued, "Elena wasn't white. She was Greek."

London smacked her lips and fired, "All I know is that she wasn't a sista!"

"Dang, London, can I finish?"

"Okay, I'm sorry. Go on."

He sighed heavily and resumed. "We share the kind of love that people search for their entire lives. I want to be the man you lean on and the one you grow old with. I want you to be the mother of my children and I want you, now and forever, to be my wife. I love you, Vanessa. Will you marry me?"

London signaled for him to wait as she wolfed down another spoonful of ice cream. "That was beautiful," she mumbled, spurting out beads of chocolate.

Bernard pushed her hand away. "And that was just plain nasty! Now I see why you can't keep a man." London fumed and rolled her eyes. "And give me back my ring!" He snatched the ring off of her finger.

"Don't get mad," she taunted. "I don't know what you're getting all worked up about. You know she's going to say yes."

"You really think so?" he asked, stuffing the ring back into his pocket.

"You've been living together for two years. You're practically married anyway."

"Yeah, but she's been on edge lately, wanting to know where our relationship is headed and if I'm really serious about us. I want her to know that I'm ready to settle down and start a family with her. She's my rib."

"That's so sweet," cooed London. "Vanessa loves you, Bernard. Why wouldn't she say yes?"

London's prediction couldn't have been more inaccurate. Around eight o'clock that night, Bernard showed up on London's doorstep disheveled and angry; a far cry from the smooth, clean-cut brother that he prided himself on portraying.

"She said no!" he announced.

London stopped munching on the popcorn in her mouth. "What happened?" she asked, letting him into her townhouse. She flipped on the light switch, illuminating the mustard walls and cosmopolitan-themed great-room.

Bernard slumped into her ivory Landau sofa and loosened his tie. "I don't know. Everything was perfect! We went out and had a romantic dinner. We came back home, listened to a little music, drank a little wine . . ."

"Tapped a little booty," sang London, sitting down next to him.

"*Whatever* . . . Anyway, afterward, I asked her to marry me."

London set the bag of popcorn down and clicked off the flat-screen television with the remote control. "And?"

"And she said that she didn't think that we were right for each other. To make matters worse, she said that her ex, Alonzo, is back in town, and she thinks she might still be in love with him. Ain't that a b—"

London broke in before he could get the expletive completely out. "Which one—the situation or Vanessa?"

"Both!"

London winced. "What did you do?"

"The usual, I guess. I packed up some clothes, called her a back-alley trick, and told her to board the first train to hell."

"That was mature," replied London.

"I wasn't trying to be politically correct at the time." Bernard closed his eyes and leaned back on the couch. His familiar dimpled grin soured into a hapless glower. "Man, I wanted to marry that girl, and she picked *that* moment to tell me that she's in love with somebody else."

"So, that's it? It's over?"

"As far as I'm concerned, it is. I don't play 'runner-up' to nobody!"

"So, what now?"

"Well, after I get my money back for that ring," he sat up, "the first thing I've got to do is find a place to crash. Technically, the apartment lease is in her name."

"Don't even worry about that," assured London, patting him on the thigh. "You know that you can stay here as long as you want."

"I appreciate that. It'll be short-term, I promise."

"So do I," replied London.

He squeezed her hand. "You know, you're about the only female out here that I can count on or trust."

"That's because you could bury me with all the bones you know I have stashed in the closet. I have no other choice but to be your friend." She giggled, shaking her head.

Bernard grew defensive. "Oh, you think this is funny?"

"Well, yeah. Look at us; we got dumped on the same day! I believe this is a first for us. I guess in this love game, it's either play or get played, huh?"

He reached into her bag of popcorn. "I'm sad to say that it looks like we both did the latter." Bernard sat quietly for a few minutes before arriving at a new revelation. "You know what? You were right; forget love! Forget love, forget Vanessa, forget all of it!"

London ran her hand over his closely-shaven head. "Now, don't tell me that you're going to become one of those bitter, I-hate-love-and-I'm-scared-to-commit guys," she teased.

He laughed in spite of himself. "Naw, just one of those women-ain't-worth-a-you-know-what guys!"

London pulled him into a playful embrace. "Aw, don't worry about ol' Vanessa. If she wasn't smart enough to realize what a good man you are, she doesn't deserve you."

"That's sweet. I know you don't mean a word of it, but it's nice of you to say."

"I do mean it, B!" she insisted. London caressed the side of his face. "Besides, that Vanessa has some big teeth. Can you imagine what the children would've looked like?"

He chuckled a bit. "Yeah, she does have a little beaver thing going on, doesn't she?"

"And you know she can't cook!" instigated London. "And remember when she had that weird Mohawk happening with her hair last year? I swear it looked like a gang of meerkats had been kick-boxing in her scalp. I just didn't say anything because she thought it was cute."

"Hey, I thought she looked pretty fly with that hairdo," he shot back. "At least it wasn't all this horse hair you keep glued in your head!" he joked, tousling her hair extensions.

London smoothed her sleek bob back into place. "Ordinarily, I would get you back for a move like that, but I'll spare you since you just got your heart stumped out."

His jovial mood turned serious again. "Yeah, I did, didn't I? You know, I sat outside in my car and cried for about thirty minutes," Bernard confessed. "I'd never let her have the satisfaction of knowing that, but I did."

London brought her hand to her chest. "Don't say that. Now, you're going to make *me* start crying."

"Naw, you'll probably do better to save those tears for Creighton's wife. You might need 'em to garner some sympathy when she shows up to deliver your beat down."

"Oh, Creighton's had his share of my tears today, but that doesn't stop my heart from aching for you. All jokes aside, I know that you really loved her, and I can see how much this is hurting you."

He tried to blink back the tears that were threatening to fall again. "I'm a big boy. This wasn't my first heartbreak and probably won't be the last. I just wish she had told me before I proposed, though. At least, then, I could have left with some dignity."

"Bern, Vanessa is the one who did something to be ashamed of, not you."

"Remind me of that the next time you see me over here crying like a little punk, all right?"

"You're not a punk for crying; just human." He nodded, smearing a tear that had managed to trickle down his cheek. Vanessa continued. "You don't have to put up a brave front for me. We're best friends. If you can't cry in front of me, who can you cry in front of?" She kissed him on the jaw. "You know what we need?" hedged London, smearing her thumb across his teary cheek.

"A stiff drink and maybe a bag of the sticky-icky," he answered.

She elbowed him in the chest. "No, we need a change of scenery! We need to get out and have some fun. Today has to be something other than the day we both got kicked to the curb!"

"I'm all for that," Bernard replied, shaking off the temporary indignation. "What are you trying to get into?"

"I don't know—what's another word for doing something crazy and spontaneous?"

"Regret."

"I'm talking about something fun that'll give us a chance to let our hair down."

He thought for a moment. "We could go down to the strip club. Nothing can cheer me up like watching Cherry Nasty sliding up and down that pole."

London hit him with a throw pillow. "I said *hair* down, not underwear, and I also said something we can *both* enjoy! What is watching some low self-esteemed table dancers poppin' and shakin' for rent money going to do for me?"

"Who says we can't both enjoy that? You know y'all females like to look." She drew the pillow back, poised to strike again. "All right, all right!" he recanted, attempting to block her attack. "No strippers."

"Thank you."

He readjusted his seat on the couch and grinned. "What then? Are you offering something . . . else?"

She frowned. "Something else, like what?"

"You know," he said, raising and lowering his eyebrows in quick motions."

London rolled her eyes at his immature transparency. "Not even if you put a gun to my head," she answered flatly.

"Well, I'm fresh out of ideas, and I don't want to spend my money on something stupid that I'm just going to regret the next day."

London's eyes lit up, and she snapped her fingers. "I got it! We should go to Vegas!"

"Okay, clearly, you didn't hear the part about not wanting to waste my money on something stupid that I'm going to regret the next day."

She slipped her arm around Bernard's, trying to coax him. "Think about it for a second, B. The one thing that we were sure of—love—turned out to be a big disappointment. So, why not take a chance on something that no one can be sure of, like gambling? It can't be any worse than sitting here, thinking about what might've been."

"Lon, I'm not trying to fly out to Vegas tonight, not to mention shelling out the money for plane tickets and a hotel room."

"No need. I took care of everything when I planned the trip for Creighton and me. Besides, we haven't gone to Las Vegas together since we graduated from college, and I know you remember how much fun we had then. All you have to do is grab your toothbrush and drive us to the airport."

Bernard wasn't quite convinced, but he hadn't dismissed the idea either. London pushed harder. "Come on, it'll be fun, I promise. We can hang out, hit the poker table and the slot machines, and just be wild and have fun together like we used to."

"How long are you talking about staying down there?"

"Just for a day or two. We can fly out tonight, spend all day Saturday doing things that'll make the devil close his eyes, and then rest and fly back home some time tomorrow so we'll be back in plenty of time for work on Monday."

She made it sound so easy. She always did, no matter how disastrous the outcome. He stroked his goatee, pondering the possibility. "Vegas, huh?"

"We can go, do whatever we want, and no one will be the wiser." When he still didn't budge, she tugged on his sleeve. "Come on, do it for me."

Every rational bone in Bernard's body screamed *no* but not loud enough to override the shrill of London's voice. Her excitement was infectious, and he was more than willing to put a few thousand miles between Vanessa and himself, even if just for a day.

"This better be worth my time *and money*," he warned, "because I already know that one way or the other, I'm going to wind up paying for this trip."

She squealed and shrouded his face with sloppy, wet kisses. "You won't be sorry we did this, Bernard. It'll be a night we'll never forget!"

Chapter 2

London was yanked back into reality, her own prophetic words echoing through her head as she lay in bed next to Bernard. But that was yesterday, when the world still made sense. Today, her mission was to find the quickest way out of her lifelong commitment to matrimony.

"Bernard," she called just above a whisper and was answered by his light snoring. She tapped him on the shoulder. "Bernard?" She huffed and gave him three seconds to respond. *"Bernard!"*

With one swell thrust, she heaved his nearly 200 pound, six-foot frame onto the floor. He met the ground with a thud.

"What's wrong with you?" he fired, rubbing the side of his head, which turned a blush red from the impact.

"What's wrong?" London leaned over the side of the bed and held her hand to his face, brandishing the wedding ring. *"This* is what's wrong!"

Bernard sprang to his feet and grabbed her hand. His eyes grew to the size of watermelons as they locked on the ring bought for Vanessa now around London's finger. He frantically panned the unfamiliar room. "What... where are we?"

"Suffice it to say, we're not in Kansas anymore. We're on what's known as our honeymoon, or as I like to think of it, in the depths of hell."

A mixture of shock and horror washed over his face as blurred images started to crystallize. Images of the two of them stumbling into an Elvis-inspired chapel and giggling through vows. "Did we—?"

"*Yes!*"

His eyes scrolled down to his boxers and back up to meet her eyes, and he nervously inquired, "Did we—?"

"No! At least I don't think so. I still had on my necessities when I got up this morning."

He peeked underneath the blanket at her toned, bare legs. "Then where are your pants?"

She snatched the covers to block his view. "I think I puked on them last night. Besides, if I'd slept with you, I'd know it. I'm sure I'd feel dirty and slightly violated."

He nodded and gripped a corner of the bedspread. "You're probably right, because if we did have sex," a devilish grin crept across his lips, "you definitely would have remembered."

She shuddered at the thought. "What I *do* remember is that we're married ... husband and wife ... life partners ... espoused ... wed ... ball and chain," she ranted.

"Okay, I get it, just stop talking so loud. This headache is a mother!" He climbed back into bed, molded his pillow to fit his head, and locked the blanket around his half-naked body.

She sat up with her arms folded across her chest. "So, you're just going to go back to sleep?"

He yawned. "You got a better way to get rid of a hangover?"

"I'm about ten seconds away from hanging *you* over the side of this hotel if you don't do something about this. How can you sleep at a time like this? Don't you realize what we've done?"

He punched his pillow into submission before settling his head back into it. "London, we were falling-down drunk, not to mention buzzed on God-knows-what from that guy at the club. The marriage probably isn't even legal."

"Oh, it's legal." London reached over on the nightstand and waved the certificate above his head. "Here's your proof." She let it sail to the floor. Bernard picked it up and skimmed over the paper. The ceremony had been officiated by Bobby Whitlet, witnessed by his wife, Agnes, and the certificate signed by both the bride and the groom.

He set the paper down. "So, it's legal—big deal. People come to Vegas and get married on a whim all the time. I'm sure they have all kinds of annulments and quickie divorces set up around the city just to handle situations like this." He rolled over, turning his back to her.

"You better hope they do, because I refuse to go home calling myself Mrs. Bernard Phillips."

"You've been called worse."

She smacked her teeth. "London Phillips . . . it even *sounds* stupid! Can you imagine how my grandmother is going to take all this? And Pop-Pop?" London panicked, her skin turning a pale yellow. She thought of her grandparents, who put their lives on hold to raise her after her parents died, and the look of disappointment that would register on their faces once they discovered what she and Bernard had done. Suddenly, she began to feel hot and dizzy. Her mouth became watery and the bile that she'd been trying to suppress rose to her chest. "Oh, God, I think I'm going to be sick!"

Covering her mouth with her hand, she made a dash for the bathroom. When she emerged, the color had returned to her cheeks. "It's official. The mere thought of being your wife literally makes me sick."

"Morning sickness kicking in already, huh?" he teased, sitting up in bed. "Are you sure I didn't drop a seed in you last night?"

"Are you trying to make me throw up again?"

"Insults? Vomiting? London, this is no way to start a marriage."

She splotched her face with a cool towel and smacked her lips. "Can you be serious for one second?"

"*Seriously*, London, I don't think this is anything to worry about. We'll get up, go back to the chapel or Justice of the Peace or whatever it was, get an annulment, and by this time tomorrow, you'll be free to go out and ruin another marriage."

She propped her body up against the flamingo-pink dresser. "You think so?"

"Do I think that you'll ruin another marriage? Of course!" She stamped her foot at his folly. Bernard followed up with, "Just like I know that we'll be out of this mess in no time."

London pointed a finger at him, issuing him a stern look to go with her warning. "Nobody can ever know about this, Bernard. I mean it!"

"I'm in no more of a hurry to send out wedding announcements than you are. Think of what it'll do to my reputation if everyone knew that I went from bootylicious Vanessa to . . . *you*."

"Going from her to me is what they call an upgrade."

He slipped his undershirt over his head. "Upgrade or not, I'm ready to get this over with before you start falling in love with me. It doesn't take long for me to have that effect on a woman, you know."

"Says who? Vanessa? By my calculation, it doesn't take long for any man to have that effect on her."

"Very funny." He arose and made his way over to her. "My shirt please."

London shielded her chest with her hands. "Do you expect me to take it off right now?"

"Why not? We're married. Going topless is the least you could do."

"Leave your fantasies out of this."

"Don't flatter yourself. I need my shirt; unless, of course, you're secretly deriving pleasure from gawking at all this sun-kissed chocolate." He playfully rubbed his chiseled torso.

"Save that for the boys at the gym," she retorted, mentally taking stock of how ripped he was. It never occurred to her to notice before. "You can have your shirt back, but you'll have to close your eyes first."

"*Close my eyes?* What are we, London, twelve?"

She hollered, "Close 'em!"

Bernard exhaled and complied. London quickly wriggled out of his shirt and scampered across the room in her underwear to grab her clothes. He stealthily peeked out of one eye. "Not bad, Mrs. Phillips, not bad at all. You finally graduated out of that training bra, I see."

"Stop looking at me!" she ordered, scourging the floor for her clothes. She ducked down beside the bed to get dressed.

"Yeah, we need to go ahead with this annulment. I can't have a wife who's this frigid."

"Let's go," she said, emerging from the side of the bed. As she darted past him, he reached down and zipped up her jeans. His touch remitted an electric sensation that she wasn't prepared for.

"Your fly was open." He flashed a mischievous smirk and opened the door. "After you, wifey," he replied, giving her a whack on the behind as she walked out in front of him, propelling her ahead a few feet. "Just wanted to know what I was working with before we got the annulment."

"And?"

"As I suspected, not a doggone thing. Let's go."

Chapter 3

"Okay, so I was wrong," conceded Bernard for about the hundredth time during the drive home from the airport that evening. "How was I supposed to know that the courthouse would be closed?"

London slapped her hand against her forehead. "It's Sunday, you idiot! Everybody knows it's closed!"

"*You* didn't," he pointed out.

London shot him a look of contempt before succumbing to hysteria again. "How could we have been so stupid?" she lamented. "Who gets married in a Baby Phat tube top and jeans?" London buried her face in her hands. "I'm never getting drunk again—make that never *drinking* again! Who cares if Jesus turned water into wine, I ain't touching the stuff!"

"Will you chill out? I've known you for practically your whole life, and this, by far, is not the stupidest thing you've ever done. We're not the first ones to do something impulsive after a break up, and the whole courthouse thing is just a minor setback. It only means that we'll have to wait until tomorrow to get the annulment. Everything will be straightened out then."

"Forgive me if I have a little trouble believing you," countered London. "It sounds a lot like the speech I heard this morning." Her cell phone rang. London looked down at her grandmother's phone number registering on the screen. "Shoot, it's Nana. What should I do?"

"I think the common practice is to answer it."

"I can't talk to her. I'm not in the mood to be grilled about missing church today, and you know how she is." London looked at him with a raised eye and added formidably, "She *knows* things."

"And?"

"She can sense when I'm hiding something. It would be just like her to have the whole thing figured out before I have time to come up with a good lie."

"Then tell her the truth."

"Humph, and have biblical scriptures thrown at me in five different languages? I don't think so."

"Well, don't just let it ring," replied Bernard, annoyed. "Something may have happened to your granddad."

London thought of her ailing seventy-five-year-old grandfather, who had been fighting a losing battle with dementia for the better part of the past year. "You might be right," she told him. She let it ring once more, praying that the call would be sent to voice-mail.

London cleared her throat before answering the phone, hoping to disguise the distress in her voice and to ward off any suspicion of trouble. "Nana, hi! Is everything all right with you and Pop-Pop?" After a moment, she nodded to Bernard to signal that both of her grandparents were fine. "Me? I'm okay, just riding around with Bernard. We're headed home now . . . Actually, we can't because— Hello? Nana?" She clasped the phone shut.

Bernard's eyes quickly darted from the road to London. "What was that about?"

London stared at the phone with her mouth gaping. "I can't believe she just hung up on me!"

"Did you piss her off?"

London dropped her phone into her purse. "She didn't give me a chance to. She said to come right over and hung up."

"Well, good luck with that," muttered Bernard. "I'll drop you off, and you can call me when you're ready to be picked up."

"Uh-uh, she said both of us, and I know you're not crazy enough to drop me off and keep going. You've obviously forgotten that you're going to need a place to rest your head tonight."

Bernard wrinkled his brow. "What does she want to see me for?"

"B, what did I tell you earlier? She—"

"Yeah, I know—*she knows things!*" he added, mocking her.

"I'm serious, Bernard. She's psychic or something, I swear."

"Just be cool," directed Bernard, exiting the interstate and turning down the road that led to London's grandmother's modest farmhouse on the outskirts of Atlanta, in Stockbridge. "We'll get in and break out before she can ask too many questions."

London exhaled and raked her fingers through her hair. "That's right . . . cool, relaxed . . ."

"Did she give you any clues about what she wanted?"

"No; only that I was in her 'spirit,' whatever that's supposed to mean."

Ten minutes later, they passed the vacant, dilapidated home Bernard lived in as a child and drove a few feet down the road, turning into Essie's graveled driveway, where they were greeted by rows of mid-summer sun-flowers and crabgrass growing sporadically in the yard. The aroma of Sunday dinner welcomed them into the brightly lit house long before any of the occupants did.

"Nana, we're here," called London as she and Bernard crept into the cramped kitchen through the unlocked door.

"I'm at the stove, baby; just trying to finish up these greens." Essie Harris set the heavy lid down on the pot and lowered the gas on the stove. "Girl, where have you been? I was trying to get a hold of you all weekend. Come on in and sit down." Essie, with her gray chignon and apron tied around her stout marshmallow frame, had a stride and way about her that was surprisingly spry for a woman of near seventy.

"We're in kind of a hurry," said London, inching into the kitchen, which was warm and humid from both the sti-fling August heat and the searing stove that caused the flowered wall-paper to shrivel up and peel.

"There ain't no such thing as being too busy to talk to your old grandma," admonished Essie. "When I've gone on to glory, you can do all the running around you want to do but while I'm here, you gon' come right here and give me a hug and sit and talk for a spell." Any references to Essie's "going to glory" always elicited immediate guilt and compliance from London, and Essie was banking on it. "You come on and get some sugar, too, Bernard." He hobbled over to her and pecked her on the cheek.

"Nana, you were kind of cryptic on the phone," mentioned London, laying her purse on the countertop. "I'm not really sure why you wanted to see us."

Essie picked up a knife and began slicing onions to toss into her turnips. "I didn't realize that I had to have a reason to see my favorite grandbaby, a child I've been raising since she was seven years old."

"I'm sorry. It's just that you made it sound kind of urgent. I thought something might have happened."

"It's like I told you, baby, you've been in my spirit."

"*In your spirit?*" echoed Bernard. "What does that mean?"

"Nothing, really, just that she's been on my mind, that's all," Essie explained and squinted her bluish-gray eyes at London with an intense, almost eerie, stare. "You ain't in no trouble, is you?"

"No, everything is great!" she lied. "Why wouldn't it be?"

"Don't you tell me no stories, gal! You still running around with that shifty lawyer fellow? What's his name . . . Satan?"

"Creighton," London filled in.

"Same thing," uttered Bernard.

"And, no, we're not together anymore. We broke up a couple of days ago," said London, still obviously hurt about it.

"Uh-huh," grunted Essie. "I never liked him anyway. Something about his eyes wasn't right." Essie turned to Bernard. "What about you? You and that girlfriend of yours still shacking up, living in sin?"

Bernard laughed a little. After almost three decades, he was well acquainted with Essie's interrogations. "No, ma'am. We've gone our separate ways, too," he said. "I've decided that the next woman I move in with will have to be my wife." London crushed his toe beneath her heel, catching the double meaning.

Essie wiped her hands on a dish towel. "That's good. Y'all didn't have no business shacked up in the first place. It ain't Christian. Don't you worry about that girl none, though, Bernard. You're a good boy, and you'll meet a nice young lady soon enough. I've been telling Lonnie for years that she's a fool for not snatching you up for herself."

"I think she may finally start listening to you," he alluded.

"How's Pop-Pop?" asked London, poking around the stove, eager to change the subject.

"He's asleep now, but he had a rough time last night." Essie's eyes fell downcast. "He, uh, was asking for Dell again."

London looked up, puzzled. "His dead sister?"

Essie nodded. "He had a fit, too, thinking I'd done something to her and wouldn't let him see her. I just don't know what to do sometimes. Pastor says that I ought to put him in a home and let them look after him." She shook her head, "But as long as there's breath in my body and the Lord keeps giving me the strength I need, I'm gon' be the one to 'tend to him."

London made her way across the kitchen and rubbed her grandmother's back. "Nana, maybe you should at least think about it. You're not as young as you used to be. What if it gets to be too much for you?"

Essie shook her head. "Hush all that! Your granddaddy'll be fine, just fine." She affectionately tapped London's hand and took a moment to compose herself before continuing to slice the onion. "You missed a good sermon this morning, Lonnie. Pastor preached up something today! You know I don't like it when you miss church. I didn't raise you like that." London lowered her head. Her penitence satisfied Essie for the time being. "Well, y'all children hungry? I got plenty to eat. You better get it while you can because once your cousins come over and eat, there won't be enough to hit a lick at a snake with." It was one of Essie's many southern colloquialisms that no one bothered to ask her to explain anymore.

"You ain't gotta tell me twice!" exclaimed Bernard, rubbing his stomach. "I haven't eaten since we boarded the plane." London cringed, and he realized his gaffe as soon as the words escaped his lips.

Essie halted. *"Plane?* Where y'all been?"

"Nowhere, we just went to do a little harmless gambling and catch a couple of shows," covered London.

"Where at?" Essie casually asked.

London mumbled, "Nevada."

Essie took a step back. "You and this boy went to Las Vegas?"

"It was London's idea," blurted Bernard.

Essie's scolded them both with burning eyes. "Good Christian folks ain't got no business being around all those heathens! What is it that they call that place?"

"Sin City," he answered.

"That's what I thought! Girl, how many times have I told you what the Bible says about the appearance of evil? And don't try to lie to me. I know what kind of depravity goes on in those kinds of places," preached Essie.

Bernard folded his arms and shook his head, siding with Essie. "That's exactly what I tried to tell her, Miss Essie. The only reason I went was to keep London out of trouble."

London waved her hand to dismiss his censuring. "You wanted to go just as much as I did, Bernard! Don't front."

Essie spotted the diamond ring gleaming on London's finger and seized her hand. "What's all this, Lonnie?"

A heart-stopping chill rushed through London's body. "Nothing," she stammered, swallowing hard and using her right hand to cover the left one as she slipped out of her grandmother's grasp. "It's just a ring."

Essie snatched London's hand again for a closer inspection. "That looks like a wedding ring to me. Girl, you didn't go off and do something stupid with that lawyer, did you?"

"No, I got it while we were in Vegas." London cleared

her throat and slung her purse over her shoulder. "Well, look at the time. We should probably go. Bernard, don't you have that thing today?"

"Um, yeah, I almost forgot." He fumbled with the keys, as anxious to dodge Essie's prying as London. "We better jet."

"Where you got to run off to?" asked Essie.

London replied, "A meeting" as Bernard said, "I've got a date."

"Well, which is it?" quizzed Essie, not about to let up on them.

London opened her mouth to form another lie but stayed quiet instead, taking a cue from Bernard, who silently stared out of the window.

"Something in the milk ain't clean," balked Essie, shaking her head. "And one of you better start talking right now!"

London turned to Bernard. He shrugged his shoulders, at a loss over what to say. Only Essie had the ability to reduce him to a quivering ten-year-old boy waiting to be told to go in the backyard and pick out a switch.

Essie drummed her fingers on the countertop. "Well, I'm waiting . . ."

London's eyes shifted from Essie to Bernard and out the door. "Um . . . you know, we really don't have to get into all this right now," stalled London. "How are your azaleas coming along this season?" She moved toward the door under the pretext of searching for flowers. "Bernard, you should have seen them last year. I keep telling Nana she needs to enter her flowers in one of those contests and win some money. She won't listen to me, though."

Essie pointed a finger at her. "Lonnie, you must either think I'm crazy or a fool, one. I know that you don't bit more care about my 'zaleas than the man in the moon. Besides, they're not even out this time of year; you need to save that excuse for spring. Now what's going on here?" She aimed her fiery gaze at Bernard. "I'm waiting!"

"Tell her," hissed London.

"*You* tell her," Bernard shot back.

Essie was starting to lose patience. "*Somebody* tell me *something!*"

When it became obvious that Bernard wasn't going to say anything, London cleared her throat and stepped forward, mouthing some choice words to him in the process.

"Well, like I told you," she began, "Creighton and I broke up and so did Bernard and Vanessa, so we decided to go to Vegas to have fun and let off some steam." She slowly paced the floor as she spoke, fidgeting and keeping her eyes glued to the green and yellow speckled linoleum. "And that's pretty much it."

Essie shook her head. "I know there's more to it than that. I want to know about this ring business and why the two of you are acting so shady."

"We were both emotional, you know? We were tired from the flight. We weren't thinking clearly and were acting impulsively. Everything happened so fast that I barely remember even being there."

"Yes, but what does all that have to do with you and this wedding ring?"

"I'm getting to that, Nana." London glanced back at Bernard. "You see, there's a lot of temptation in a place like Vegas, and while I know that it's not right, but we did do a lot of drinking when we were down there, too—"

"So, you and Bernard were running around Nevada drunk and acting a fool. Now, you know I taught you better than that!" thundered Essie.

"I know you have, Nana. It was wrong and completely out of character for me."

Essie shook her head and moaned, "Umph, umph, umph! Go on."

"And Bernard and I got to talking, and then we saw this wedding chapel," London continued, nervously wringing her hands together.

Essie stopped her. "Wedding chapel?"

"Yeah, Nana, and people were going in and out, getting married. And they just seemed in love and so happy—"

"It's not like we planned it or anything," offered Bernard. "And I guess we were just too out of it to think about the consequences."

Essie started to put the pieces together and clamped her hands onto her hips. "Are you trying to tell me that you and this boy done up and got yourselves married?"

"I know that it was reckless and stupid and never should have happened," London professed quickly.

"We're going to fix it, though," inserted Bernard.

"First thing tomorrow!" finished London.

Essie closed her eyes and began humming a hymn to herself, as she often did whenever she was upset. She toddled to the sink and started rinsing dishes.

"Did you hear what I said, Nana? We're going to fix this!" promised London, putting her arms around her grandmother.

Essie nodded her head slowly. "Yes, I guess there's only one thing you can do about it now."

Bernard rested his hand on her shoulder. "Don't worry, Miss Essie. Once we get the annulment, we can put all of this behind us."

Essie was taken aback. "*Annulment*? Who said anything about an annulment?" She wriggled out of their arms and stood before the two of them. "You all went before God and said that you wanted to be man and wife, and the Lord's going to hold you to that!"

London blinked, speechless for a second. "Nana, you can't be serious. I can't be Bernard's *wife*. I don't even love him. Not like that, anyway."

"Well, how many different kinds of love do you think there is? It ain't but one kind, honey—real love."

"Nana, you don't understand—"

"No, *you* don't understand. You made vows to be this man's wife." Essie wagged her finger at London. "Now, I don't care how drunk you were, a part of you, even if it's a part that you don't even know exists yet, wanted to marry him." Essie turned to Bernard. "And a part of you wanted to marry her, too, or you wouldn't have done it. Now you owe it to each to try to work this thing out."

London formed her lips into a forced smile. "You're kidding, right?"

Essie peered into London's face with a stiff frown. "Do I *look* like I'm kidding?"

Bernard gulped.

"This is crazy!" said London, more to herself than anyone in the room. "Nana, you don't stay married to the guy you eloped with while downing shots of Patron in Vegas. That just doesn't happen."

"Oh, yeah? Hand me that Bible," commanded Essie, pointing to the old, battered New International Version that rested on her countertop. Bernard brought it to her. "Now, let's see here." She began flipping through the pages then set the book down in front of him. "Read it."

Experience had taught him that it was best not to defy her. Bernard took a deep breath and began reading. "*I instruct married couples to stay together, and this is exactly what the Lord himself taught.* First Corinthians, chapter seven, verse ten."

"Uh-huh, now go on to . . . uh, uh, Corinthians seven and thirty-nine. Let Lonnie read that one." Bernard passed the Bible to her.

"*A wife should stay married to her husband until he dies*," London rambled hastily. "Nana, I know this, but—"

" 'Nard," broke in Essie, ignoring London's protests. "You read verse ten."

He cleared his throat. "*And a husband should not leave his wife.*" He re-read the verse to himself.

"There it is, in black and white, just as plain as day," declared Essie. "The second you two took those vows and made a covenant with the Lord, He started holding you accountable to honor it."

"There's got to be some kind of contingency clause," argued London, flipping through the Bible. "I refuse to believe that God expects me to stay married to a man that I don't love."

"There is," replied Essie. "It's called death. That's the only contingency I know about."

London shoved the Bible into Bernard's hands. "Nana, you're being closed-minded and unreasonable. We need to think about this rationally."

"You can do all the rationalizing you want, Lonnie, but ain't nothing gon' change the fact that you married him. Now, y'all just go on home and work this thing out." She shooed them toward the door and walked back to the sink.

"*Bernard, say something!*" whispered London.

Bernard looked up from the opened Bible in his palm. He didn't respond at first but finally said, "I think she's right."

London whirled around, her eyes bulging. "What?"

He reached for her hands. "Everything she's saying is true, babe. Don't you think we owe it to each other to try? Hey, it can't hurt, right?"

"We'll discuss this in the car," she muttered through clinched teeth.

"You better listen to your husband, Lonnie," warned Essie, scouring a pot. "He knows what he's talking about."

Bernard laid his hands on London's shoulders. "London, think about it. People are always saying that you should marry your best friend. Well, I did and so did you. We know each other better than any two people ought to. In fact, the only thing that's been constant in all of our other relationships is each other. I believe we can do this. Babe, I know we can."

"Bernard, do you honestly expect me to believe that you want to spend the rest of your life with me?" London asked. "And stop calling me babe!"

"I know that you can't process the thought of being together forever right now, but what about baby steps, giving it a shot for a few months? I mean, what's six months out of about eighty years of your life going to hurt?" Bernard reasoned.

"I think you should at least try for a year," interjected Essie.

"A year?" cried London.

"We owe it to ourselves." The verse he read from the Bible rang in his head again and filtered into his heart. "We owe it to God."

London shook her head. "Don't go dragging God into this."

"God *is* in it!" affirmed Essie. "And He's watching you— you better believe that. So is your mama. You know, I sat right there in that hospital after the accident, watching that girl dying, and I promised her that I was going to raise you up right, get you through school, and see to it that you married the kind of man that they'd be proud to call son-in-law. And you know that I don't go back on my promises!"

"And look." Bernard picked up the Bible that was still turned to Corinthians. "*Even when we don't know what to do, we never give up.* We have to have faith that God will lead us through this."

London covered her ears. "Both of you stop, *please*! I

can't think with the two of you ganging up on me like this."

"I'm not trying to pressure you, London. I'm only asking that we think about this before we rush out and make another rash decision," Bernard said.

She pulled him aside, out of earshot from Essie. "We talked about this, remember? We both agreed that getting the annulment was the only thing that made sense. Don't be taken in by Nana's emotional and spiritual blackmail."

"London, right now, trying to be your husband *is* what makes sense to me. I can't explain it, but I know that if we get this annulment tomorrow that we're going to regret it for the rest of our lives."

"So, now *you're* psychic, too?"

"I don't know what y'all are over there whispering about, but, Lonnie, you better not be over there trying to get that boy to change his mind," scolded Essie.

"Miss Essie, I agree with you. I think we should give this marriage a shot, but I'm not going to force London to do anything that she doesn't want to do," he stipulated.

London threw up her hands. "Forget it—you win! We'll do it your way. Just don't say anything when this whole mess blows up in everybody's faces."

Essie shook her head. "I declare, if you ain't the most ornery thing I've ever seen—"

"No, Nana, I'm not ornery, I'm realistic. But if you want to play God with our lives, you go right ahead. You're the one in control here, right?"

"Don't start smelling yourself," warned Essie. "You ain't never too old to get slapped."

"You can slap me and you can yell at me and you can even bring my dead mother into it, none of it matters." London yanked up her purse. "Nothing is going to change the fact that this is a mistake, and, trust me—things are going to get a whole lot worse before they get any better."

Chapter 4

"You want me to carry you over the threshold?" asked Bernard as London unlocked the front door to what was now their home.

"I'm not in the mood for jokes, Bern."

"Who's joking?" He bent down to scoop her up.

"Stop it!" she snapped, pushing him off of her.

"You don't have to bite my head off. I'm only trying to lighten things up a little. What's your problem?"

She flung the door open and walked in with Bernard trailing behind her. "My problem is that you're acting like this is some kind of game."

"No, I'm just trying to make the best of a difficult situation. Yes, we're married and, no, this is not what either of us planned, but it's what we've got. And let's face it," he said with a grin, "you could have done a lot worse." London rolled her eyes. "So, where do you want me to put all this?" He dropped his duffle bag at his feet.

"I guess you can put your stuff over there." She pointed to a closet in the hallway. "We can work out the sleeping arrangements later."

Bernard flinched a little. "Sleeping arrangements?"

"Yes, I only have one bedroom now since I turned the other one into my office, but the couch in there is pretty comfortable. I don't think you'll have a problem falling asleep on it."

"Darn right, I won't," replied Bernard, "because I don't intend to sleep there. I plan to be in the bedroom with you, my wife."

"Are you kidding me? There is no way I'm going to share a bed with you."

"Why not? We slept in the same bed all of the time in college. Shoot, you just slept with me last night."

"This isn't college, and I'm sober now. Besides, I know what this is about, and I want to make it very clear to you right now that, married or not, I have no intentions of having sex with you *ever*."

"Oh," he said. The disappointment showed on his face. "That's cool. I won't touch you, but I'm not sleeping on that rock you call a couch either."

"Don't you think that it would be better that way? I want to keep things as normal and uncomplicated as possible."

"There is nothing *normal* or *uncomplicated* about this marriage."

"Will you stop calling it that?" she barked. "This is not a real marriage."

"What I am supposed to call it then?"

"It's an *arrangement*," she enunciated, "a temporary arrangement that we're just doing this long enough to appease my grandmother. After that, you'll do your thing and I'll do mine."

He capitulated. "You're the boss. Although, spiritually speaking, I'm the boss because, as your husband, I am the head of this household."

"Will you kill all the husband references? I know what

that certificate says and what my grandmother says, but we know the truth."

"And what truth is that?"

"The truth is that getting married was a huge mistake. All we can do now is roll with the flow until we're able to move on with our lives."

"So you're determined to end this marriage no matter what?"

"Aren't you? I mean, two days ago, you were on bended knee proposing to Vanessa."

"And yesterday, I married you. We made vows, London. Granted, they're just a drunken blur to me right now, but you know we did. Your grandmother's words really hit home with me. She's right. We ought to at least try," implored Bernard.

London massaged her forehead to ease the looming migraine. "Let's be real for a minute, shall we? You still love Vanessa, and I'm still in love with Creighton. If we hadn't both gotten our walking papers, we wouldn't be standing here having this conversation."

"I'm not denying any of that, but who's to say that all of this didn't happen for a divine reason?"

"Sweetie, the only reason this happened is because we were both drunk and heartbroken— end of story. There's nothing celestial or prophetic about it. In fact, it's the opposite. We're making a mockery of what it means to be in love, committed, and united in matrimony."

"It doesn't have to be that way. This marriage can be whatever we make it," he maintained. "I know that it's a long shot, but so was quitting my job to open a health-food restaurant and making it a success; so was your losing both parents in the same night and still becoming a killer real estate broker instead of some drug statistic. And who would have thought that after I hid your lunch-box on the bus that first day of school in second grade that we'd end up as best friends? We've always beaten the odds and put the long shots within arm's reach."

"It's not the same thing," refuted London. "Back then, we both had goals that we wanted to achieve. Marrying you wasn't a goal. It was a ridiculous, irresponsible lapse in judgment." She saw in his eyes how much her words had hurt him, but there was no point in deluding him or herself.

"So, it's like that, huh? Are you giving up before we even try?"

London shirked his question. "Bernard, I've seen it happen too many times. Marriage changes everything for the worse. Look at my parents—do you know what they were doing right before the accident? Arguing about my mother wanting a divorce. Look at Creighton's marriage; look at your folks' marriage. Think about your brother. I stopped keeping count of his ex-wives years ago. Except for Nana and Pop-Pop, I don't know anybody who's happily married. Why would we be any different?"

"It won't be like that with us if we don't let it. We can make it work. We can be that exception."

"I don't understand why you're even pushing the issue. We've always been just friends. That's all we're meant to be."

"Says who?"

London exhaled and closed her eyes. "Bernard, you just don't get it, and I'm not in the mood to argue with you until you do. I'm too exhausted." She headed to her room. "Go on and make yourself at home. I'm going to bed, and I would appreciate it if you left me alone."

"London, wait," called Bernard. She stopped but didn't turn around. "We're still cool, right? I mean, this doesn't change the way we feel about each other as friends, does it?"

"I wouldn't want it to, but how can it not?" She faced

him. "When I look at you, I don't see my husband. I don't even see my best friend anymore. I only see a man who's jacked up my life."

He laughed, hoping she would join in. "Okay, this is over-the-top, drama-queen London, right? You don't really mean that, do you?"

Her hands fell to her sides, defeated. "What do you want me to say, Bernard? I don't think that we can come out of this unscathed. Somebody's going to get hurt." She lifted her head, and he thought he saw the tears rising in her eyes. "I don't think that things will ever be the same for us again."

Bernard watched her figure retreat down the hall. It was the second time within forty-eight hours that a woman he loved managed to break his heart.

Chapter 5

London had every intention of sleeping in the following morning. Her first client wasn't scheduled until eleven, and she wanted to make up for all of the sleep that she didn't get over the weekend. She had almost managed to forget that she and Bernard were married or that he was down the hall, asleep. The last thing she needed was to be awakened at five o'clock in the morning by rapper Ludacris, calling her the B-word and demanding that she get out of the way.

She sat up, startled. "What the—?" London flung the blankets off the bed and started down the hall, tightening the belt on her terrycloth bathrobe. She found Bernard glistening, fresh out of the shower and wrapped in a white towel from his waist to his knees, bobbing his head to the beat.

He smiled when he saw her. "Hey, babe."

"*Hey*, yourself!" she fired and stomped over to the stereo, kicking his shirt and shoes out of her path. She snatched the plug out of its socket. "Some of us are trying to sleep!"

"Oh, was the music too loud?"

"I don't know." She pinched his forearm, digging her nails into his skin until it began to turn red. "Did that hurt?"

"Ouch! All right, I'll keep it down." London slammed the door shut behind her, praying and resisting the overwhelming urge to strangle him. Before she could reach her bedroom, bass permeated the walls once again. Boiling over with rage, she marched back to his room and pounded on the door.

"What now?" Bernard asked with agitation. "I turned it down."

"I can still hear it. I want it off."

"Don't worry. I'll be out of here in about ten minutes," promised Bernard, hoping to pacify her.

"You're going to be out a lot sooner and for a lot longer if you can't respect my rules," she warned.

He frowned. "Rules? London, my mama died eight years ago."

"I'm not your mother, just your landlord. And look," she scooped up a damp washcloth hanging over her computer monitor, "you haven't even been here a whole day and it looks like a tornado ripped through here! Vanessa may have let you live like a pig, but I'm not Vanessa!"

"That's for sure," he mumbled under his breath.

She rolled up the comforter that had fallen from the sofa bed onto the floor. "This is ridiculous! I refuse to live like this."

"London, when have you ever known me to be neat and organized? You're the Type A in this marriage, not me."

London pinched one of his socks and tossed it into the wastebasket. "Bernard, you are an *A* in more ways than you know."

"Why are you messing with my stuff?" he shouted.

"Why are you messing up my house?"

Bernard exhaled, shaking his head. "I never knew you were such a witch first thing in the morning. If this is how I can look forward to starting off every day, I will start looking for a place immediately," he said half-jokingly.

"Good!" Again, London slammed the door shut and crawled back into bed. As soon she had begun to drift back off to sleep, she was distracted by Bernard knocking on her bedroom door.

She groaned. "What?"

"I just wanted to let you know that I was leaving," he answered softly, approaching her oak sleigh-bed.

"Thank God."

"After work, I'll probably stop by the apartment to get the rest of my things, so I might be a little late coming home."

"You don't have to give me a run-down of your schedule, Bernard. You'll get here when you get here."

"I just wanted to let you know in case you needed me."

"The day I need you, Bernard, will be the day I need a hole in my head. Now go on. I'm trying to sleep."

"London, I don't want to leave like this. I won't be able to focus at work if I know you're still angry. This is only our third day of marriage, after all. We're still supposed to be on the honeymoon," he joked.

"I'm not angry; I just want you to go."

He leaned down and tried to kiss her on the cheek, but she shrunk away from him and buried her head beneath the satin comforter.

"Do you want me to call you later on? Maybe we can grab a bite for lunch today."

She shook her head. He lifted his hand to touch her but stopped. "Well, I'll see you tonight when I get home. Don't oversleep, all right?" Slowly, he retreated toward the door, pausing to give her a chance to say something—anything. When she didn't, it began to dawn on him that the bond that had sustained them since they were in second grade was starting to unravel, and he was powerless to stop it.

Chapter 6

London sat down at her desk and kicked off her shoes. She rubbed her feet and vowed, as she did every morning, to start leaving the business suits and high heels at home and start coming to work in jeans and tennis shoes. She helped make up the staff that was comprised of a small but efficient bloc at Taylor Realty, a boutique agency set in the heart of Fulton County. London's small office, which scarcely left room for her desk and neatly arranged rows of real estate periodicals and journals on makeshift shelving, left a lot to be desired, but featured a wall-sized picture window that flooded the space with natural sunlight and a spectacular view of the city.

She smoothed back her bone-straight hair, which had been neatly parted and drawn into a sleek ponytail. She then pulled out her notebook and began tackling the day's agenda. No matter how much of a mess her personal life was, she was determined not to let it interfere with work.

"London, line one," paged the office receptionist.

She picked up the telephone. "Hello? London Harris speaking. How can I help you?"

"So, how long do you plan on rejecting my calls?" asked the familiar raspy voice on the other end of the phone.

London briefly closed her eyes and cringed. "I thought I asked you not to contact me."

"I tried. I just couldn't go another day without hearing your voice."

She felt her pressure rise. "What do you want, Creighton? What could we possibly have to talk about?"

"Us—what else?" he answered, as if everything was normal.

"Which 'us' would that be: me and you or you and your wife?"

"You've got it all wrong about Yolanda and me, baby, but you keep hanging up on me before I have a chance to explain."

"Then it should come as no surprise when I do it now. Good-bye, Creighton."

"Wait a second, just let me say one thing," he pleaded.

"What?" she asked, hating herself for wanting to hear it.

Creighton paused then cleared his throat. "I love you."

London would have been lying to herself if she didn't admit that hearing those words come from his lips jolted something in her that had been lying dormant since their relationship ended. She smiled to herself.

"I know you love me, too," he continued. "There's got to be a way for us to work this out."

"Creighton, I can't. Things have changed now, and there is no point in dredging up the past." She couldn't bring herself to reveal to him that she was now married.

"You don't know everything that's going on, London. If you meet me somewhere, I can explain and get everything out in the open."

It was tempting, but she knew she couldn't. London leaned back in the chair. "Did you mean it when you said you loved me?"

"Of course I did."

"Then let me go. This relationship isn't healthy for either one of us. We're through."

"Baby, I'm sorry that I hurt you, but you and I both know that we are far from over."

"Good-bye, Creighton. Please don't call here again." London slammed the phone down and cursed at her imaginary image of him and his too-little-too-late apology.

"That kind of language calls for a closed door," advised her co-worker and self-appointed, conservative older sister, Cassandra Hicks, who was standing in the doorway of London's office. As usual, she was impeccably dressed in a tailored suit and matching pumps. Not one strand of urchin-cropped hair, which was trimmed and colored perfectly to complement her mahogany skin, dared to stand out of place.

"Sorry about that. My morning seems to be going from bad to worse. I'm mad as the devil, I didn't get enough sleep, and that phone call from Creighton just elevated me to the heights of pistivity."

"I guess I don't have to ask how your weekend was," presumed Cassandra, letting herself into the office. "Whenever you start making up words, I know there's trouble brewing."

"Trouble doesn't even begin to describe it. If you wanna hear about my weekend, you probably *do* need to close the door for this one."

Cassandra shut the door. "What happened?"

London swiveled around in her desk chair. "Well, let's see . . . I went to see my grandmother, saw a couple of shows, lost about two-hundred dollars. Oh, did I mention that I also got married?"

Cassandra's mouth flew open. "*You what?*"

London held up her ring finger. Cassandra adjusted her glasses and zoomed in for a better look. "Is this for real?"

London nodded. "Yep. Pretty stupid, huh?"

"I knew that you and that guy Creighton have been seeing each other for a while, but I had no idea that it was so serious."

"It's not. Last week, I found out that Creighton already owns both a wedding ring and a wife, which was why I was so upset." She paused. "I'm married to Bernard."

"Girl, shut up!" roared Cassandra. "*Shut up*! Bernard? *We're-just-friends-and-that's-all-we'll-ever-be*   Bernard? How in the world did that happen?"

"It's a long story."

Cassandra pulled up a chair to London's desk. "Oh, I'm making time for this one! Spill it."

London filled her in on everything from finding out that Creighton was married to finding out that she was, too, and their run-in with her grandmother and the promise to devote at least a year to trying to make the marriage work.

"Wow," said Cassandra at last. "A whole year?"

"Yep—two days down and 363 to go."

"Dang . . . all I did this weekend was my laundry."

"We're already fighting. I'll be impressed if we haven't killed each other by Christmas."

Cassandra wrinkled her nose. "Is it that bad?"

London nodded. "If there was ever a marriage made in hell, this is it."

"You guys just need to get used to each other, that's all," consoled Cassandra.

"I *am* used to Bernard. What I'm not used to is having boxers on the floor and rap blasting in my ears at five in the morning and having what amounts to a fifteen-year-old boy in the house. You know me, Sandra. I like order. I like keeping things neat and clean. None of that describes Bernard."

"You said that you're the one who invited him to live with you. What did you expect?"

"I extended the invitation thinking that he'd be staying a few days, a week, tops, not until death do us part."

Cassandra stared at London. "I still can't believe it. You and Bernard just hopped on a plane and got married. That's crazy!"

"A lesson to the wise: never go to Vegas drunk and newly-dumped."

"Hey, look at the bright side," offered Cassandra. "On your silver anniversary, you'll both look back on this day and laugh."

"At least now I have something to look forward to," she replied sarcastically.

"And you've got to admit it, Lon: Bernard is very easy on the eyes," Cassandra added, twirling a lock of her hair around her finger.

"Yeah, easy on the eyes, but hard on the nerves."

"I think you just described every man I've ever dated," Cassandra quipped then leaned forward. "All right, moment of truth . . . while you two were in Vegas all liquored up and freshly married, did you and Bernard," her eyes fluttered, ". . . you know."

"Did we what?" London asked, frowning.

"Did you, um, *consummate* the marriage?" supplied Cassandra with a smirk.

"Sandra!"

"Well, did you?"

London grimaced and threw her hands up. "*Eww*—of course not! I could never sleep with Bernard—too much of an *ick* factor. It would be incestuous or something. He's like my brother."

"Well, according to the law, he's your husband now. And if you think that pretty thing is going to spend the next year practicing some kind of warped celibacy as a married man, you're crazier than I thought."

London covered her eyes. "I don't know what he's going to do because, husband or not, I'm officially placing everything on lock!"

"That's what you should have said when you were fooling around with Creighton," piped in Cassandra.

"Amen," retorted London with a laugh and leaned back in her seat. "San, I really messed up big time, didn't I? I don't know how I'm going to get out of this one."

"You might not have to. Who's to say that Bernard won't turn out to be the love of your life?"

"He won't in *this* lifetime." London shook her head. "As much as I hate to admit it, my heart is already spoken for by a man who's already taken."

Cassandra cocked her head to the side. "You're talking about Creighton, aren't you?"

London nodded. "It's still hard for me to believe that our whole relationship was just one lie after another."

"Welcome to Dating 101! Don't be so hard on yourself, though. It's happened to the best of us. He'll get what's coming to him soon enough."

London picked up a stack of folders. "Well, it's a moot point now. It's over between Creighton and me."

"Fortunately, you have that fine husband of yours to help you pick up the pieces," Cassandra reminded her.

"Bernard is a sad consolation prize, like winning a lifetime supply of tomato soup instead of the trip to Europe. Creighton is midnight strolls in the park and French wine and jazz," she relayed with a faraway smile. "And Bernard is a basketball game with beer and onion rings. Not exactly my idea of romance."

"Romance is a poor substitute for honesty and respect," observed Cassandra. "And he makes you laugh, and you know that he'll do anything in the world for you."

"Great—he can start by moving out of my house."

"What's wrong with him staying at your house?"

"The fact that it's *my* house. It's become painfully obvious that neither one of us is roommate material."

"You sure you're not trying to keep the bed empty for ol' Creighton?"

"Creighton is out of my life and my bed for good this time. I just wish . . ."

"What?"

She shook her head. "It doesn't matter."

Cassandra squeezed her hand, understanding. "Letting go is a lot easier said than done, isn't it?"

"You know, when I met him, I thought that after dating for thirteen years, I'd finally found the one. What a joke!"

"Don't miss the forest for the trees, girl." Cassandra looked down at London's ring. "Maybe you have found him."

"Girl, Bernard is just something to do until I have something better to do. I wouldn't count on us even making it six months, much less a whole year."

Cassandra stood up, preparing to leave. "Stranger things have happened, London."

"What could be stranger than me running off to Vegas and marrying Bernard?"

"Falling in love with him."

Chapter 7

Later on that night, London glanced out of her living room window at the cars zooming down the neon-lit street and then eyed the clock. It was 10:48, well past closing at Bernard's restaurant, and he still hadn't made it home. Cassandra's words were still resonating through London's mind. Suddenly, the thought of Bernard and Vanessa being alone together was met with a baffling twinge of jealousy. She slapped her hand against her forehead.

"Snap out of it, girl. You're losing it," London chided herself. She peeped through the blinds once more, hoping to spot Bernard's car. When she heard his key jiggling against the lock, she scurried to the sofa and tore open a magazine, hoping to appear indifferent to his late arrival.

" 'Sup?" greeted Bernard, closing the door behind him.

London didn't look up from her magazine. "Hey."

"How was your day?" he asked.

She nodded and turned the page. "Fine."

He tossed his keys into an empty space on the book shelf. "Did you tell anyone?"

"Not really. Just Cassandra. It's not something I'm really proud of or am going around broadcasting."

Bernard masked his irritation. "I told Rod. He took the news okay."

London continued skimming through her magazine. "He's your brother. He's supposed to be supportive." Casually, she broached the subject that had been weighing on her for the last two hours. "How did it go with Vanessa today?"

"All right, I guess. I haven't even gotten all my stuff out the apartment, and she's already moved that fool in."

London lifted her head. "You didn't try to beat him up or anything, did you?"

"No, I didn't have to. It was enough to watch her ego drop down about twelve notches when I told her that I was married to you."

"You told her?" London asked, astonished.

"It was priceless!" he boasted. "The kicker was when I told her that you were wearing her ring. That drove her crazy. Then she started accusing me of being in love with you all along." He shook his head. "She's probably over there still picking her face up off the floor."

As a woman who'd just found out that her lover was married, London couldn't help feeling sorry for Vanessa. "Bern, that wasn't very nice of you."

"Forgive me if I'm fresh out of compassion where she's concerned."

"I can't say I blame you. Creighton called, all contrite and apologetic, of course. I took great delight in telling him what he could do with his apology."

Bernard was impressed. "I underestimated you, London. I didn't think you had it in you to walk away, but you've proven me wrong. I'm proud of you."

"It has to be a lot tougher for you, though. We weren't

together nearly as long as you and Vanessa were. I know you miss her."

Bernard couldn't deny it. "I guess the manly thing to do would be to lie and say I don't, but I can't front, especially not with you. It's hard, you know? In the middle of the night last night, I reached out for her, just like I have every night for the past two years . . . except she wasn't there. I can't even remember what it feels like not having her lying next to me."

"It'll get easier, B."

He went on. "Do you want to know what the worst part was about seeing her today? Having to see her wearing that red dress I bought her for her birthday last year, knowing that she was wearing it for him."

London hugged him and kissed him on the cheek before letting go. "You don't have to try to be strong. If you need a shoulder, I'm here. I'm still your friend, you know."

Bernard shook his head. "No, I'm cool. You've seen me shed all of the tears I plan on dropping for a long time." The glint of sadness in his eyes fled after a moment. "The best way to deal with something like this is to keep it moving and do what you have to do. I can't get caught up in what could've been."

She nodded in agreement. "We have to focus on the future."

"And let the past stay where it is."

"You know, one day we're going to wake up, and it's not going to hurt so much anymore," London predicted. "All we can do now is look at it as a learning experience and try not to be bitter."

He shot a simper in her direction. "And just what have you learned from this, old wise one?"

"I've learned that love is overrated and to not put my heart into someone unless I want it to get broken."

"Spoken like a true spinster," remarked Bernard. "I

don't blame love. I blame falling in love with the wrong people. Love itself is a beautiful thing."

"How can you say that when you just saw your woman shacked up with another man?"

He shrugged his shoulders. "Hey, I've still got you, right?"

London smiled. "We've come a long way in three days, haven't we?"

"Yeah, I think this moment deserves a toast."

"Sounds good, but no wine," she insisted. "I'm sure I don't have to remind you about what happened the last time we drank together."

He returned from the kitchen with two champagne flutes and a pitcher of lemonade with lemon slices floating at the top.

"To moving on instead of hanging on," proposed London after he filled the glasses.

"I couldn't have said it better myself," concurred Bernard. They tapped flutes.

"This is nice," she acknowledged. "We're sitting down, having a drink and talking about our day. Nobody's fighting."

"Yeah, it's kind of like old times. You see, being married to me ain't so bad after all," touted Bernard, stretching out on the sofa.

She joined him. "Don't get ahead of yourself." She took another sip.

"It can't be too bad. You haven't kicked me out yet."

London set her glass down on the coffee table. "Speaking of which, I have great news. I found you a place. You're gonna love it, too. It's got a huge master bedroom, a covered deck and skylights. It's a rental, but I think that the owner might be interested in selling very soon." Bernard looked away, not saying anything. "What's wrong? I thought you'd be thrilled."

"You said that we were going to try," Bernard reminded her, feeling his frustration rising to the surface again.

"And we are, just from separate addresses."

"Separate homes, separate lives—what kind of marriage is that?" he struck back.

"I think this is the best way for us right now. Things are moving way too fast. The separation will give us a chance to step back, look at the bigger picture, and decide where we want to go from here."

"Separate but equal doesn't work, London. Remember Brown versus The Board of Education?"

Her mouth dropped. "Are you seriously trying to compare our marriage to the Civil Rights Movement?"

Bernard let out a deep breath. "I'm only saying that if we want this marriage to work, we need to be under the same roof."

"Just this morning, you said that you were going to start looking for your own place."

"I was frustrated and said the first thing that came to mind. I was just blowing smoke."

"Well, I'm not," she stated firmly. "I've made my decision, and it's final."

"So you're throwing me out?" he asked in disbelief.

London folded her arms across her chest. "It's for the best."

"London, if your heart isn't in this and you're going to put a halfhearted effort into making this marriage last, then say so," demanded Bernard.

"It's not that I don't want it to work. I just don't think it will. I don't feel like your wife, Bernard. I probably never will."

His countenance morphed into a scowl. "Why do you have to be so negative all the time?"

"I'm being pragmatic. One of us has to be."

Bernard looked at his glass then tossed it aside. "I'm

going out," he grumbled and stood up. "I need a real drink."

"Didn't you learn anything from that this weekend?"

"Yeah, I've learned that the only way a man can put up with you for more than twenty-four hours is if he's drunk."

His words stung. "Then go!" she fired as he moved toward the door. "Maybe then I can finally have some peace and quiet around here."

Bernard grunted something and slammed the door shut.

"And don't be slamming my door either!" she blared after him, hurling a pillow at the door in vain. As much as Bernard's assertion burned her, it hurt even more to see him leave. As friends, they couldn't stay mad at each other for more than five minutes. Now, it seemed like they couldn't agree for that long. London stared at the door waiting for him to walk back in, apologize, and pretend like the fight never happened. He didn't and, for the first time, she feared that he never would again.

London had already gone to bed by the time Bernard returned. She wasn't asleep but pretended to be when he poked his head into the door to look in on her. He whispered, "Good night, London" before retiring to his room. The part of her that loved him and missed her best friend wanted to reach out to him. Instead, she turned over in her bed, dreading the challenges and disappointments the rising of the sun would bring to both of them.

Chapter 8

London knew that something was wrong before she even approached her grandmother's house. It wasn't like Essie to not answer her phone, especially at eight in the morning, and she rarely left the house before noon unless she had a doctor's appointment. After three unanswered phone calls, London sped to the farmhouse bracing for the worst.

Standing at the front door, London could hear a loud commotion echoing from the living room. Then she heard something crash to the floor. She barged in through the unlocked door leading to the kitchen, running in the direction of the screaming voices.

"I want Della!" yelled her grandfather in a voice unfamiliar to her. "Y'all hiding her—I know you are!" Remnants from a broken vase and glass were scattered across the hardwood floor.

"Just calm down, Frank," soothed Essie in a reassuring tone. "You're getting yourself all upset."

"Is he all right?" asked London. Her grandfather, once a

brawny, towering man who never knew fear, now looked old and frightened.

"Go on back in the kitchen, Lonnie," instructed Essie. Frank stared at London through restless, vacant eyes. He had no idea who she was. The fear in his eyes gave rise to repulsion as he studied her face.

"Devil—you're the devil!" he spewed. "Go away—away, I tell you!"

"Sweetheart, that ain't the devil. That's Lonnie, your grandbaby!"

"I rebuke you, Satan!" he fired, raising his arms above his head.

"Pop-Pop, it's me." She reached out to touch him, but he quickly drew back his hand All of a sudden, he seemed fearful again and childlike.

"He got her. He took Della Ray," he whimpered.

"Come on, now. Let me take you to bed," said Essie, cowering him in her arms.

"Dell?" He looked up at Essie. "Where's Dell?"

Essie reached behind a throw pillow on the sofa and pulled out a tattered baseball. They had discovered that it was one of the few things that would calm him down. "Look, here's your ball."

He cradled it in his hands. "It's my baseball," he replied softly.

"Yes, now let's get you back on to bed." She began steering him toward the bedroom.

"Where's Dell?" he asked once more.

"Della Ray is just fine, you hear me? She says she wants you to lie down and have yourself a good, long nap."

He clutched his ball as she led him to the back of the house. He was still asking about his sister.

"How is he?" asked London when her grandmother returned.

"He's sleeping." Essie lowered her body onto the sofa. "He's all right now."

"How often does he get like that?"

"It's been happening a lot lately," she revealed. "But we manage."

London sat down beside her. "Doesn't it scare you when he does this?"

"Child, I've been loving that man more than forty years. There ain't too much Frank can do to scare me. Besides, God didn't give us the spirit of fear."

"Nana, I hate to ask, but . . ." London held her breath, "how much longer do you thinks he has?"

"Tomorrow ain't promised to none of us, Lonnie. I just thank the Lord for every second we do have together."

"It's funny . . . you and Pop-Pop are on borrowed time, and Bernard and I have all the time in the world and—"

"And you're wasting it!" reproved Essie. "I look at y'all, and I just shake my head. You and that boy could have it all and you're throwing it away."

"It's not the same, Nana. You two love each other."

"So do you and Bernard."

"In your way of thinking, I know that should be enough, but I'm looking for my true soul mate. I refuse to settle for anything less than that, and being married to Bernard is settling."

"What do you want, Lonnie? Some flashy, smooth-talking joker who ain't 'bout nothing like that shyster you've been running around here with? And don't think you're his only woman either. A man like that always has more than one. I wouldn't be a bit surprised if you found out he was married with a house full of children."

London wanted to ask her if she really *was* psychic. "I'm not saying that Creighton is perfect, but the feeling that I get when I'm around him is the way I want to feel about the man I'm committing the rest of my life to. I need that excitement; I need the butterflies."

"Honey, is that what you think marriage is all about? *Umph!* Just keep a-living, that's all I got to say."

"Nana, I've lived long enough to know what I need to be happy and fulfilled. As a friend, Bernard can do that. As a husband, he can't."

"How do you know that when you won't even give the man a chance?"

"I know *me*—that's enough. Bernard and I can't agree on simple things anymore. I'm starting to think that we won't even be friends by this time next year. Being his wife and being Bernard's friend are two vastly different animals. Marriage is hard enough under the right circumstances."

"You keep saying that the marriage is doomed and that you can't get along with your husband. Watch what comes out of your mouth, Lonnie; you're speaking death on your marriage without even realizing it. If you changed your doom-and-gloom attitude, things might work out better than you think."

"Nana, all the positive affirmations in the world can't make my marriage to Bernard be anything other than it is: a big, fat mess that keeps getting bigger."

Essie gave up. "I'm tired, Lonnie. I can't argue with you 'bout this today. Read your Bible and stay in prayer, and everything will work out the way it's supposed to. And stop nagging that man all the time. Matthew 12:25 says the town or family that fights will soon destroy itself. Now you remember that, you hear?" She stretched out on the sofa to relax her weary mind and body.

Watching Essie's quiet strength made London realize how petty and immature she must seem to her grandmother. "You rest, Nana. I'll straighten up in here before I go back to work."

Essie nodded, already half asleep. It dawned on London how exhausted her grandmother must be between trying to run a household and taking care of her grandfather, who had become almost infant-like with her having to bathe, clothe, and feed him. But London couldn't remember having ever heard her grandmother complain, not even once.

As she swept the broken glass into a pile, London spotted her grandparents' forty-year-old wedding picture on the floor. It, too, had fallen, but it didn't break.

"So this is love," she said to herself, gazing down at the picture. The photograph was bittersweet. She was elated to know that this kind of love was possible but crushed to think that, despite her best efforts, love that strong might elude her forever. Then she thought of Bernard, and for the first time, began to see their marriage as a union that might just work out after all.

Bernard unleashed a sigh of relief as the last of the morning rush exited his diner, *The Manic Organic*, too exhausted to trifle with the pub stools and coffee cups that were left out or the napkins strewn across the tiled floors. His brother and co-owner, Roderick, greeted the wait-staff as he entered into the restaurant three hours late.

"You finally decided to come through, I see," playfully scolded Bernard. "I've been here knee-deep in smoothies and fruit cups and complaining customers while you were somewhere hitting the snooze button on the alarm clock."

"Man, it was one of those nights," growled Rod, an older, leaner version of Bernard, though not quite as handsome.

Bernard swept bread crumbs off of the countertop. "So who was she this time—Kayla? Rhonda? Destiny?"

"Rhonda and Kenya . . . and not in a good way either."

Bernard winced. "Ouch."

"Plus Danielle's been sweatin' me about this child support and alimony. I've been ducking and dodging deranged females all morning!"

"I tried to tell you not to marry that girl." Bernard shook his head. "Married for eighteen months and you let her get you for half."

"I wouldn't be so quick to judge if I were you," he retorted. "I can't think of a bigger mistake you could have made than marrying that looney-toon, London, and you gave up Vanessa's fine self to do it."

"Hey, now—that's my wife you're talking about."

"That's still funny to me." He laughed, but his smile vanished when he spotted Vanessa's Camry pulling into the parking lot. "It looks like I came in just in time."

"What?"

Rod motioned his head toward the door. "Guess who's coming to breakfast?"

Bernard's bottom lip fell as Vanessa strolled in. She wore a scarf tied around her spiraled hair as a makeshift headband that matched her black and white houndstooth mini-dress. She was carting a large cardboard box. Seeing her looking so beautiful made it impossible for Bernard to hate her, but knowing that another man had taken his place in her heart allowed him to come dangerously close to doing so.

"We're closed," he grumbled, refilling the napkin holder.

"The sign on the door says differently. Besides, I didn't come here to eat. I wanted to give you something."

He occupied himself with mundane tasks to keep from looking at her. "Does your boyfriend know you're here?"

"Alonzo is the one who insisted that I come. He says that we need closure if we're ever going to move on."

"Doesn't seem like you're having any trouble moving on to me," stated Bernard.

"I'm not the one who's already married, now am I?" she fired back.

"It's just a matter of time, though, right?" He finally met her gaze. "Look, why are you here, Vanessa? I thought we said all we needed to say the other night."

"This is all your stuff," she plunked the cardboard box down into his hands, "CDs, razors, a few old shirts, pictures of your mom, and your lucky socks."

He set the box on the counter, showing no emotion. "You didn't have to come way down here. You could've just thrown it away."

Vanessa nodded. "I could have, but I wanted to see you."

"Why?"

"To apologize and to talk. I don't like how we ended things between us."

"How we ended things or how *you* ended things?" He walked behind the counter.

"Okay, how I ended things," she conceded, propping herself in front of him. "But it's not like I didn't love you, Bernard, or that I don't still care about you."

"Vanessa, you're living with another man. How can you look me in the eye and say that?"

"I can say it because it's true. Bernard, I never meant—"

"Yeah, you never meant to hurt me, right?"

"I didn't," she asserted.

He muttered, "Whatever, Vanessa."

Vanessa huffed and rolled her eyes. "I can see that I'm wasting my time here. Have a nice life, Bernard."

Bernard's conscience began to gnaw at him as Vanessa started to exit. "Vanessa, wait a second." She turned around. "There are no hard feelings, all right?"

"Thank you." She came toward him. "Bernard, I'm not even going to ask you if we can be friends; I know it's too soon for that. I just hope—"

The sincerity in her voice touched him. "What?"

"I just hope that one day, you won't hate me so much," she added.

"I couldn't . . . I could never hate you, Vanessa," he admitted.

She smiled and touched his hand. "It really was difficult for me, too, Bernard. I loved you; I still do, probably always will. Just because we didn't make it doesn't mean that what we had wasn't special."

He pushed the cardboard box aside. "How special could it be if all we meant to each other can fit into an old box? Is this all we have to show for the last two years?"

"I know that you're married now, and I'm back with 'Zo, but nothing can ever replace what we shared. This box doesn't define what we had. The only place big enough to hold our love, and our life together is my heart." Her eyes welled with tears.

Vanessa's words and tears melted the lingering animosity in his heart toward her. Bernard came to her and held her face in his hands. Just as he blanketed his arm around her as she sobbed into his chest, London, still on a high from her new revelation about her marriage, parked her car and headed into the restaurant. When she pulled back the glass doors, the first image she saw was her husband cradling his ex-girlfriend. Their embrace was followed by a tender kiss on the lips. To Bernard and Vanessa, it signaled good-bye; to London, it was a kiss a death on her marriage.

The sight was almost as crushing to her as learning that Creighton was married. Other men, she expected to be liars and cheaters, but not Bernard. He was supposed to be different, at least in that capacity, especially when it came to her.

She eased out without Bernard ever seeing her. It was just as well, London told herself. She knew that the marriage was a mistake and now she had proof. Any part of her heart that she'd been willing to share with Bernard was closed, possibly for good.

Chapter 9

Bernard walked into the townhouse that night exhaling the spicy aroma flowing through the living room. His mouth began to water. A long day of stock ordering, ending his relationship with Vanessa, and running interference for his philandering brother had prevented him from breaking long enough to eat, and biting into a savory meal would be the perfect ending to a hectic day. He spotted London seated on the couch surrounded by small white cartons and a hearty plate with mounds of food heaped on top of it.

"What do you have over there that's smelling so good?" he asked.

"Wok 'n Roll. I've been craving this General Tao chicken all day today." She licked duck sauce off of her finger.

Bernard settled down next to her, rubbing his hands together in ravenous anticipation. "I haven't had anything to eat all day. I'm starving." He looked around the table. "So, which one of these boxes is for me?"

She stopped chewing long enough to answer him. "I guess yours is the one still at Wok 'n Roll."

"What?" He stood to survey the cartons and found that they were all empty. He angrily flung one across the room.

"What is wrong with you?" she shrieked, shocked by his reaction. "Are you crazy?"

"I'm well on my way, thanks to you!"

"What's your problem?"

"Why would you go out and just get food for yourself, huh? Did it ever occur to you that your husband might be hungry, too?"

"*Hello*—you own a restaurant!"

"That's not the point." He glared at her. "You're selfish, you know that? You don't ever think about anybody but yourself."

"Oh, so now I'm selfish because I stopped to pick up something to eat? Grow up, Bernard!"

"*You* need to grow up and start thinking of someone other than London."

"How can you say that to me when I just spent the past two hours helping Nana with Pop-Pop after putting in a full day at work?"

"It would be great if you'd put in at least *half* that much effort into our marriage."

"I give one hundred percent to the people and things I care about. Obviously, this marriage isn't one of them." London was still bitter about the sight she walked in on at the restaurant and took pleasure at taking shots at the places she knew would hurt him most.

"You know, I'm really starting to understand why you can't sustain a relationship for more than a couple of weeks. My brother was right about you."

"And he's the resident expert on relationships? If Rod is your source for understanding women, you're better off being gay. Maybe if you listened to him a little less, your girlfriend wouldn't be sleeping with another man. So before you try to advise me on how to keep a man, learn how to keep a woman." Bernard couldn't say anything, but the veins creasing his forehead said it all. "What's wrong—truth hurt?"

He shook his head. "You're cold, London, a selfish, cold-hearted b—"

"I wish you would!" she hissed, getting up in his face.

He backed away. "I don't have to," Bernard replied, scooping up his car keys. "You already know what I'm thinking. You look in the mirror everyday. You know what you are. I'm out."

"So this is your M.O? When you don't get your way, you storm out of here like a big baby? Not man enough to stick around?"

He continued toward the door. "You're the one who said you wanted me gone, right? This is what you asked for, you ought to be happy."

"Then, on that note, you've got until this weekend to leave for good. Now, I can be ecstatic." She brushed past him.

"Don't get it twisted, London. You ain't all that," he lashed out at her. "I can go out to the mall right now and find ten just like you. Lonely, desperate chicks with an attitude are a dime a dozen." She shot lethal glares into him, but that didn't stop Bernard from continuing. "I don't have to put up with this bull. You say you don't want me, huh? Fine, you won't have me!" He snatched up his wallet and stormed out.

Chapter 10

"What storm blew you over this way?" asked Essie when she looked up and saw Bernard standing in the doorway.

"Hurricane London." He sat down at the counter as she moved about the kitchen finishing dinner.

"Don't tell me y'all are at it again? Lord, that girl won't listen to a thing I tell her!" She reached into the cabinet and pulled out three plates. "Now, you can eat, but I ain't fixing your plate!"

Bernard chuckled. "Yes, ma'am." He stood up and began loading mashed potatoes onto a platter. "It's all so confusing, you know?"

"What is?"

"Marriage. If you read the Bible, you'd think that marriage is supposed to be this sacred and honorable institution. There's nothing in there about what to do when your spouse just buys dinner for herself or throws all your mistakes in your face."

"Sure it does, baby. That's why the Bible says 'in all your getting, get understanding.' You just have to know where to look and how to read in between the lines. It would help if both of you put in an appearance at Bible Study once in awhile."

"I'm trying, Miss Essie. I want to be a good husband, but I don't know if I can. I never saw that when I was growing up. My dad left when I was two, forcing my mom to raise six kids by herself, so what could I learn from him?"

"Well, merely having the desire to be a good husband is a step in the right direction. A lot of marriages don't even have that."

"But most couples will at least *try* to make it work. London is just going through the motions, counting the days until this marriage is over."

"Yeah, she's a stubborn one, all right. It's in her nature, I suppose. Her mama was the same way. But be patient with her; she'll come around."

"Maybe we're just not meant to be," he concluded.

"Or maybe y'all are and you just don't know it yet."

Bernard sat down at the table with his plate and asked the blessing over the food. "Tell me, Miss Essie. Are all you Harris women as pig-headed as the one I have?"

"Watch it, boy. You're talking to one of those Harris women!" They both laughed. "We all got a mean streak, but we love hard, too."

"I think that London's got a little more of the mean streak than the love one."

"It might seem like that now, but, child, there's always two sides to a story. Did you think about things from her point-of-view before you rushed over here?"

Bernard realized that he hadn't, but he wasn't ready to concede yet. "No matter how you look at it, she was in the wrong," he argued.

"Was she, baby?" She poured him a glass of iced tea.

"Yeah. With her, it's all about London all the time.

Would it really have been asking too much for her to call and say that she was stopping by the store and to see if I wanted something to eat?"

Essie set the pitcher down, dismayed. "Is that what you're mad and huffing and puffing around here for?"

He felt silly. "Yes; partially, anyway."

"Well, what's the other part?"

He pushed the potatoes around on his plate. "It's not so much about the food as it is her attitude about everything, especially our relationship. I'm not a factor in any of her decisions, even something as simple as getting some dinner. I just wish that she would put forth a little more effort." He looked up at her. "Am I being unreasonable? Am I really asking too much?"

"No, but is that what you told her or did you make her think you were upset about the dinner?" He didn't say anything. "You see, Bernard, if you gon' fight, you at least got to know what you're fighting about. You weren't mad because she didn't get you any food; you're mad because you feel like she doesn't care about you the way she ought to. If that's the case, then you need to tell her; not blow up over something stupid. You see, this is what happens when you try to be all fast and get married without some kind of pre-marital counseling with the pastor. That poor girl probably doesn't know what to think, and it's obvious that neither of you know the first thing about being married."

"I still say she should have gotten me some food," he grumbled, digging into the mashed potatoes. "Vanessa would have never done that."

Essie stopped what she was doing. "Boy, I hope to God that you weren't stupid enough to say that to Lonnie. You don't ever want to compare one woman to another one, not even as a compliment. Anyway, you're the one who works at a restaurant. You can't get mad at her because you didn't have enough sense to fix you a plate on the way out. If anything, she should be mad at you for not asking if *she* wanted *you* to bring some food home."

"I suppose."

"And did you ask her about her day before you decided that she was being selfish and inconsiderate? I bet you didn't. You don't know what that girl has gone through today. If you had asked, maybe you'd understand why she didn't get you anything. And you've got to remember that Lonnie ain't never lived with nobody but me and her granddaddy, and she moved out of here years ago. It probably never occurred to her to ask you because she's so used to just having to look out for herself. If you ask me, Lonnie is not the one being selfish in this situation—you are."

He bit into his chicken. "You don't cut corners, do you?"

"Ain't no need to. No time for it either. I believe in calling a spade a spade. And I ain't just telling you this because she's my granddaughter. When she's in the wrong, I get on her just as hard. But I'm gon' tell you when you're wrong, too, especially when you come over here eating up all my food."

Bernard laughed. "I can't help myself when I get in your kitchen, Miss Essie, but I appreciate you for kicking my butt about London. I feel bad about the way I left things. I shouldn't have walked out on her like that."

"You didn't even tell her where you were going, did you?" He shook his head. "That's your wife, Bernard, and you can't go running out every time there's a problem. All that does is prove to Lonnie that she can't trust you to be there when she needs you or when things get rough. Women need that security. They need to know that you're going to be there no matter what, especially a girl like Lonnie. I don't think she's ever really gotten over her parents' death. As hard as me and her granddaddy tried, we could never love her enough to fill that hole left in her heart."

"London knows that she can count on me."

"How is she supposed to believe that if you're over here, leaving her just like everybody else?"

"I tell her that I'm here for her all the time, Miss Essie."

"A woman don't care nothing about what you say. A mouth can say anything. A woman is looking at what you do and how you treat her. And don't ever leave without telling your wife where you gon' be. How do you expect to establish trust? Son, Lonnie has always had a real hard time trusting people, but she does trust you—*did*, anyhow."

He dropped his head and exhaled. "I guess I blew it, didn't I?"

"You can always go home and make amends, but you can't do it sitting here eating up all my dinner. You know where you need to be."

"You're right." Bernard stood up and handed her his plate. "If it's okay with you, I'd like to take the rest of this to go." He thought for a moment. "Maybe I ought to get a little of that peach cobbler for London. I know it's one of her favorites."

Essie covered his plate in foil and handed it back to him with a smile. "You're learning. Keep living, you'll get there. I'm praying for ya'll. You keep praying, too."

"Yes, ma'am."

"And, honey, your wife is your gift from God. When a man gets himself a wife, then he finds favor with God. You need to honor Lonnie, and don't you ever put anything ahead of her needs, you hear me?"

"I do, Miss Essie, and I thank you." He bent down to hug her. "We're both very blessed to have you in our lives."

"Well, you're family now, and I want you to do right by

my girl. I know she's hard-headed, but she's still my baby.
Try to get along with her. The Word says to patiently try to
put up with each other and love one another. That's
what's kept me and Frank going all these years, and it'll
work just as well for you."

Bernard left Essie's house with a new determination to
be a better husband. He only hoped that the time apart
had inspired the same thing in London. When he walked
in, he found her asleep on the couch. He was overcome
with remorse the moment he saw her.

"I'm sorry," he whispered and leaned down to kiss her
on the cheek. "I shouldn't have said those things, and I
shouldn't have tripped about the food. Can you forgive
me?"

She stirred a little. "It's fine."

"No, it's not. You're my wife, and it's my duty to honor
you and to put your feelings first. And what I said about
you being lonely and desperate—nothing could be further
from the truth. You're one of the most unique and beautiful people I know. Any man would be lucky to have you as
a wife."

She sat up, rubbing the sleep from her eyes. "Bernard,
you're taking this whole wife thing way too seriously. I'm
your homegirl, remember? We always fight and then we
get over it."

"It's different now that we're married, at least it should
be."

She yawned. "You've been talking to Nana again, haven't
you?" London shook her head. "She almost got me today,
too. I love my grandmother with all my heart, but she
doesn't understand our circumstances. She only sees
black and white."

"To her, it doesn't matter how or why we got married,
only that we are. I'm not so sure I disagree with that."

"Bernard, you're no more in love with me than I am

with you. Let's just go to bed and call it a day. I'm tired."
She rose from the sofa.

"Hold up. I brought you something." Grinning, he pre-
sented her with the peach cobbler.

She lifted the aluminum foil and smiled. "Thanks."

"It's my way of apologizing." She pinched off a piece of
cobbler and ate it. "So am I forgiven?"

"Definitely," she mumbled, breaking off another piece.

"Well, you know what the best part about fighting is,
don't you?"

She raised her eyes. "What?"

"Making up." He leaned into her and, without warning,
slid his lips over hers and stole a kiss. His kiss left her
speechless, and for the first time in a long time, breathless.

Chapter 11

London walked in from work, and as she had the night before and on her way out the door that morning, scuttled past Bernard without so much as throwing a glance in his direction.

"Are you still giving me the silent treatment?" he asked.

She laid her briefcase on the sofa and stepped out of her heels. "That depends on whether or not you plan to assault my lips like that again?"

"Assault?" he bucked.

"Yes, *assault*! What were you thinking when you kissed me last night?"

"I wasn't, really. But you have to admit, London, it wasn't that bad. Truth be told, it was kind of hot," he added with a smile.

"If by 'hot' you mean uncomfortable, invasive, and un-provoked, then, yes; it was scorching."

"Why are you acting like kissing me was the worst thing in the world?"

"No, there are worst things—nuclear holocaust, starving babies in Africa, September 11th, Hurricane Katrina, to name a few."

Bernard traced the line of her lips with his finger. She shivered a little. "London, there was a spark in that kiss, and you know it."

London grew uneasy and defensive. "What I *know* is that this house is a wreck!" She stepped over his boots lying on the floor. "Look at this place! Didn't you take the day off?"

"No, I worked from home. It's not the same thing. I spent most of the day on the phone with distributors and my accountant, not to mention bill-paying and teleconferences. I was just as busy here as I would have been at the restaurant."

She checked the washing machine, livid to find the same clothes still in there from the day before. "Would it have killed you to bother to check the laundry?"

"Did you hear what I just said I've been doing all day?"

London began unloading the dryer, flinging the clothes into a basket. "I don't see how anyone who goes through as many towels and wash cloths as you do can sit around here all day and not so much as fold a sock."

Bernard joined her. "Fine . . . move. I'll do it."

She pulled away from him. "No, don't try to help me now."

He reached for the basket. "Will you stop being so stubborn?"

"I said I've got it!" shrieked London.

"And I said I'll do it. Go sit down." They both tugged on the basket, neither giving in to the other.

"Bernard, I don't need your . . ." The basket capsized and all of the clothes tumbled to the floor. ". . . help."

London stooped down to pick up the clothes and snatched a shirt from his grasp when he tried to pitch in. "Will you leave me alone? Haven't you *helped* enough already?"

"You think I don't know what all this attitude is about?" he asked, amused by it all.

"It's about what an inconsiderate and lazy pig you are," she replied.

"No, it's about your not wanting to talk about the kiss."

She brusquely folded a towel. "Of course I don't want to talk about it. I don't even want to *think* about it. Knowing that it happened is sickening enough without having to relive the moment in some long, drawn-out discussion. In fact, you'd be doing me a huge favor to never bring it up again."

Bernard realized that it was pointless to pursue that conversation with her. "Why don't I give you a hand with some of these socks over here?"

He rolled up a pair of socks and playfully tossed them at her, striking the side of London's head. She retaliated by rolling up a towel and chucking it at him. A corner of the terrycloth scratched his eye.

"Hey, that hurt!" he bellowed.

She sneered. "Good."

"Oh, yeah?" He balled up a shirt and aimed it at her face, barely missing her.

"This isn't funny, Bernard," she wailed, side-stepping him.

"It is to me. *Take that!*" He laughed as she unsuccessfully tried to dodge another flying garment.

London scrambled to her feet and hurled a pair of jeans at him. "Do something!" she dared him, drawing back a pillow case.

He snatched up a bath sheet. "Oh, I'm going to do something, all right!" He charged toward her, but instead of hitting her with the towel, he swept her up in it, pulling her into a kiss with the same intensity and passion as he had the night before.

She broke away and pounded his chest. "Why do you keep doing that?"

"Why do you keep fighting it? What are you afraid of?"

"I'm not afraid of anything, least of all you."

"Are you denying that you feel something between us? I know you won't admit it, but I felt something in that kiss, London."

"You should be more concerned about what you'll be feeling if you pull another stunt like that. Never underestimate my right hook or a knee to the crotch." She was moving erratically and breathing hard.

"Look at you—you're all worked up. The only time you get like that is when somebody's gotten next to you," noted Bernard. "If you can't be honest with me, be honest with yourself."

"You're deluded." Fuming, London began picking up the clothes again.

"You have to admit, it felt kind of good, though," he persisted.

She rolled her eyes. "It was nothing to write home about," she told him.

He stooped down to pick up her bra, suspending it from his fingers. "Can you believe that after all these years that last night was the first time we ever kissed?"

London snatched it away from him. "And if you don't mind, I'd like for today to be the *last* time that it ever happens."

He sidled up to her, pressing his lips against her cheek. "Why can't we just let nature do its thing?"

"There's nothing natural about kissing you or," she pushed him off of her, "doing anything else with you that requires your body to be near mine."

"So you're not the least bit attracted to me? Not the least bit curious?"

"No."

"Look at me. You know I can tell when you're lying." He

tilted her chin up to make her face him. "Now answer the question again."

She moved his hand. "Bernard, this is stupid."

"Humor me, all right? Did you feel something when we kissed?"

"You mean other than the nausea?"

He rolled his eyes. "Yeah, other than the nausea."

London refused to look directly at him. "No, I didn't feel a thing."

He snickered. "You're lying."

"*I am not!*"

"Then kiss me again." He postured himself inches from her face. "Come on, I dare you."

He teased her lips with his tongue. She could feel her resolve faltering. She quickly regained it and not a moment too soon. "That's enough playing," London replied, breaking the spell. "Let's get back to work." She tore herself from him. She closed her eyes and touched her lips. It was almost as if she could still feel him kissing her. It was a memory that her lips wouldn't soon forget.

As she continued picking up the overturned laundry, she discovered that her heart was doing something that it hadn't done in a while. It was racing, proving to be a much weaker liar than her words were.

Chapter 12

"I guess I don't have to ask what you and Bernard were doing last night," teased Cassandra when she spotted London dozing off at her desk.

London grudgingly sat up and yawned. "I can't tell you what he was doing, but I was up all night torturing myself in the name of soul-searching."

"Why? What happened?"

London sighed. "He kissed me."

"Ohh, did he carry your books home from school, too?" mocked Cassandra.

"Go ahead, make jokes. This is serious, Cassandra."

Cassandra apologized for being insensitive and sat down. "So, he kissed you. Where's the crime in that? He's your husband."

"Kissing is only the beginning. Next, he's going to want to go out on dates and have sex and fall in love and become this whole mushy couple thing that I'm not trying to be a part of."

"Again, I ask, where is the crime?" Cassandra shook her head. "Lon, it's just me and you right now. What's going on here? You're married to a great guy, and you're one of the few women lucky enough to actually like the man you're married to. Any girl in her right mind would kill to be in your position, including me, so what's the deal? Why are you hell-bent on sabotaging it?"

"I know how it looks on the surface to you and everybody else, but it's much deeper than that. I can't just snap my finger and create a happy marriage out of nothing. Nobody seems to understand that part of the equation."

"Then explain the problem to me. Is this about Creighton?"

"A little," she admitted.

"A little or completely?"

"San, Bernard isn't any more ready to be committed than I am despite whatever he says. I saw him all over Vanessa the other day at his restaurant."

"What were they doing?" pumped Cassandra.

"Let's just say that the service he was giving was not on the menu. And to think that I'd actually gone over there to work things out."

"What did he say when you confronted him?"

"I didn't tell him, and I don't intend to. It's just as well anyway, especially since God knows I'm not over Creighton."

"I thought you were working on that."

"I'm trying, but I loved him. I mean, I *really* loved him."

"And he ground your heart into crumbs," weighed in Cassandra. "Not even crumbs, more like unidentifiable traces of dust."

London exhaled. "But you want to know what the really sad part is? A part of me still wants him. How sick is that?" She shook her head. "Maybe Bernard *is* the one for me. I deserve someone who's just as dysfunctional and demented, and he's the only other person I know of who's more screwed up than I am."

"You're not sick, London. You fell in love with a man-whore, and who hasn't done that? But you do deserve to be happy and to be with a man who will cherish you. I think Bernard wants to be that person if you'd let him."

"I know that he's a good man, and I do love him in my own way. I just don't want to be his wife."

"You'll never know until you try."

"I'm still there, San. That should count for something."

Cassandra picked up a photograph of Creighton that was laying face-down on the desk. "You want to know what I think is really going on here?"

"Not really, but that won't stop you from telling me."

Cassandra looked down at the picture. "I think you're scared, London. I think that Creighton broke your heart so badly that you're afraid to trust anyone else with it."

"This isn't about fear," clarified London, snatching the picture and stashing it in her drawer. "Even if it was, who wouldn't be scared in my position? Bernard and I got married for all the wrong reasons. The worst case scenario is that I'll get hurt all over again. The best is that I'd lose the best friend I've ever had. Who wants to deal with odds like that?"

"The best case scenario is that you and Bernard could have a wonderful marriage, make lots of babies, and live to see a hundred years together. Did you ever consider that one?"

"No, I stopped believing in fairy tales when I was seven. Losing both parents at the same time tends to do that to a person."

"So, now you're afraid to let anyone get too close," surmised Cassandra.

"Will you stop trying to psycho-analyze me? I'm fine," insisted London, her voice rising in pitch. "I don't have some sort of commitment phobia. I *want* to be in a good relationship, but life has shown me that 'happily ever after' doesn't exist."

"London, if you're holding out for perfection and guarantees, you might as well give up now."

"I know that, but I do believe that I can do a lot better than Bernard."

Cassandra crossed her arms in front of her. "What's better than a man who practically worships the ground you walk on?"

"Creighton. Our relationship was as close to perfection as I've ever gotten."

"He treated you like dirt."

"I'm not talking about that. I mean the way I felt so alive when I was with him."

Cassandra shook her head. "Lust can be a powerful drug."

"It was more than that, San."

"Was it really, Lon? Was there any deep sharing going on between the two of you? Do you know his fears? His dreams? Did you ever pray together?"

"When two people connect the way we did, you don't need to do all that," she disputed.

"There is no real connection if you *don't* have that."

"Talking can be overrated. Bernard and I talk all the time. I know every insipid thing he's ever done, said, or thought, but with Creighton, we didn't need words. We just knew."

"You sound like a woman who got a hold of some great sex and decided to confuse that with love, which is one thing while you're lying in bed sweating your weave out with him. But what about afterward, when you realize that in exchange for giving this man your heart, body, and soul, all you're left with is the guilt, a sore back, and a broken heart? I know you want more from life than that."

"I do, but not with Bernard."

"London, I think you're walking away from your blessing and don't even know it. And for a creep who didn't even respect you enough to tell you he was married. If Creighton was all that, he wouldn't have lied about his situation and made a fool out of you the way he did. Even if he left his wife tomorrow, what's to stop him from cheating on you like he's done to her? You know what they say—if he'll cheat with you, he'll cheat on you."

"You're acting like I'm about to go crawling back to him. I'm not."

"Umph, you'll be back with him before this year is out. I can see it in your eyes." Cassandra shook her head. "And I couldn't be more disappointed."

Chapter 13

"Well, look a-here! It's about time you two decided to come over for dinner. You been married almost a whole month and ain't bothered to cross my table yet," said Essie, letting Bernard and London into her house.

"I've been over plenty of times. We both have," contradicted London.

"I'm talking about together. Put your purse down over there. I tell you, there's nothing like a big old Sunday dinner after a good sermon. I was mighty pleased to see the two of you in church today."

"Well, you've dropped more than enough hints about our attendance," murmured London as Bernard removed her blazer.

"Then maybe you should stop giving me a reason to have to do that."

London waltzed over to her grandfather seated at the far end of the table. She kissed him on the forehead. "Hey, Pop-Pop, how are you feeling?" He raised his right hand slightly to acknowledge her presence.

"Bernard, you go on over there and sit down. London,

you come over here and fix his plate," directed Essie with a ladle in hand.

London smacked her lips. "Bernard can fix his own plate. Let's see what you've got over here in this pan that's making my mouth water." She snatched the lid off of the roaster and inhaled the aroma of hen, spices, and onions.

"Gal, did you hear what I said? Now, all that feminist stuff gets checked at the door when you pass under my roof. Around here, we honor our men, so go over there and fix your husband's plate like I told you."

London pouted and obeyed as Essie set a plate down in front of Frank.

London brought her plate to the table, but left Bernard's at the stove, to his chagrin. Perturbed, Bernard sighed and got up to retrieve his plate, then led them all in grace.

"Lonnie, guess who I saw at the grocery store yesterday," began Essie after all of the "amens" had been said. "Dena Wilson—you remember her, don't you?"

"Yeah, she was our valedictorian," replied London, swallowing a forkful of collard greens.

"I ran into her a couple of years ago," said Bernard. "They were talking about making her assistant D.A. back then, one of the youngest the city's ever had."

"Oh, she gave all that lawyer stuff up after she had the twins," informed Essie. "Now, she and her husband's got two of the prettiest little girls you ever want to see and another baby on the way. She says they're praying for a little boy this time."

London shook her head and muttered, "That's such a waste."

"There's power in prayer, Lonnie, and I won't have you talking that way in my house!"

"I'm not talking about prayer. I mean this fake 1950s life she's trying to lead. Dena has one of the most brilliant minds I know. She belongs in that courtroom, not sitting at home baking cupcakes and trotting off to play groups."

"I think it's cool that she wants to stay home and raise her family." Bernard directed his words at London. "I admire any woman who wants to put her children and her husband first."

"*You* would," London shot back.

"The world was a better place when more women did that. The Bible says that the woman's place is in the home. The man is the one charged to go out and work," voiced Essie, feeding her husband.

"Yes, and while she's at home changing diapers and watching Jack and Jill go up the hill for the millionth time, her husband will be somewhere making deals and sharing ideas with other women who can stimulate him in ways she no longer can. Then what is she left with? A divorce and a lifetime subscription to Dr. Seuss books. No, thank you. I have goals and a career to think about, too."

"Your plans might not necessarily be the Lord's plan, sugar. We make our own plans, but the Lord decides where we will go."

"Amen," seconded Bernard. "And if nothing else, if he did leave, she'd be entitled to half and child-support. Just ask my brother!" Bernard sat down to the table. "But no man in his right mind is going to up and leave with some chick on the side when he's got a woman who's the mother of his children and taking care of him and the house. Now, I'm not saying that he won't do *other things* with the chick on the side, but he ain't leaving home."

"Tell that to all the women who have had that very thing happen to them," retorted London. "But what else can you expect when you turn your whole life and financial independence over to a man like that? I would never give any man that kind of power over me *or* my money."

"When you get married, it's supposed to be the household's money, not mine and yours," Bernard barked back to her.

"Me and your grandfather never did anything separate when it came to the money. When it's all in one pot, nobody can complain." Essie wiped Frank's mouth as he sat drooling.

"You know, money is the number one cause for divorce in this country," threw in Bernard.

"That's why I believe that what's yours is yours and what's mine is mine and that everybody should leave with what they came with. I'm all for pre-nups and whatever else you need to do to protect yourself," proclaimed London.

Bernard frowned. "Why would you go into a marriage planning for your divorce?"

London sprinkled some pepper on her food. "In today's world, why wouldn't you? Marriage is a big joke nowadays."

Essie shot her a menacing glare. "Does this look like a joke to you?" she asked testily, sitting next to Frank.

"I don't mean you, Nana. You know that," London stated.

Essie exhaled. "In a marriage, you take care of one another, plain and simple. Whether it's financially or physically or emotionally, you look out for each other and act as one unit. The sooner the two of y'all realize that, the better off you'll be."

"Well said," concurred Bernard. "It's not about scheming and trying to take advantage of somebody like you're trying to make it seem, London. You could learn a lot from Dena."

"All I could learn from Dena is how to be somebody's doormat," she fired.

"Bernard, what did I tell you about making comparisons?" said Essie.

"You don't have to tell him nothing, Nana. That's what's wrong with him now. He's got all the answers on how to be a good wife, but can answer none of the questions about how to be a good husband!"

Bernard turned to London. "And you're the definition of a good wife?"

"Stop it, both of you!" broke in Essie. "I won't have this fighting, not over my table."

"I'm sorry," apologized Bernard.

"Yeah, you bet you are!" mumbled London, who flung her napkin on the table and walked out.

Chapter 14

"Here," said London, dropping a slip of white paper into Bernard's lap as he watched the football game following their visit with her grandparents. It was the first word she'd said to him since their argument at the dinner table.

"What's this?"

"Your half of this month's bills."

"Bills?"

"After all that trash you were spouting today about couples and money, you didn't think that you were going to come up in here rent-free, did you?"

"No but," he scanned her list, "a hundred dollars in groceries? I don't even eat any of that stuff you buy."

She crossed her arms. "Oh, really? Because there are about two full bowls of my frosted flakes that are unaccounted for."

He continued to inspect the list. "And why do I have to pay half of your credit card bill?"

"Because I've had to charge household items on it."

"The new shoes that you were parading around in last week were not for the household; those were for you."

"That was a quality of life decision. With all of the stress that I am forced to endure as your wife, I need to splurge every now and then."

"Okay, all right." He scribbled some numbers on the back of the paper and handed it to her.

"What am I supposed to do with this?"

"Follow through on it. That's your bill from me."

She read it and laughed. "You're charging me for your cell phone?"

"Most of the calls are made to you anyway."

Her eyes bulged at the next item. "And eighty dollars in gas? I don't drive your car."

"No, that's for all of the times I filled up your car whenever I saw you getting low. Include half of the insurance premium while you're at it. I forgot to write that down."

London tossed the list at him. "I'm not paying that! You're the one who begged me to switch over to your company for the couples' discount."

"But you're the one who wants everything split down the middle."

"What would you prefer—that I pay for everything?"

"No, but I wish you would have sat down and talked to me before deciding how to spend my money."

"I thought you said it was *our* money," she replied, needling him. "And don't you fool yourself into thinking that I'm going to have you freeloading off of me."

"I don't want to!"

"I don't know what kind of arrangement you had with Vanessa, but around here, you have to pay up. I'll die before I finance you or any other man," she declared, rolling her neck.

"Vanessa and I didn't have to have any kind of arrangement because I paid for everything from the rent to her personal feminine products. I would never have a woman taking care of me, but I'm not going to have one trying to dictate to me either."

"If you're so accustomed to paying for everything, why are you giving me such a hard time about it?"

He turned down the volume on the television. "London, I had every intention of paying all of our bills, but as usual, you wanted to takeover and decide how everything was going to go down and expected me to just go along with it."

She sat down beside him. "I don't need your money. I make plenty of my own and can take care of myself. I just want you to hold up your end financially."

He held her hands and spoke softly. "I already know that you don't need me to take care of you; I *want* to do it. You're my wife, so taking care of you is at the top of my job description."

"So, what are we going to do about these bills?"

"Just let me handle it, and we'll use your check for savings."

London shook her head. "I wouldn't be comfortable with that. I think it should all be fifty-fifty. Nana always says that when you let a man start paying for things, he thinks he owns you."

He chuckled. "This from a woman who never worked outside of the house a day in her life."

"Obviously, Pop-Pop was more evolved than most men. He never tried to control her."

"And you think I want to control you? London, we're equals; that was the whole point I was trying to make earlier. Having my name on the check that goes to the mortgage company doesn't change that."

"Look, it's sweet of you to offer to pay everything, really. But, come on, Bernard, do you honestly think we need to start a routine like that only to stop it a few months from now?"

He was confused. "Why would we put a stop to it?"

"Do I have to say it?"

"Yes, you do."

"Bernard . . ." He waited for her to finish. "I mean, does either one of us really think we're still going to be married a year from now?"

He stood up, suppressing his urge to say something wrong out of anger. "London, I have about had it with your negativity and pessimism about this marriage."

"Well, it's the truth, isn't it?"

"And you won't let me forget it for a second, will you?"

"Bernard—"

"No, squash it. We'll do it your way; we always do. Fifty-fifty, just like you said." He shook his head and sneered. "And you talk about me being controlling."

London could tell that he was starting to shut down emotionally. "I don't want to end the conversation like this, Bernard."

"London, right now, I don't really care what you want, but I do know one thing: The next time you bring up getting a divorce or anything like that, you better be ready to go through with it. Now, I don't know what kind of arrangement *you* had with Creighton, but you don't have to worry about me chasing after you. I've done about all the running I'm going to do."

"Bernard, don't act like this."

"Try telling yourself that, London," he fired before slamming the door shut to his bedroom.

She exhaled, and after a few seconds, made her way to Bernard's room. She opened the door and found him sprawled across the sofa-bed with his eyes closed and his hands pinned behind his head.

"A penny for your thoughts," she ventured quietly.

"Dang, you charge for that, too?"

"I'm sorry, okay?" She settled down next to him. "I shouldn't have said all those things."

"London, I know that this marriage isn't what either of us had in mind, but it's what we've got. We can do this if we work together, but not if you keep pushing me away. I can't be in this marriage by myself, which is how it's been since the moment we stepped off the plane."

"I know. I haven't been fair," she confessed. "But I am willing to try if you don't mind taking it slow."

He sat up. "We can go at whatever pace you feel comfortable. I just need to know you're willing to try, even a little. I need to know that we're in this together."

She sighed. "I want to, but no matter what we do, we always end up arguing. I don't know how to fix that."

"I know one way." He reached out for her hand. "Pray with me, London."

She snickered. "What?"

"I think we should pray. If nothing else works, we know that prayer always does. Maybe it's time we got a little divine intervention."

"Stop playing, Bernard. This is serious."

"Who's playing?" He closed his eyes and bowed his head. Reluctantly, she followed suit. "Lord, we come to you right now giving you all glory and praise. We love you, and we honor you as our Lord, Savior and our provider."

"We thank you for this union, Lord, and for all of the blessings that come as a result. And we ask for forgiveness for the sins we've committed against you and against each other."

"Lord, right now, we ask that you look down upon us. Give us direction. Give me the ability and the desire to love my wife as Christ loved the church. Help me to be everything she needs in a husband. Make any changes in me that are necessary to make me better for her. Keep your angels camped out around her and protect her, Lord. Help us to be a living example of what marriage is supposed to be. In Jesus' name, I pray. Amen."

"Amen," replied London, overcome with emotion. "That was beautiful, Bernard. I've never heard you pray like that before."

"I believe in us, and I'm willing to do whatever it takes. I just hope that you are, too."

She wiped tears from her eyes. "You're going to see some changes in me starting today; I promise."

"So does that mean you're ready to move me into your bedroom?" he asked hopefully.

"I said *changes*, not total insanity." Bernard slumped back onto the couch. "Let's give it a couple of months and see what happens," she bargained.

He cut his eyes over to her. "What about a couple of weeks? I would hate to have to sic the Lord on you about this matter, but I'll do what I have to do."

London thought about it. "Hmm. . . . Are you willing to sleep on the floor?"

"How about a chair pulled up real close to the bed?"

They laughed.

"You might have yourself a deal."

He nodded, pleased with himself. "You see, compromise is a beautiful thing—that and persistence."

"You really think we can do this?"

"I don't *think*," Bernard stated, braiding his hand into hers, "I know we can. We've got God on our side. We can do anything."

"You know, you might make me a believer after all," said London, actually meaning it this time. "I'm starting to feel hopeful again. I had almost forgotten what that felt like."

He crept closer to her and licked his lips. "I bet that you've forgotten what a lot of other things feel like, too."

"True, but I haven't forgotten what regret feels like, and I'm in no hurry to do anything that might trigger that feeling either." She sidestepped him.

He grabbed her again. "What if I could guarantee that regret is the *last* thing you'd be feeling?"

"Will you stop?" she pleaded, shoving him. "Your horns are showing."

"Can't you cut a brother some slack? We've been married almost two months now."

"That's why the world created hookers."

"Is that what it's come down to?"

London tried to reason with him. "Bernard, look. I've thought about it, and I don't think we're anywhere near ready to take that step. We can't even decide on whose turn it is to do dishes."

His eyes twinkled. "So you *admit* that you've thought about going one-on-one with the great one," he pressed.

"I wouldn't read too much into that if I were you. I can't tell you the number of times I've thought about killing you, but you're still breathing."

"What about all that talk about wanting to give the marriage a shot? You haven't even let me get to second base yet," he whined.

"Patience, my dear." She patted him on his chest. "All in due time."

Bernard pinned his hands against her back, drawing her to him. "I've never had to ask a girl more than once, and I am practically begging you. You've got to give me something. Work with me already," he pleaded.

She thought for a moment and batted her eyes at him. "So you want to get down and dirty, huh?"

His eyes brimmed with anticipation. "What exactly did you have in mind?"

"How can I put it?" She licked her lips. "I think it's time that we both get a little wet, don't you?"

His lips curled into a smile as he slid his arms about her waist. "Yeah, now that's what I'm talking about."

She caressed the back of his head. "You want to get all lathered up and do it standing over the sink?"

He was delighted. "Dang, London, I didn't know you had it in you!"

She giggled. "Then let's go."

Bernard snatched his shirt over his head. "I'm right behind you, baby."

London tenderly kissed his neck as she spoke in low, seductive tones. "I'm thinking maybe start off in the kitchen and work our way to the bathroom . . ."

He closed his eyes, aroused by her nibbling his ear. "We can do it in the bathroom, kitchen, bedroom—wherever you say."

"Does that mean you're willing to do anything I want?"

"You just name it, and it's done." He gawked at her subtle curves and firm body. "Hey, enough with all this talking. Let's get down to business."

"That's fine with me, but I think you're going to need this." She handed him a used coffee cup.

"What, you want me to pour it on you or something? We don't need coffee. There's whipped cream in the fridge, baby."

"No," she brought his head down to her, just shy of kissing him, "you're going to need it because it's your night to wash the dishes. You might as well clean the bathroom, too, while you're at it."

His mouth dropped. "You're joking, right?"

"You said you wanted to get down and dirty in the kitchen and bathroom, remember? Here's your chance." She roared with laughter on her way to the bedroom.

Bernard couldn't help laughing about it himself. "Yeah, she wants me," he told himself. "Even if she doesn't know it yet."

Chapter 15

"Hey, you wanna get out of here and get some lunch?" asked London, poking her head through the door of Cassandra's office. "I'm starving."

"Can't—I have a showing in thirty minutes." Cassandra shut down her computer and slipped the laptop into her bag. "Why don't you use this opportunity to surprise your husband and invite him to lunch? That would make his day."

"We're going out tonight as it is. I don't want to risk going into quality-time overload, especially since we're starting to make some headway."

"Come to think of it," replied Cassandra, "it *has* been awhile since you came in here whining and complaining about your marriage."

"Honestly, I haven't had anything to complain about. I'm actually almost used to having him around. We're still moving cautiously, of course; taking it one day at a time. But things are definitely getting better."

"Great. At this rate, you all should be holding hands by next summer."

"Ha, ha. You sound like Bernard. He's in heat and starting to get restless. I may have to start locking my bed-room door at night."

"Wouldn't it be easier to just stop stalling and put the man out of his misery? It's been a while for you, too, hasn't it? You ought to be about ready to ravish him."

"I'd be lying if I said that the thought hasn't crossed my mind," professed London.

"You need to quit all this playing and go on and give that man what both of you obviously want."

London moved into the office, closing the door behind her. "I don't think I'm ready to deal with the repercussions of that yet. Weren't you the one who warned me about having a broken heart and a sore back?"

"Yeah, I said that, but a girl has needs. Bernard is not some cat you met at the club; he's your husband. Even the Bible says you owe the man a little sumthin'- sumthin' every now and then."

London raised an eyebrow. "And just what chapter and verse did you read that in? Uncle Luke, 69?"

Cassandra giggled. "Hush. You know what I mean."

London mulled the possibility. "Do you really think we're ready to take that step? There's no coming back from that, you know."

"Only you can answer that, London. I just know if it was me married to a man that fine, we'd be taking steps, ladders, staircases, and everything else in between!"

London laughed. "He is kind of sexy, isn't he? I caught a glimpse of him coming out of the shower the other night, and the brother is definitely working with something!"

"Then what are you waiting for?"

London shrugged. "I don't know—a sign, I guess."

"Once you get him alone in that bedroom, he'll provide all the signs you need—*trust*."

"Me and Bernard, though?" London shook her head. "I feel weird even thinking about it."

"Girl, he's your husband now. He loves you, and, in some bizarre, twisted way, you love him, too."

London covered her face with her hands. "This is so embarrassing. I don't even know what to do. Should I call him up and say, 'How would you like to spend the night in London?' That sounds so corny."

"Just go home, light some candles, and set the mood," urged Cassandra. "I doubt that you'll have to *say* too much of anything."

"This is so unlike me," said London, thinking it over. "He's really going to think I've lost it."

"He'll be too busy waiting for you to lose your layers of clothing to be worried about whether or not you've lost your mind." Cassandra looked down at her watch. "And I must've lost mine to still be sitting here talking to you when I have a client to get to. Some of us are still single and have to depend on Ben Franklin to give us our thrills."

London opened the door. "Go make that money, girl. And thanks."

Cassandra grabbed her purse and files. "All right, go get him. And I do mean that literally and figuratively."

London's heart fluttered. She was no virgin, but the thought of finally consummating her marriage to Bernard made her more nervous than she'd been in her entire life. But the time had come, and by the end of the night, she would become Bernard's wife in every sense of the word.

London left work early that day. The occasion definitely warranted a half-day off and a lingerie splurge. The leopard print negligee trimmed in black lace that she'd selected struck the perfect balance between elegant matron and untamed kitten. London lit white tapered candles and set them all over the house; then she revved up the jazz and dabbed perfume on her neck and chest. She slipped into her matching satin robe, hoping to string out the final unveiling until the last minute. Her heart began pumping when she heard Bernard unlocking the door.

The smile that she had waiting to invite him into her boudoir deflated the second he stumbled into the living room. "You look awful!" she cried.

Bernard sniffed and wiped his nose with his sleeve. "Then you already know how I feel."

He was pale and languid. London pressed the back of her hand to his forehead. "My God, Bernard, you're burning up." She felt the side of his face. "Go lie down while I look for the thermometer."

"I'm fine, just need to get something to eat." He doubled-over in a coughing fit.

"Are you all right?" she asked, alarmed. He nodded. "Okay, to bed, Mister," she ordered. "I mean it."

"Babe, I—" He nearly lost his balance and stumbled. London caught hold of him. "On second thought, maybe you're right." He sneezed.

"Come on, let me help you. You can barely even walk." He leaned against her for support.

" 'Preciate it," he mumbled and crawled into bed. She tucked him in thinking that this was not the scene she had in mind when she'd planned their evening in bed together.

After locating the thermometer, she sat at his side and pointed it toward his mouth. "Open sesame."

"I can't read that thing. Don't you have a digital one?"

"You know, I could go get the rectal one," she threatened.

"Go ahead, that'll be the most action that I've gotten in weeks."

Peeved by the irony, she jammed the thermometer into his mouth, taking it out after a few minutes. "It's 103.7," she read. "That's pretty high."

Bernard sank down into the covers. "I'll be all right after I sleep it off."

"Bernard, you can't *sleep off* a fever! What have you taken for it?"

"Real men don't take medicine."

"We're not talking about real men; we're talking about you! Now, I'm getting you some aspirin and a bowl of soup. I can't have you dying on me. The light bill is due next week, and I haven't gotten your half yet."

He cracked a smile, but his droopy, darkened eyes worried her. She went into her medicine cabinet, snatching out every tablet and bottle of medicine she could find. When she entered the bedroom, she found Bernard shaking uncontrollably. "It's so cold," he stuttered.

She pulled off some of his blankets. "You can't wrap up like this. It'll only make the fever worse."

"It's freezing in here, London."

"Here, take this." She handed him a few tablets and a glass of water. "Try to get some sleep."

He swallowed the pills. "This ain't enough. What else you got?"

"I found a couple bottles of cold and flu medicine, but I don't think you should be mixing medicine like that. It could be dangerous."

"I'll live. Hand it here." She unwillingly passed him the bottle, and he took a swig of it.

"You didn't even measure it, B!" she exclaimed. "You're taking too much." London snatched the bottle out of his hands.

He settled into the bed, flinching in jerky motions. "I feel so weak."

She rubbed his head the same way she'd seen Essie do for Frank when he was having one of his fits. She asked God to let Bernard's fever break. As she tended to him, she started singing softly to calm her nerves.

"I didn't know you had such a nice voice. The only thing I've ever heard you use it for is screaming at me."

"What can I say? You bring it out of me."

"What, the singing?"

"No, the screaming." She felt his chest. "You feeling any better?"

"A little, it's still cold, though."

London draped one of the blankets over him. "How's that?"

He nodded, feeling light-headed. She could tell that the medicine was starting to take effect. "I'm going to go and let you get some rest, okay?"

Bernard grabbed her hand. "No, please stay, just for a little while."

London blotted his face with a damp washcloth. He lapsed into a semi-conscious state, awake one minute and asleep the next. After he'd been resting a couple of hours, she woke him up briefly to check his temperature. "It's a little over 102. Still kind of high but at least it's going down."

He stared at her out of half-closed lids. "London, you're so pretty, you know that?"

She snickered. "Dang, how sick are you?"

He mustered up the strength to speak, though his voice sounded airy and faint. "I'm serious. Your eyes are all big and sparkly . . ."

"*Sparkly?*"

"You know what I mean . . . and your smile . . . it's gotten real pretty since you took your braces off . . ."

"I'm glad you noticed. I've only had my braces taken out for the last fifteen years," she deadpanned.

He tried to sit up but was too weak. "You remember that time we went skating, you know, that time after senior cut day?" he slurred.

"Yeah, I remember."

"And your ride left you at the rink 'cause she caught you kissing her boyfriend."

"Curtis Denson—how could I forget?" she recalled, giggling. "Charlene was *pissed*! She came after me with a pair of skates and tried to strangle me with the laces."

"I saw you hugged up in the corner kissing him, too. I never told you that."

"Why not?"

"Because then I would've had to tell you the other part, too."

"What other part? Did you have a crush on ol' Curtis, too?"

He yawned. "When I saw you together, I got kind of jealous 'cause I wanted to kiss you myself."

"You did?" This was news to her.

Bernard rolled over on his side, nodding off again. "You knew I liked you, girl . . ."

"This has got to be the medicine talking," decided London, disregarding his ramblings.

"I knew one day I was gon' marry you, and I did."

"Bernard, what are you talking about? If Vanessa hadn't dumped you, you would've married her."

"You remember . . . how you used to come over to my house . . . . and use our computer?" His tone was airy and detached.

"Yeah, I never could convince Nana and Pop-Pop to buy one. Nana doesn't like computers to this day. She says they make people lazy."

"One time when you came over, my mama said, 'Bernard, you and that girl are going to make me lots of pretty grandbabies one of these days. The Lord's already told me that she's gon' be your wife.' "

London was stunned. "Your mother said that?"

"Uh-huh. She never said that about any other girl but you. I guess she was right. That's the reason my sisters never liked you. They were jealous because Mama liked you so much and so did I."

London was blown away. "Why am I hearing all of these things for the first time, Bernard?"

He sniffed. "I got one more thing to tell you for the first time."

"I'm almost afraid to ask what it is."

Bernard closed his eyes and slipped into a deep sleep, but before he dozed off, he uttered, "I'm in love with you."

Chapter 16

When the morning sun pierced through the blinds, Bernard awoke to find London curled up at the foot of the bed, asleep.

He gently roused her, "Paging Dr. Phillips."

London yawned and stretched. "Good morning. How do you feel?"

"Much better, thanks to you."

"I'm sure that all those pills you popped and that bottle of cough syrup you guzzled down helped a lot more than I did."

"You ain't lying!" Bernard exclaimed. "They need to start demanding a cover charge with that stuff."

London threw the empty medicine bottles into the trash can. "I'm glad to see that you're lucid again because you were completely out of it last night."

"Did I say or do something crazy?"

"Well, you were going on about Curtis Denson and my braces and your mother." She popped the thermometer into his mouth. "You really don't remember any of it?"

He shook his head. "I don't even remember how I got

home yesterday. Everything that happened after ten that morning is a blur. Feel free to jog my memory."

London debated with herself about whether or not she should reveal anything about his professing his love for her. "You might not want to hear it. It's sort of embarrassing."

"Don't tell me that I was going on and on about Vanessa," he groaned.

"No, actually, you were talking about—"

"You know, I dreamed about her last night," he recalled, cutting London off. "She was sitting right there where you are now, just appeared out of nowhere like an angel or something. Then I told her that I loved her. Weird, huh?"

"I suppose it's not that strange," she replied, camouflaging her true feelings. "You loved her. Apparently, you still do."

"I wouldn't take it that far. Of course, I still have feelings for her but—"

"You should probably stop talking until I read this," she snapped. After a minute, she removed the thermometer, pleased that his temperature was down to 100, but riled that he had mistaken her for Vanessa.

"So, you think I'll live, Doc?"

"It looks like you've been spared this time. Now that you've been given a second chance, you can go on out and chase after your dream-girl. I'll even help you pack."

Bernard snatched the blanket off of himself. "Can you let me get out of bed before you start trying to kick me out again?" he huffed.

"Bernard, obviously, this isn't where you want to be if you're still pining away for Vanessa."

"I never said that I was pining away for anybody."

"No, you only *dream* about being with her. That is, of course, when you're tonguing her down in the middle of your restaurant."

Bernard was thrown. "What? What are you talking about?"

"Are you denying that you've kissed her since we've been married?"

"I haven't even seen—" Bernard thought back and exhaled. "We kissed once, just to say good-bye. How did you even find out about that?"

"It doesn't matter."

He frowned. "Why are you trippin' on who I kiss anyway, especially when you've made it clear that you'd rather I kiss anybody other than you?"

"Yes, Bernard, blame me. This is so typical of you," London charged, raising her voice.

He was mystified. "You're crazy, you know that?"

She didn't respond, taking a few seconds to collect her thoughts, not wanting to reveal too much emotion or her disappointment at his questioning her sanity. "Well, it's clear that my work here is done. I'm going to the office, a place where my efforts are appreciated."

Bernard could tell she was upset. A calm, rational London was much more of a threat that a melodramatic one. "Lon, don't leave like this."

"No, I'm the crazy one, remember? I must've been to think—"

"To think what?"

She shook her head and exhaled. "I don't want to talk about it. I need to get out of here."

"London, wait . . ." He tugged at her robe.

"Stop—let go of me!" In her haste to break free of him, her robe flew open, revealing the barely-there teddy underneath.

Bernard was speechless. "What the—" He gazed at her as if seeing her for the first time. "Are you trying to lower my temperature or raise it?"

"That's a question you should have asked last night, when I was willing to do the latter."

It was then that he remembered the romantic scene that he'd come home to the day before and started putting the pieces together. "Did you put this on for me?"

London didn't answer him as she knotted the robe back together. He stood up, pressing his hands against the sides of her arms. "Does this mean what I think it means?" he asked softly and brushed a strand of hair from her face.

She couldn't look at him. "It means nothing, okay? For a split second during a momentary lapse in judgment yesterday, it might have meant something. Then you got sick and—"

"I'm feeling much better now," he quickly assured her.

"I'm not." She stepped away from him. "Bernard, I had a lot of mixed feelings about taking things to the next level, and I wanted a sign that becoming intimate with you was the right thing to do. I think you getting sick like that was the sign I was looking for. Let's face it—we're better off keeping things the way they are."

"London, we're married. And by the looks of it, you're as ready as I am. Let's just do it and let the chips fall where they may."

"Bernard, I can't do that. I'm sorry. We've already made one mistake. Sleeping together would be another one."

She dashed out of the room, ignoring his pleas for her to return. She was in over her head and knew it. It was time to either sink or swim. Not knowing what to do either way, she simply panicked.

Chapter 17

"Can I get some service please!" demanded London. She was on edge after running out on Bernard, and the crowded restaurant and incompetent waitress weren't making things any better. "All I want is a freakin' cup of coffee!"

"You haven't had your caffeine fix either?" observed a man who was sitting alone at the table next to hers.

"And it doesn't look like I'm going to get it anytime soon." She turned to see who had spoken to her and her heart stopped. There he was in a tailored fawn suit that accentuated his Cognac skin and athletic build. "Creighton!"

"In the flesh," he replied as the frazzled waitress made her way, with coffee pot in hand, to his table. "Ah, right on time." The waitress apologized for taking so long while filling up his cup. "Do you mind filling up that beautiful woman's cup while you're at it? I think her claws are going to show if she doesn't get some coffee soon." The waitress smiled and tottered over to London's table and filled her cup as requested.

"Thank you." London closed her eyes and raised the

mug to her lips, anticipating the soothing jolt of the first sip.

"I score you a cup of coffee and all I get is a lousy thank you? I thought that we were better than that. You could at least offer me a chair." Creighton didn't wait for her to extend an invitation before planting himself in the empty seat across from her.

She eyed him as she stirred cream and sugar into her coffee, determined not to be seduced by either his charm or hypnotic eyes.

"Well?" he prodded.

"What do you want, Creighton?"

"Besides this cup of coffee, the same thing I've wanted since that day we met at the bank last February . . . *you.*"

He flashed his spellbinding smile that had a way of turning London's insides into jelly. She tried her best to ignore it. "Sorry, I'm not on the menu."

"That's because you're on my mind. Not even somebody as fine as you can be in two places at once."

They stared each other down until London broke the tension with her cackling. "Okay, that has got to be the lamest pick-up line I've ever heard," she declared, sipping her coffee.

"Do I at least get points for trying and for making you smile?"

She caught herself slipping and tensed back up. "Shouldn't you be saving all of your smiles and jokes for your wife?"

He chortled a little. "I don't know why. She's saving all of hers for our gardener."

London smacked her lips. "Yeah, right."

"I'm serious. Apparently, I've been paying him to cut more than just the lawn." He swallowed some of his coffee. "I've moved out."

"It serves you right, you know. You haven't exactly been the poster child for fidelity."

He winked an eye. "She doesn't know that."

"Still the same ol' Creighton, I see. It's comforting to know that some things never change." London dabbed her lips with a napkin. "Well, thanks for the coffee. I have to run." She gathered her purse and portfolio.

"Where to?" he asked.

"That's none of your business, Creighton. Good-bye." She stood to leave.

"Hold on!" He grabbed her hand and inadvertently zeroed in on her ring. "What's this?"

London snatched her hand back. "What does it look like?"

"It looks like a wedding ring—not a very expensive one, but a ring, no less."

"That's right, you don't know, do you? I'm married," she announced. She couldn't help being smug about it. "Aren't you going to congratulate me?"

Creighton's eyes nearly popped out of their sockets. "You're what?"

"That's right," she boasted. "You're not the only one with secrets."

He laughed nervously and pointed at her. "Good one, London. You almost had me going for a minute there."

"You don't have to take my word for it. I can call my husband, Bernard, and let him confirm it for you."

"Bernard?" he sputtered. "That goldfish looking . . . *that's* who you're married to?" He hooted raucously. "I thought you were talking about somebody." He caught his breath and slapped his thigh. "That was funny. I needed a good laugh; thank you."

London glared at him. "You can laugh, you can cry; frankly, I don't care what you do anymore."

His demeanor morphed into something more sinister. "Since when, London? Wasn't it you who called me bawling when you found out I was married? *How could you do this to me, Creighton?"* he said, mocking her. *"I loved you!"*

"Needless to say, I was a lot stupider then, too. Rest assured that you never have to worry about me doing that again. Now, if you'll excuse me, I have business to take care of. Have a nice life."

Creighton rose from the chair and propelled his body against hers. "So, what's this about, huh? Pay back? Rebound? Do you honestly believe you can convince me to think that you lie in that bed at night and not think about all the nights we shared there?" He stroked her cheek. "That you're not thinking about it right now?"

She slapped his hand away. "Don't touch me that way or talk to me like that! You can call it rebound or whatever you want but as far as you and I go, I call it *over*." She pushed him aside and walked away.

"Hey, London," he called after her, "marriage can get very old and very boring very fast." She paused long enough for him to catch up with her. He leaned into her ear and whispered, "And there's nothing like a good ol' affair to break up the monotony, know what I'm saying?"

"I know that's how slimes like you operate, but I'm not interested."

"Oh, you're interested," he countered, drifting his eyes over her frame. "You're definitely interested. But, hey, you know the number. Don't hesitate to use it." He passed his hand over her waist and kissed her lightly on the mouth, sending a tingle through London's body that she wasn't expecting to have. And certainly not at the same level of potency that it had at their first kiss. He winked at her and walked to the cash register while she quickly sprinted away in the opposite direction.

Chapter 18

"**D**id you hear what I said, Lonnie?" asked Essie after London had been at her house for twenty minutes without uttering more than two words or answering her questions.

London snapped out of her daydream and looked up at her grandmother. "I'm sorry; what?"

"I said that the family can't wait to see you and your new husband at the Christmas Eve dinner. What's the matter with you, baby? It ain't like you to just show up out of the blue during the middle of a work day. What's going on?"

"Nothing," she replied, gliding her finger around the rim of Essie's cake-batter bowl. "I just wanted to see you."

Essie peered up at her over the rim of her glasses. "Girl, you know I can smell a lie from across the room. You and Bernard still having problems?"

"What makes you say that?" London asked, forming a fake smile.

"Lonnie, I've known you longer than you've known yourself! When you gon' learn that you can't hide nothing from your old nana?"

London exhaled and admitted, "Things aren't going so well between us. He wants something that I'm just not ready to give him."

Essie shook her head and continued stirring the batter. "I was afraid of that. Well, baby, marriage is hard work, but hang in there. Sooner or later, y'all will figure everything out."

"I don't think so. I mean, just how long and how hard am I supposed to try?"

"Until you get it right, child!"

"But we *have* tried. We—"

"You tried talking to the pastor? Counseling?" London shook her head. "Then, honey, you ain't tried at all."

"You don't get it, Nana."

"Oh, I get it, Lonnie. *You* don't. That's the problem."

"What do you mean?"

"Well . . . how are things in the bedroom?"

"Nana!" she gasped.

"Aw, hush, girl. You think I don't know about that? If I didn't, neither you nor your daddy would've been here. Now, granted, I don't know as much as I used to, but I do know that your marriage won't survive without it."

"Nana, we don't . . . he's my friend. It's just better if we keep things the way they are."

"Well, you better step up before some other hot-tailed thing does! Friend or not, he's still a man."

"I can't even think about sex after being stressed and tense like this all the time."

"You know of a better stress reliever?" murmured Essie.

"*Nana!*"

Essie stopped stirring. "Look, the Bible says to be glad when you have trouble. You get stronger whenever you have your faith tested. You've just gotta learn to endure, that's all."

"But aren't you the one always telling me that God

wants us to have an abundant life? This isn't abundance. This is unnecessary aggravation!"

"Just keep a-living, child. Just keep a-living."

London went to the refrigerator and brought out a pitcher of tea. "I ran into Creighton this morning."

"Oh, Lord; please don't tell me that you've let that slippery-tongued snake reel you in again. You're supposed to run when you see trouble, not be a fool and walk right into it."

"He didn't reel me back in, but seeing him again did remind me of something."

"What's that?"

"What it's like to be in love, to feel that rush of excitement and nervousness when the man you love walks into a room. I don't have that with Bernard." London poured a glass of tea for herself and one for Essie.

"What you're talking about is lust and don't have a thing to do with love. That's what's wrong with you young people. You get so caught up in emotions that you forget all about what's real and lasting."

"But, Nana, there has to be chemistry and attraction for a relationship to work."

"All that is well and good, but I haven't heard you say a thing about commitment and respect and trust. Those are the things that are gon' carry you year after year, not all that soap opera mess you're talking about. Of course, you could have all that, too, with Bernard if you tried."

London shrugged her shoulders and swallowed her tea. "If you say so . . ."

"Keep the faith, honey. I don't think—" Essie looked up and spotted Frank limping to the kitchen leaning heavily on the cane at his right side. "Frank, what are you doing out of that bed?"

"How are you doing, Pop-Pop?"

"Oh, I'm making out all right; can't complain." Today appeared to be one of his good days.

"Honey, why don't you sit down and let me fix you something to eat?" extended Essie.

Instead of sitting, he approached his granddaughter and rested his hand on her shoulder. "You're not happy, are you, Lonnie?"

London smiled at him. "I'm all right, Pop-Pop. At least, I will be when you're up and back to yourself."

"You don't need to wait on that. You shouldn't let nothing or nobody keep you from being happy, baby, not even yourself."

"I won't."

His eyes roamed around the kitchen. "Where's your husband? He here?"

She looked away. "I don't know where he is. At work, probably."

"She and Bernard been at each other's throats again, Frank."

He coughed. "You need to find him and make things right. Do it before it's too late."

"Some people make better friends than lovers. Not everybody can be like you and Nana. I'm just so thrilled to see you up and moving around," rejoiced London. "You look good!"

"The Lord ordained marriage, child. He put it here so man would have a help-meet and wouldn't have to be alone. I don't know what's going on between you and your husband, but promise me you'll work it out. I want to go home knowing that my grandbaby is happy."

She smacked her lips. "Pop-Pop, you're not going anywhere no time soon, and you know it."

"Just promise me, Lonnie," he insisted. There was a strange look in his eyes.

"I promise," London swore somberly.

"Now, Frank, you get on back to that bed. I'll bring your supper out directly." He turned and treaded back down the hall to their bedroom.

"Pop-Pop must be feeling better. He's out of bed and looking stronger. It was kind of weird for him to be asking about Bernard, though."

"He's just trying to get things in order."

London was uneasy. "You don't think—"

"Didn't you see his eyes, child? God's getting ready to call him home."

Chapter 19

"Delivery for London Harris," announced Cassandra, carting a large array of pink and white tulips to London's office. "It looks like somebody wants you to have a *very* happy birthday."

London was overjoyed. "Are these for me?"

Cassandra set the vase on London's desk. "Yeah, a guy was headed to your office with them. I told him I'd save him a trip."

"Aren't they pretty? I wonder who sent them."

"Whoever it is obviously wanted to show me and my birthday earrings up."

"Don't say that. I love the earrings. They're beautiful." London reached in and tore open the small envelope tucked inside of the arrangement. "*I hope this brightens your day as much as you've brightened my life. Happy Birthday. Love, Creighton.*" London's smile dissolved, and she balled up the card and dumped the flowers into the trashcan.

"What are you doing?" cried Cassandra.

London rolled her eyes. "Isn't this what we do with all the trash?"

"These flowers are too beautiful for you to just throw away. If you don't want them, give them to me."

"Take 'em!"

Cassandra recovered the vase and flowers. "At least he remembered that it was your birthday. You have to give the guy credit for that."

"Yes, it seems that Mr. Graham can remember everything except that he has a wife at home. He's called me at least five times today."

"Did you talk to him?"

"No. Entertaining his phone calls is the quickest way to get sucked back in." She shook her head. "Please—let's just talk about something else. I don't want to waste any more energy thinking about him."

"Fine with me. So, do you and Bernard have big plans for tonight?" asked Cassandra.

London stared at the crumpled card. "Does he really think that a few phone calls and some flowers can erase everything he's done?" she asked, flinging the card and raising her voice.

"I thought that we were changing the subject."

"He lied to me, he broke my heart, and he lured me into this adulterous affair that I knew nothing about. Now, I have to live the rest of my life knowing that I slept with another woman's husband. I don't know how anyone can be that cruel. I have a good mind to call up his wife right now and let her know what he's been up to."

Cassandra peeked out of the doorway to make sure that no one overheard. "Calm down, London. The walls have ears, you know."

"I'm too pissed to calm down, and I don't care who hears me! The world needs to know what kind of scum we have lurking around out here. Just who does he think he is anyway? I wish you could have seen him strutting around the coffee shop, practically daring me to resist him. Does he think I'm so desperate to have him in my life that I'd let a few raggedy tulips do what all his apologies and excuses couldn't? Does he honestly believe that I'd take him back that easily? The whole thing gets my blood boiling whenever I think about it," ranted London.

There was a knock at the door, and a massive bouquet of yellow and red roses loomed toward them, blocking the carrier's face.

"I don't want them. Go away!" barked London.

"Then I guess you're in no mood to hear the birthday rap I made up on the way over, huh?" The man lowered the vase. It was Bernard.

"Hey, Bernard," spoke Cassandra. "Those are roses are gorgeous."

"I sure hope the birthday girl thinks so." London rolled her eyes and faced her computer.

"London, say something," urged Cassandra. "I'm sure you want to thank Bernard for being so thoughtful." Cassandra sniffed the bouquet. "They smell as good as they look."

"The roses are fine, just put the vase down somewhere," said London was an obvious lack of enthusiasm in her tone.

"Where do you want them?" Bernard asked, searching for clean spot on her desk.

London proceeded to roll and click the computer's mouse. "I don't care as long as they're out of my way."

Bernard glanced over at Cassandra, who offered a weary smile. "Baby, if you're free, I was hoping you'd let me take you to lunch today," proposed Bernard. She didn't respond. "London?"

"Huh?"

"He said he wanted to take you to lunch," filled in Cassandra. "Isn't that sweet?"

"I'm not hungry," she replied gruffly.

"Come on, let me take you out in honor of the occasion. It's not everyday that my wife turns 29. So where to, Mrs. Phillips?"

"You know I hate it when you call me that."

"With the way you're acting, I'm tempted to call you something else," he joked.

London failed to see the humor. "I don't need this, not today. Why don't you pack up your little flowers and trot on back to where you came from."

Bernard set the roses down. "London, it was a joke—dang!"

She shook her head. "You men are all alike. Marriage, relationships, emotions—it's all just one big joke to you. The other person's feelings don't even matter."

"London, he said he was kidding," noted Cassandra, disturbed by London's conduct toward Bernard. "Cut the man some slack."

"That's what's wrong with him. He can't be serious for more than five minutes."

"Do you want me to come back when you have a little less hell in you?" he asked.

London rolled her eyes. "That's so typical. A woman wants to speak her mind and the man can't handle it, so he has to high-tail it out to the nearest bar or the nearest woman. You all can't cope when a woman calls you on your crap and if she does, she's automatically labeled crazy or a female dog."

Bernard was completely dumbfounded. "Look, I don't know what kind of PMS venting session I walked in on, but all I wanted was to take you to lunch and bring you some flowers."

London slammed her hand down on the desk. "And just why do you men act like flowers are some kind of global panacea for all that is wrong in the world? *Baby, sorry, I cheated on you, but look—I brought flowers.* Or *after stringing you along for ten years and impregnating you a few times along the way, I've decided not to marry you after all but don't worry because I picked up these lovely roses on the way back from my girlfriend's house!*" she shrieked. "A woman doesn't want your flowers. She wants your respect and honesty."

Bernard shook his head. "London, you lost me at hello. What in God's name are you talking about?"

She opened her mouth to respond but changed her mind. "You know what? Never mind. It's not in you to understand. You clearly lack the mental capacity to understand anything I'm talking about. Now, I see why Vanessa had to replace you."

Her words hit below the belt. He glared at her with seething animosity. "I swear I wouldn't wish you on my worst enemy, London. You can cancel the lunch invitation, and you know what you can do with those flowers." He charged out, slamming the door shut behind him.

Cassandra looked at her friend with confusion and concern. "You know you owe him an apology, don't you?"

London pulled out one of his roses, sniffed it, and placed it back in the vase. "I'm sure *he* thinks so, but it's my birthday. I can fuss if I want to."

"Why did you go off on him like that? He was only trying to be thoughtful, and you go flying off the handle. One thing's for sure: no one can ever accuse you of knowing how to keep a man happy."

"You're single. One could make the same assessment about you."

Cassandra was taken aback. "Oh, you're snapping at me now, too?"

London sighed. "No, I'm sorry. It's not you; it's not even Bernard, really." She sank down in her chair. "It's Creighton."

"Isn't it always about Creighton?"

London screamed in frustration. "Why do I keep letting him get to me like this?"

"I don't know but if you don't get it together soon, you're going to end up losing Bernard. You can't keep pushing him away and expect him to stick around for the abuse."

"I can't help it! Creighton's not here, so I end up taking everything out on Bernard."

"You're not being fair to him, and he doesn't deserve that kind of treatment." Cassandra paused a moment. "In fact, I'm starting to think that maybe he doesn't deserve to married to someone like you."

"What's that supposed to mean?"

Cassandra secured Creighton's flowers in her arms. "It means, young grasshopper, that Bernard is one of the good ones and if you're not careful, you're going to lose that man. And when that happens—and it will happen— you'll have nobody to blame but yourself."

"What are you doing back here?" asked Rod when he saw Bernard coming into the restaurant. "I thought you wanted the rest of the day off to spend time with London."

"Don't even mention her name around me," grumbled Bernard.

"Oh, it went that well, huh?"

"You know there's only so much trying that a man can do, only so much bull that a man can put up with!" he let out.

Rod slapped his hand on his brother's back. "Do you remember when you came up with the brilliant idea of having frozen vegetables slushies?"

Bernard corrected him, "It was smoothies, man."

"Smoothies, slushies—either way, it didn't sell. Despite all your free samples and your hype and your promotion, nobody was buying. Eventually, you decided to cut your losses. You had given it your all, but you knew when it was time to give up. You might want to think about that now."

Bernard nodded his head. "I hear you. Hey, look; you get on outta here. At least one of us should enjoy a night at home."

"You sure? I could stick around 'til closing if you want."

"Go on. I need to do some thinking, know what I mean?"

His brother nodded and left through the kitchen. Bernard was propped behind the counter when a pretty doe-eyed woman breezed into the restaurant with a gym bag draped over her shoulder. She sat down at the bar and unfastened her barrette, allowing the auburn ringlets to tumble down her exposed shoulders and caramel skin. He was struck by her natural beauty and grace.

"What do you recommend after a long workout?" she asked breathlessly, dropping her bag down beside her. "I want something decadent and filling but without the calorie guilt."

"Then you want to try our peach and strawberry smoothie," he proposed, cranking up the blender. "It's our biggest seller."

"Thanks." She smiled.

He handed her the cup. "I hope you're not trying to lose weight. Everything seems to be right just like it is," replied Bernard, admiring her svelte figure. "No man wants to be hugged up with an ironing board at night."

"Nobody wants to be hugged up with a parade float either."

He laughed a little, surprised to catch himself smiling. "So do you work out around here?"

She nodded. "Yeah and my apartment is about two blocks away. I don't know why I haven't come in before, especially since this place has such good drinks . . . and such cute waiters."

He blushed. "I haven't been a 'cute waiter' since I was in high school. Now, I'm just a cute owner."

She seemed intrigued. "You own this place?"

"Yeah, my brother and I opened up about three years ago." He gestured his head toward Rod as he sped out of the front door. "That's him right there."

"Really? I never would have guessed it. Both of you look so young."

"Twenty-nine isn't that young, and Rod's pushing forty. Besides, I never knew that there was an age-restriction on starting your own business."

"No, I guess not. So, what made you go the health-food route? You look more like a beer and burgers kind of guy."

"Oh, don't get me wrong. I can enjoy a fat, juicy steak as much as the next guy. But my mother passed away when I was in college—heart attack. She was only 46-years-old, but she was overweight and didn't really watch what she ate. The restaurant was my brother's and my way of making up for that."

"Cool," she replied, nodding. "So do you have a name or what?"

"Yeah, I'm Bernard." He extended his hand to her.

"Nice to meet you, Bernard. I'm Rayne." Her hands were soft, and he liked touching them.

"So, Miss Rayne, what do you do with yourself when you're not working out?"

"Oh, I'm a grad student; international finance."

"That sounds . . . boring."

Rayne laughed. "It's fascinating, actually. I also work part-time at Outwrite."

"What's that?"

"It's a bookstore over on Piedmont."

"I've driven by there a few times," recalled Bernard.

"Well, the next time you're over that way, you should come in and say 'hello.' " Rayne kept her eyes fixed on Bernard as she sipped her drink. "That is, of course, if it's okay with your wife or girlfriend."

He sneered and started wiping down the counter.

"So I take that there is a wife or girlfriend somewhere," she inferred.

"It's complicated."

"It always is," Rayne replied sarcastically. "So which is it—wife or girlfriend?"

"The first one." Rayne pursed her lips together. He could read the blighted hope on her face. "Trust me. I'm not some philandering husband trying to seduce young ladies with drinks and sympathy. It really is complicated."

"Well, you're married, right?"

"Yes."

"So where's the complication?"

"The marriage was a mistake," Bernard admitted out loud for the first time. "It was a drunken, knee-jerk reaction to getting dumped."

"Your wife isn't some stranger you just picked up, is she? I mean, you did know the woman, right?"

"Sure, we're best friends . . . we *were* anyway."

"Are you getting a divorce?"

"Probably," he revealed, feeling that divorce, which had only been an option before, was now the chosen course of action. "We were supposed to have it annulled the day after we got married, but her grandmother convinced us to hold off on it. Anyway, we tried to give it a shot, but it's not working out. I'm afraid that if we stay in it much longer, we won't even be friends anymore."

"That's sad."

He shrugged. "What can you do? She wants out, and I'm starting to agree."

"You don't have any kids, do you? I was crushed when my parents split up."

"You can't have kids if you don't have sex, can you?"

"You don't have sex?" Rayne blurted out. "I'm sorry. I'm getting all up in your business, and we just met. Honestly, you don't have to answer that."

Bernard shook his head. "The problem isn't that you asked; the problem is that I have nothing to report. The marriage has never been consummated. Believe me, it's been a long, frustrating three months."

She winced. "Are you serious? Never?"

"Nope, not even close."

"You poor baby!"

"Don't worry about me. I'll live." Bernard couldn't help staring at her supple, pink lips wrapped around the straw.

Rayne slurped the last of her smoothie and cleared her throat. "That was every bit as delicious as promised."

"Well, we aim to please."

She placed a couple of dollars on the counter and picked up her gym bag. She stood up and slung it over her shoulder. "I better get out of here. It was nice meeting you, Bernard. You're a good guy to have around when you need a sugar fix."

"That's what all the girls tell me—excuse me." He turned away to answer his cell phone. When he finished his conversation, he spotted Rayne scribbling on the back of a piece of paper.

"You were so engrossed in your conversation there that I was just going to leave my number on the bar." She handed it to him.

"I suppose one good turn deserves another." Bernard

handed her his card. "Now you have someone to call the next time you're the victim of bad restaurant service or watered-down frothy, fruity concoctions. You just let me know, and I'll swoon in and save the day."

"I might just do that." They both smiled, acutely aware of the chemistry brewing between them. "And don't be afraid to use that number either."

"I won't be; neither should you."

"I should go," she repeated. "Otherwise, I might do something stupid like start flirting with you."

"I like a girl who's not afraid to do a little flirting," he told her. "To be honest, I wish you didn't have to rush off just yet. I was enjoying our conversation and your presence."

"I wouldn't want your other customers to get jealous if I'm monopolizing all of your time."

He leaned down as if to say something secretively. "Believe it or not, there are these people called employees that we hire to handle that sort of thing."

"You don't say!"

"See, there's one now," he replied, gesturing his head toward one of the wait staff. "So, you see, I've got my end covered."

"In that case, I suppose I can spare a few more minutes." She slid back onto the bar stool. "It's not like I have anyone waiting for me at home."

"That makes two of us," he retorted, refilling her glass.

"Hey, I only ordered one!"

"This one's on the house."

"What for?"

"For helping me to remember what it's like to have a conversation with a woman that doesn't involve yelling or telling me everything I'm doing wrong or sarcastic remarks."

Rayne dipped her straw into the smoothie. "There's a lot more where that came from."

"I bet there is."

She paused and took another sip. "You wanna get out of here?"

He grinned. "I thought you'd never ask."

Chapter 20

"What time did you get in last night?" asked London, rummaging through the refrigerator the next morning.

Bernard was sitting down reading the newspaper. "Were you waiting up for me?" he asked with sarcasm.

She pulled out a gallon of orange juice and closed the door. "Not really. When I woke up around two, I noticed that you weren't here."

"That figures. I guess it's too much to ask that you should actually miss your husband." She didn't say anything. "But fear not, you may be getting your wish soon."

"What do you mean?"

"I met someone last night. Someone who, surprisingly, enjoyed my company. We talked until about four this morning. Then we drove out to the lake and watched the sun come up. And you know what? I didn't think about you or this jacked up marriage the whole time."

"I'm glad that you had a good time. Maybe you should see her again."

"So, now my wife is encouraging me to date other

women! I guess I should be grateful. Most men would kill for their wives to tell them that."

"I think I'm more of your friend than your wife, Bernard."

"Yeah, you keep telling me that. But you don't have to worry about me fighting you on it anymore."

"Good. I want you to be happy and if you think that this girl can make you happy, I say go for it."

"Whatever, London."

She stood over him. "Will I have the pleasure of meeting the new woman in your life?"

"We just met. It's not like we're sending out wedding invitations or anything."

"Neither did we, but I ended up married and in bed with you just the same."

"I already made one mistake," he said, glaring at her, "I'm in no rush to make another one. After a couple of months with you, I'm wondering if I ever want to get married again." His words were like a punch in the stomach.

"The important thing is that we're both looking toward the future and are making plans for what comes next."

"Yeah, we shouldn't have let it go on this long."

London wasn't expecting that or the sting of realizing that Bernard no longer wanted to be married to her.

Bernard grinned inside and out the moment he looked up and saw her. "Didn't I just leave you about twelve hours ago?"

Rayne climbed onto the barstool at the counter. "Getting tired of me already, huh?"

He smiled. "Not a chance."

"Truth be told, I wanted to see you so I could have actual proof that last night wasn't a dream."

"If it was, it was the best one I've had all year." He turned to pour her a cup of coffee. "What's on your plate for today?"

She shrugged and brought the cup to her lips. "I have class at ten, but my schedule's pretty clear after that."

"Do you have to work today?"

"Not until Thursday so, you see, I'm all yours."

"You better not say that too loud. I wouldn't want your boyfriend to hear that and come up in here trying to start something. We try to keep it professional in here."

"In case you didn't notice last night, it takes a certain kind of man to capture and maintain my attention, and I haven't run across one in some time. That is, not until yesterday."

"I imagine that a woman like you has more than a few men vying for her attention, though."

"What can I say?" He liked her slight arrogance and confidence. "I'm very selective, though. Besides, I don't have to wait for any man to choose me. I'm the kind of girl who sees what she wants and goes for it."

"A go-getter . . . I like that."

"Stick around and you'll find many more things to like about me."

The flirtatious tête-à-tête was interrupted by Rod's arrival.

"What's up, man?" said Bernard.

" 'Sup." He nodded toward Rayne. "Is this chump treating you right?" he asked her.

"Best waiter this side of the Mississippi," she replied.

He extended his right hand. "I'm Rod, the better half of this brother duo."

"Rayne—pleasure meeting you."

Rod didn't want to let go of her hand. "Didn't I see you in here yesterday? I usually don't forget a pretty face."

"You better watch out for this one," warned Bernard. "He's on the prowl for wife number three."

"Hey, third time's the charm!" he retorted. Rod's phone rang, and he disappeared into the kitchen to answer it.

"I didn't get you in trouble with your wife, did I?" asked Rayne, stirring her coffee. "A lot of women wouldn't take too kindly to their husbands coming home with the sun."

"She barely even noticed. Believe it or not, she said that I should keep seeing you."

"Are you sure it wasn't a threat?"

"No, she'd rather I spend time with any woman other than her."

Rayne made a face. "Things must be pretty rocky between the two of you."

"It's hard to imagine how they could get any worse. It doesn't matter now. As soon as we get everything resolved and I find a new place, it's over."

"I guess the important thing is that you tried. Nobody can ask more of you than that. The sad reality is that marriage doesn't come with any guarantees. Whether or not it lasts can be a toss-up."

"I can't worry about it anymore. I'm taking my happiness where I can get it, with or without London. I'm sure she feels the same way."

"So, you and your wife have an open marriage then?"

"Open, uncommitted, no strings—call it whatever you want, but it all means the same thing: I don't care what she does, and she doesn't care what I do."

"And she doesn't mind if you see other women?" she pried.

"She admitted that much to me. Besides, I'm almost positive that she's still messing around with her ex."

"Does that bother you?"

"At this point, I'm pretty much immune to any of London's antics. If he wants her, good riddance!"

Rayne loosened up. "Well, then, if that's the case, I don't see the harm in our continuing to see each other. Do you?"

"It wouldn't matter either way. Being with you is like a long overdue vacation after dealing with London all day."

"Well, you are welcome to book a trip to me whenever you get ready."

"I'll have my travel agent get right on it." He looked up and let out a deep breath. "Speak of the devil . . ."

Rayne turned around just as London entered the restaurant. She had come to make amends for their fight that morning and treatment of him on her birthday. She changed her mind when she saw Bernard conversing with Rayne, a scene not unlike the last time she stopped by for a visit. It was too late to duck out this time; he'd already spotted her.

"So, is this what you do all day?" London asked jokingly.

Bernard didn't return her smile. "What are you doing here?"

"Do I need a reason to drop in on my husband?" The look he shot her said "yes." He was obviously in no mood to play along, so she stopped. The last thing she wanted was to look like a fool in front of this other woman. "Actually, I just stopped by for one of those breakfast smoothies. I didn't have time to eat this morning."

"Hi," said Rayne with a smile as Bernard mixed the smoothie.

"London, this is my friend Rayne that I was telling you about. Rayne, this is London," introduced Bernard, obviously doing it more out of protocol than desire.

"Rayne? I'd say it's more like *Sunshine* with the way he's been glowing since he came home last night, or rather, this morning."

"We had a good time. I was just telling Bernard that I was hoping that I didn't get him into any trouble for getting in so late."

"No, that's okay. The only thing that matters is that he

did come home . . . to me." The inference wasn't lost on Rayne, who was now uncomfortable. "When you have time, I think we should talk about what happened yesterday."

"Which part do you want to talk about? The part where you blew me off in front of your friend when I was just trying to do something nice for you? How about the part where you threw Vanessa all up in my face again?"

Rayne was at a loss. "It looks like you all have some things to hash out, so I think I better go before it starts to get awkward. Bernard, I'll see you later." She began gathering her things.

"You don't have to leave," entreated London, not meaning it one bit. "As soon as Bernard finishes with that smoothie, I'm out of here."

"Be sure to give Creighton my regards," snarled Bernard, snapping a lid on London's drink.

"I'm not going to see him. I'm showing a couple of houses on this side of town this morning."

"Oh, you're in real estate?" asked Rayne. London nodded. "My boss is looking for a house. If you have a card, I'll tell him to give you a call."

"Where do you work?"

"Over at the bookstore on Piedmont."

London plastered on a smile. "So you're a book clerk—how nice."

"She's also a grad student at Georgia State," added Bernard.

"Is that how the two of you met?"

"No, we met right here," answered Rayne. "Apparently, you and I have the same taste in smoothies."

"And other things," muttered London. "So you came in for a smoothie and left out with my husband. Isn't that something?"

"Excuse me?" asked Rayne.

"Relax, I'm kidding." She really wasn't. "Bernard is his own man. He's free to see whomever he wants."

"I'm glad to hear it because we intend to see a lot more of each other," Rayne replied condescendingly. It was her subtle way of letting London know that she would not be intimidate or bullied.

"Just don't do anything that I wouldn't do or that the laws of Georgia don't allow. You know, sodomy and all that."

"London, wasn't there some place you needed to be?" hinted Bernard. He handed her a napkin and straw.

"As a matter of fact, there is. It was nice to meet you, Rayne. I'm sure we'll be seeing a lot more of each other as well. Feel free to drop by the house anytime."

"I might just take you up on that."

"I'll see you at home tonight, Bernard." Rayne waved goodbye to her. London pretended not to notice.

"Wow, that was . . . strange," summed up Rayne after London's departure.

"That's London for you."

"Am I paranoid or was she taking shots at me?"

"She probably was. Then again, who knows with her?" He watched her drive away.

"She's a character all right."

"You only got a glimpse of it. Try living with her." He passed a smoothie to her.

Rayne pulled the straw out of the cup and licked the residual froth. "I'd rather try doing that with you."

"You're quite the little flirt, aren't you, Miss Hollis?"

"I don't hear you complaining."

"And you won't."

"Well, I better get out of here and on to class before any more of your slightly off-kilter wives come in."

"That's the last one, I promise. Will I see you later on today?"

She winked at him as she stepped off of the barstool. "I'll call you."

"Okay, I'm going to hold you to that."

"Why don't you get a head-start on that now?" She opened her arms for a hug, and he happily complied. "I better go, don't wanna be late." She eased out of his arms.

"Take care," he said, "and have a good day."

She tossed him a smile over her shoulder as she sauntered out. "I already am!"

Chapter 21

"That witch!" cried London, barging into Cassandra's office after leaving Bernard and Rayne.

"Did a buyer stand you up?"

"No, I'm talking about Bernard's new *friend*." She said *friend* as if it was a debilitating virus.

Cassandra was intrigued. "Oh, Bernard has a friend, does he?"

"You should have seen her, too; just waiting to sink her talons into my husband."

"When did you start getting so possessive about Bernard and actually referring to him as your husband?"

"I'm not. I just thought the way she was drooling all over him was desperate and embarrassing. And her shoes were the ugliest, greenest sandals I've ever seen in my life," she added for good measure.

"Then I'm guessing they weren't the lovely shade of green that your eyes are turning."

"What are you talking about?"

"London, you're jealous."

"I am not. I don't care who Bernard is friends with as

long as they don't bother me. Humph, if he likes it, I love
it."

"Then why are you so upset?"

"It's the way she said everything. *We had a lot of fun.
We're going to be seeing a lot more of each other. I hope I
didn't keep him out too late,*" she emulated, still fired up.

"Since when did they become a *we*?"

"This sounds an awful lot like jealousy to me, London.
Was she pretty?"

London sulked, "Gorgeous . . . and younger . . . and thin-
ner."

"I believe you've gotten a little sweet on Mr. Phillips.
You better tell him now before things go any further with
this chick."

"I can't tell him that. I'm not ready to make the kind of
commitment he wants, so I don't have the right to keep
him from being happy."

"You have every right! He's your husband."

"On paper, but that's about it." London sighed. "Maybe I
should give Creighton a call," she pondered aloud. "If
Bernard has a friend, why can't I?"

"London, don't reach out to Creighton. That's going
backward."

"Not necessarily. My future could just as easily lie with
Creighton as it does with Bernard. He's getting a divorce,
you know."

"Yes, and you can totally believe that because Creighton
always tells the truth."

"I actually believe him this time, San. Apparently,
Creighton's not the only one with wandering eyes. His
wife has been having an affair of her own."

"I wouldn't make any moves until it's in writing," cautioned Cassandra.

"What am I supposed to do in the meantime?"

"You need to try to work things out with your husband.

As you can see, these women are on the prowl. You don't have the luxury of biding your time."

"How can I fight for someone who I'm not even sure I want?"

"So you're just going to let this other chick take him?"

"She's not *taking* him," London told her.

"You're right," agreed Cassandra. "It sounds like she already has him."

Chapter 22

"So, this is your place," said Bernard, scoping out Rayne's chic apartment. Large bay windows overlooking the city bathed the room in sunlight, and hardwood floors shined underneath their feet. It had been two weeks since their initial meeting.

"Yep, this is it."

"And you can afford this on your cashier's salary?" Bernard asked, surprised.

"I'm a customer service representative, thank you very much. But I do get a little supplementary income from my parents. They have it to spare, and I'm more than happy to help them spend it; at least until I finish school."

"It pays to be daddy's little girl, doesn't it? Will you be looking for another roommate any time soon? I could be very comfortable here."

She shot him a seductive smile. "Are you making an offer?"

"You never know." He picked up an oddly-crafted object. "What's this?"

"It's an African artifact I picked up in Ghana last summer."

He picked up another figurine. "And this?"

She grabbed it and flipped it over, wrinkling her forehead. "I'm not exactly sure what that is. I saw it a little junk shop in New Delhi and had to have it."

Bernard set it back into place. "I see you're a well-traveled young lady."

"Yeah, but ATL is home, you know? Sit down." She led him to her plush sofa and sat down beside him.

"There's no place like home," he agreed. "My sisters are spread out everywhere—New York, Houston, Phoenix, L.A—but my brother and I never strayed too far from here."

"So what, or shall I say *who*, has kept you around this long?"

"Well, the restaurant for one . . . my brother . . . London."

"London . . . right." She squirmed uneasily in her seat.

"She's been my best friend for years, Rayne. She's like family."

"She's your wife. She *is* family." They were silent a moment, both feeling a bit guilty. "So, tell me about her. What's she like? I don't think I got the full range of her when we met."

He exhaled. "London is sort of the high-strung, melodramatic type. Everything has to be this big production with her, and it's always, *always* all about London. She's extremely myopic. She's got a good heart, though. She's actually pretty cool once you get to know her."

"You two never dated?"

"Nope. As much as I love her, we have absolutely nothing in common."

"That can be good, I suppose, if you balance each other

out. What about the ex-girlfriend you told me about . . . Vanessa?"

"Vanessa is this big ball of energy, always unpredictable and spontaneous. You know, the kind who says the first thing that pops into her head and doesn't give a flip about what anyone else thinks. To tell you the truth, she reminds me of you."

"She sounds like my kind of girl. We even have the same taste in men."

He was flattered. "What about you? What are you looking for in a man?"

Rayne looked into his eyes. "Everything I've found in you."

"Under different circumstances, London would probably be the main one cheering us on and telling me how stupid I must be if I let you get away." He dropped his head. "Things would be so different if we hadn't gone to Vegas that night."

"If nothing else, I wouldn't feel like an adulteress every time I thought about kissing you."

His gaze met hers. "You've thought about kissing me?"

"Well, yeah," she admitted bashfully. "I like you, Bernard."

"I like you, too. You're good people."

"*Good people!*" she decried. "Whatever happened to words like fun and sexy and exciting?"

Bernard grinned broadly. "You're those things, too."

Edging closer to him, she said, "I could tell you what I think of you." She teased him with another coy smile. "Or I could just show you." She leaned into him, planting a kiss on his lips.

He opened his eyes and gently pushed her away. "Rayne, I—"

Rayne held up her hand. "You don't have to say it. You're married, and I need to respect that." He nodded.

"But don't you feel anything toward me? I can't believe that feelings this intense are completely one-sided."

"You already know that I'm attracted to you." She reached over and touched his hand. "But I'm still married."

"It's a marriage in name only, right? I mean, it's just a matter of time before you file for divorce. You're not even in love with her; you told me so yourself. And it's clear that she's not in love with you."

"She's my wife, and I can't just pretend like she's not."

"Then why are you here?" she challenged. "Why do you keep calling and spending time with me? You're making it almost impossible for me *not* to fall in love with you."

He held her hands in his. "Rayne, I'm at a point in my life where I really need a friend, and I apologize if I've been selfish or made you feel like I'm taking advantage of you or the situation. I would hate to lose your friendship right now, but I'll understand if you think that that is what's best for you."

"I don't want to lose you either. I just want to know that when the smoke clears, that there could be a chance for us."

Bernard shook his head. "I can't make you any promises, and I don't want to lead you on. And you know that the last thing I'd want to do is hurt you."

She playfully punched him in the chest. "Hey, lighten up, will you? Let's just kill all the serious talk and just enjoy the ride and see where life takes us. I'm not going anywhere and neither are you, okay? Let's just enjoy the day like we planned."

"I'm serious about not wanting you to get hurt, Rayne."

"I'm a big girl; my eyes are wide open. Just don't be alarmed if I try to steal a kiss every once in a while when you're not looking."

"Just let me know if all my drama gets to be too much for you."

"You don't have to worry about me, Bernard." Then she thought to herself, *Your wife, on the other hand, may have to.*

Chapter 23

The day, which had started out sunny and promising, ended with a tornado watch and a powerful thunderstorm. Bernard rushed home amid the pouring rain and flying debris, worried about London. He knew that storms triggered bad memories for her and grew concerned when he arrived home and didn't find her there.

"London?" he called out, praying that she wasn't out in the storm. "London, are you home?"

He cracked open her bedroom door and spotted her on the bed, hugging her knees close to her chest, shuddering whenever the thunder rolled and crackled outside. "Are you okay?"

"I don't like thunderstorms," she answered, rocking back and forth. "I've been afraid of them ever since I was little."

Bernard moved into the room. "I know."

London nodded, jerking her head toward the window when the lightening flickered outside. "It was storming just like it is now on the night of my parents' accident. I remember wondering how Daddy was going to be able to see in all that rain. Deep down, I knew that something bad was about to happen." She hugged herself tighter. "Thunder and lightening always make me think of death."

He slid next to her on the bed and draped comforting arms around her. "I'm here now, and you don't have to be afraid anymore," he whispered and kissed her cheek. "Don't you remember how I used to run across the street and climb through your window and sit with you until the storm passed?"

Having him at her side relaxed London now as it did then. "Will you stay here with me and hold me like you used to, just a little while?"

"You know I will if that's what you want." She lay back in his arms and closed her eyes as he stroked her head. A blinding flash of lightning surrounded the room, and the power zapped off. "That's great," he mumbled. "You got any candles?"

She nodded. "There are about four over on the dresser. There should be some matches over there, too."

He groped the furniture until he felt the plate holding four multi-sized candles. He struck the match. "Let there be light," he commanded and lit one of the candles. It emitted a warm, romantic glow in the room and splashed elongated shadows on the wall.

He quickly lit the rest of the candles and returned to London's side, enveloping her and running his fingers through her hair. "Your hair is so soft," he murmured.

She let out a sigh. "That feels good."

"You know, maybe it isn't the storm itself that scares you as much as the memories that you have associated with it. Maybe it's time for some good storm memories."

"Like what? Being in here with no power and no heat?"

"Well, we've got each other to keep warm and the candles for light. It could be worse."

Another streak of lightning pierced through the window followed by an ominous roar of thunder that shook the room. Hail and rain pounded against the roof. London clung tighter to Bernard. He could feel her trembling. "It's all right; I've got you. You're safe."

"I just wish the storm would pass already." She dropped her head. "It's kind of humiliating for me to let you see me acting this way."

"I don't know why. This isn't nearly as embarrassing as the time you tripped off the stage at graduation."

She smacked him. "You promised me that you'd never bring that up again!"

He kissed her on the cheek. "I'm sorry."

"It's bad enough that you were laughing louder than anyone else in the crowd," she recalled.

"Hey, you know that I would have caught you if I could. Don't I always?"

"Yes, you do," she admitted, looking up at him. "You're like my ghetto knight in platinum armor."

"I hope that I always will be." He smiled and tilted her chin a little and leaned down to kiss her, softly and gently. She closed her eyes, swept up in the moment.

When London opened her eyes, Bernard didn't see the fear that had plagued them before. He leaned down and kissed her again, this time more intensely. She returned his passion with her own ravenous kisses.

Her body tensed upon hearing the thunder rumble outside again. He could hear her heart racing. "Don't be afraid," he whispered. "I won't let anything happen to you."

She grew calm again. She liked the way his body felt against hers. She shivered at his touch, and each kiss he planted seemed to charm her body into submission. She drank him in, becoming intoxicated with desire.

He lowered her onto the bed, and she moaned softly as he peeled back her blouse and consumed her neck and chest. "Are you sure about this?" he asked.

"Yes . . . no . . . I mean, I don't want to confuse things even more."

"We won't." He kissed her on the forehead and weaved his hand into her fingers. "And we will do or *not* do whatever you want." He gently brushed his lips across her fingertips.

"What do you want to do?" she asked, ready to yield to him.

"I want you," he replied softly.

"Then it looks like we want the same thing." He locked his strong arms around her body. She was a willing prisoner of his raw passion. They kissed and touched, greedily devouring the other until their bodies quaked from the results thereof. They fell away from each other, breathless and spent. Rather than rack her brain trying to justify her actions or mull over the consequences, she blamed it all on the rain and drifted off to sleep.

Chapter 24

Her head assured her that nothing had to change, but, in reality, everything had.

By morning, the electricity had been restored, and the aroma of freshly-brewed coffee circulated throughout the townhouse. Bernard glimpsed at his watch on the night-stand. It was 7:43. If he hurried, he could still meet Rayne in time for their morning workout before heading to the restaurant.

As he drew up his pants, he noticed London standing in the doorway with a breakfast tray made up of juice, coffee, and fresh fruit.

She was wrapped in a pink satin robe and greeted him with a scintillating simper. "Good morning, sleepyhead. Why don't you get back in bed? I made breakfast."

"Can't," he replied, pulling his shirt over his head. "I'm already late as it is." He whizzed by her, pausing only long enough to grab the coffee. "I'll take this, though."

London trailed him down the hall into the bathroom. "Do you have to leave right now?"

"Yes, I wish you had woke me up when you got up," he

added gruffly. He splashed some water on his face and brushed his teeth. London looked on anxiously. Surely, he was not going to act as if their night of passion never happened.

"I was hoping that we could talk about last night," she revealed to him.

"What about it?" He hardly paid her any attention as he loaded up his gym bag.

"Bernard . . . I mean," she stumbled, unable to articulate everything that she wanted to say.

"Are you still embarrassed about the whole storm thing? Don't worry about it. I've seen you embarrass yourself much worse than that," he added with a smile. "So you're afraid of storms—everybody's got to have a fear of something, right?"

"No, I'm not embarrassed about that. I'm just . . . what you did for me last night . . . it was amazing."

He stopped and looked at her. "Are we talking about comforting you during the storm or something else?"

She desperately wanted to tell him how connected she felt to him and how, for the first time, she actually felt like his wife. How their night together solidified her feelings for him and how more than anything she wanted to give their marriage a try. As she geared up to tell him that, she chickened out before the words fell from her lips.

"I was talking about you staying with me during the storm, what else?" she lied. "I know that things went a little further than either of us expected, but I want you to know that everything is cool. I know that this doesn't change anything between us. Last night was just a freak of nature or something."

"So what you're saying is that whatever happened in your bedroom stays in the bedroom, right?"

She gave him the thumbs up and squeaked out, "Right."

"No problem. Look, I've got to go."

"Do you think we could finish up this conversation later on tonight?"

"Yeah, sure." He looked at her again. It was obvious that there was more that she wanted to say. "Are you okay?"

She nodded. "You better get going." He jogged out without waving good-bye. She climbed back into bed alone and full of regret.

"There's something different about you, girl." Essie gripped London's chin, turning it left to right to inspect her profile. "Uh-huh . . . what you and that husband of yours been up to? Been making me a grandbaby by the looks of it."

"Nana, what goes on in the bedroom is a private matter, don't you think?" argued London, biting into one of her grandmother's freshly-baked buttermilk biscuits.

"So, does that mean that y'all finally got *something* going on in the bedroom?"

She was flushed. "You could say that."

Essie threw up her hands in jubilation. "Well, praise the Lord!"

"You're thanking God for sex?"

"Shoot, yeah!" crowed Essie. "It's about time you started acting like a real wife."

"Don't get carried away. It was just one night. It's not like it was planned or anything; it just sort of happened. Nothing's changed between us." London shrugged her shoulders. "I don't think Bernard's even given it a second thought."

Essie became serious. "But you have, haven't you, baby?"

"Of course not." Essie stared her down. "Maybe a little."

"It's like that for us women, you know. When we make love to a man, we become soul-tied; the Lord just made us that way. That's why you can't go around jumping in the bed with everybody. That feeling is reserved for your husband and him only."

"But what am I going to do, Nana? I've spent so much time screwing up my marriage that I don't think he'll ever give me another chance."

"Did you tell him how you feel?"

London shook her head. "I tried, but I punked out. It's probably for the best. Who knows how I'll feel about him tomorrow? Hopefully, these feelings will all be gone by then."

"Tomorrow won't make a difference. You'll still love him just like you always have."

"What about Creighton? I have very strong feelings for him, too."

Essie frowned up at her. "I told you to leave that man alone, Lonnie! You're just asking for trouble."

"Bernard's seeing someone, too."

Essie shook her head. "I don't understand why y'all are disrespecting God this way. Don't you know that this is a slap in the face to Him? Marriage is supposed to be honorable, and look at what you are doing with it. It breaks my heart, Lonnie, to see you acting like this."

"You act like I'm sleeping with Creighton."

"If you keep hanging around him, it's only a matter of time. The sin starts in the mind long before you carry it out. You and Bernard are blocking your blessings and for what—some cheap little thrill you get off of sneaking around? Both of you should be ashamed of yourselves." As she was blasting London, they both heard a knock at the door. "Come on in," called Essie.

Bernard strolled in as surprised to see London as she was to see him. "I didn't know you'd be here," he stammered.

"And I thought you had to go work out," said London.

"I did. I cut it short, though. I couldn't stay focused."

London nodded. "I know what you mean."

They watched each other silently. Essie could feel the tension. "Um, I better go check on your granddaddy, Lonnie," she said, wiping her hands on her apron. "I'll give y'all a minute to talk." Bernard thanked her and watched her retreat into the living room.

"So, what's up?" asked London after hearing the door close behind Essie. She suspected that he was as apprehensive as she was.

"I can't stop thinking about last night," he admitted.

"I know what you mean. Believe me, sleeping with you was not on my 'to-do' list yesterday either. I don't know what came over me."

"I know what came over me—*you*. That summer you spent at Girl Scout camp taking horseback riding lessons has paid off," he cracked. She tried to strike him in fun, but he caught her hand. "Listen, London, I don't want you to think that I was trying to take advantage of the situation. The last thing on my mind when I came home was us ending up in bed together."

"I'm sure it wasn't the absolute *last* thing on your mind." She tried to smile.

"Well, no, that would be seeing Miss Farley, our three-hundred pound art teacher, in a thong, but you get the idea."

"Any regrets?"

"In a way. I mean, I pictured our first time being a lot different from what it was. I thought that we'd do the whole romance thing with dinner and roses when the time came. But other than that, no, I don't regret what happened between us."

"Maybe it was meant to happen that way. For months, we've been trying to orchestrate something, and nothing ever came of it. Maybe this was God stepping in to do the work for us."

"Yeah, when I was telling Rayne about it this morning—"

She jerked her head back. "Excuse me—you what?"

He could see a change come over her and scrabbled to find the words to diffuse the situation. "I mentioned to Rayne that—"

"You told Rayne my personal business? You had no right to do that, Bernard," she reprimanded, gesturing her hands as she spoke. "One night—all I wanted was one night and one memory of my marriage to you that I could think back on with a smile, and you couldn't even give me that! Are you so sprung off this chick that you have to tell her every single thing that happens during the one or two seconds that you aren't glued to her side?"

He jumped to defend himself. "Weren't you here giving your grandmother a play-by-play when I got here? Do you think I wanted her to know all the dirty details of what I did with her granddaughter? I can barely look her in the face now. She probably knows more about what I've got going on down south than I do."

"I didn't tell her; she just guessed. Anyway, she's family. Rayne isn't."

"If you would shut up for a minute and let me explain—"

She put her hands on her hips. "Who do you think you're talking to like that? I'll shut up when I get good and ready! You better watch your tone."

They bickered back and forth with one another until their shouting could be heard throughout the house.

"What in the world is going on out here?" demanded Essie, rushing into the kitchen. "I can hear y'all all the way in the back."

London took a deep breath and lowered her voice. "I didn't mean to upset you, Nana."

"Me either," said Bernard. "Did we disturb Mr. Harris?"

"He's all right, but y'all got to move past all this arguing," warned Essie. "You ought to see by now that it don't solve nothing, neither does not listening to what the other one has to say."

"He told Rayne about last night," said London. "How could you do that to me, Bernard? I'm a very private person. You of all people should know that."

"If you would let me get a word in—"

"There is nothing you can say that will make me be cool with this," she asserted, interrupting him. "You violated my trust, don't you get that?"

"Lonnie, hush up and let the man talk!" ordered Essie. London crossed her arms in front of her and turned her head, refusing to look at either of them.

Bernard stepped in front of her, forcing London to face him. "All I told her was that you were afraid during the storm and how it gave us a chance to reconnect again as friends and how grateful I was to be there to comfort you. That's it."

London softened a little toward him. "So you didn't tell her about—"

"No, why would I? I respect you too much to do that. What goes on between us is our business and no one else's." He briefly looked in Essie's direction.

London stared down at her shoes, embarrassed. "I'm sorry. I guess I jumped to conclusions . . . again."

Bernard grinned. "That's what you do, London. You wouldn't be you if you didn't. Come here." He took her into his arms and squeezed her.

Essie smiled at them. "Now that you two seem to be acting your age again, I'm going back in the room with Frank. London, I want you to look in on that cake in about ten minutes," instructed Essie before leaving again.

"Okay, just what's going on between you and this new girlfriend anyway?" inquired London as she broke away from him. "I know that you've been seeing her a lot lately. Is it serious?"

"She's my friend, Lon, nothing more, nothing less. You can ask her yourself. I really want you to get to know each other better."

London looked sideways. "Why?"

"Because you're both in my life and your opinion matters to me. I want you to like her."

"Wouldn't that be a little weird—the wife befriending the girlfriend?"

"She's not my girl, but she is my friend and I don't think that's going to change any time soon."

London exhaled. "If it's that important to you, then I'll make more of an effort to get to know her. Maybe we can all hang out or double-date or something."

"Double-date? Are you seeing someone that I don't know about?" She shook her head, dodging eye-contact. "Please tell me you're not dealing with Creighton again, not after everything he did to you."

"I won't tell you then."

"London—"

"I'm entitled to have friends just as much as you are." London decided to let him think that there was more going on between her and Creighton than there really was, hoping to spark a little envy.

"You're still my wife, London, and as long as that's the case, I think we should be faithful."

"And what's your definition of infidelity? Sex? Kissing? Flirting?"

"You know what I mean."

"Yeah, I do, but don't fret. I don't intend to do anything with Creighton that you aren't doing with Rayne. That seems fair, doesn't it?"

"I already told you that I'm not having an affair with her. You believe that, don't you?"

"I believe that you're not sleeping with her, but an emotional affair is still an affair. But, hey, what's good enough for you is good enough for me, right?"

Bernard knew she was right. He didn't have a leg to stand on or the authority over London to forbid her to see Creighton. He also knew that Creighton wouldn't be satisfied until he had London back in his bed. He just didn't expect to be so jealous about it.

Chapter 25

The last thing London wanted to see upon returning home from an eleven-hour workday was Bernard with another woman cozied up on the couch, which was precisely the scenario she walked in on. She stopped in her tracks, mortified, watching Bernard and Rayne tossing popcorn at one another and laughing so hard that their happiness rang from room to room.

London cleared her throat to gain their attention. Bernard was the first to notice her. "What's up, London? Did you get my message?"

"No," answered London, still in shock.

"I called and told you that Rayne was coming over tonight. You remember Rayne, don't you?"

London dropped her things, "Sure."

"Hi, London." Rayne threw up her hand to wave at her. "This is a great place you've got here."

"Thanks," she muttered in return. "Bernard, what's going on?"

"That was the other part of my message. There's a *What's Happening* marathon on tonight, and you know I wasn't about to miss that! Turns out that Rayne's a big fan, too. I was hoping that we could all watch it together."

"Isn't that show a little before your time?" she asked Rayne. "You look so young."

Rayne balked at the notion. "Are you kidding? Dwayne was my first crush."

Bernard slapped one of the sofa cushions. "Come over here and join us," he offered, scooting closer to Rayne to make room.

"We've got plenty of popcorn and snacks," added Rayne.

London shook her head. "No, I think I'm going to sit this one out. You two kids have fun, though," she said, rallying all the excitement of a dried potato.

"See, babe, I told you she was cool," said Bernard. London felt the heat rising to her face. How dare he call *her* "babe"? That was London's pet name. She grabbed her keys and headed toward the door.

Bernard turned around. "You're leaving?"

"Yeah, I forgot that I was supposed to meet someone tonight. I'll see you later."

" 'Bye," called Rayne, with just a little too much zest for London's liking. "It was good seeing you again." London responded with a tight half-smile and left. "I hope we didn't run her off."

"I doubt it. London is not the kind who scares easily."

"I don't think she likes me very much," noted Rayne.

"Don't take anything London does or says personally. She's weird with everybody."

"She's not weird with you."

"Yes, she is, but I get her. We have sort of an understanding."

Rayne reached into the popcorn bowl. "It sounds like your feelings for her are a lot stronger than you want to admit."

"I love London; I've never denied that." Bernard adjusted his seating and allowed his arm to fall on Rayne's shoulders. "But right now, I'm kind of focused on other things."

"Oh," she said, blushing. "And just what are those *other things*? Inquiring minds want to know."

"The 'inquiring minds' will find out soon enough." He turned up the volume on the television. "This is one where Dee makes the hamburger commercial. It's one of my favorite episodes."

"Forget Dee! First she took Mama's attention away from Raj; now she's taking yours from me," stated Rayne, lying back on his chest.

"Dee Thomas ain't got nothing on you, girl. Nobody does."

Nobody except London. Bernard sat quietly and stared at the screen with the realization that he couldn't deny that either.

London wound up at a dimly-lit cocktail lounge, sitting across from her second worse mistake in her relationship history.

Creighton swirled the brandy in his tumbler. "I knew you'd call."

"Then you know more than I do," replied London, already feeling guilt-ridden. "I swore to myself that I'd never dial those seven digits again."

"But you did," he remarked, raising his glass. "And we both know why."

"Do we?" She signaled to the bartender to pour another round for her.

"This thing between us is just that powerful, London. It refuses to die out. No ring or piece of paper is going to change that."

She brought her glass to her lips. "If you say so."

"But enough of this small talk. Which is it going to be—my place, a hotel, on the desk in my office that you used to like so much?"

She narrowed her eyes at him. "That's not why I called you, Creighton. I just wanted to talk."

"That's *exactly* why you called me; your pride just won't let you admit it." The bartender refilled his glass. "It's okay, though. We'll play it your way until I get bored."

London shook her head. "Still the same smug character you've always been, I see."

"Funny, you weren't saying all that when—"

"When what?" she interrupted. "When I found out that you were married? Believe me, I said that and a whole lot worse. I can share some of those choice words with you now if you'd like."

"No need," he took a swig of his drink, "unless you're just looking for a reason to pick a fight with me."

"Why would I do that?"

"So we can make up, why else? I'm sure that you can remember we had some very memorable make-up sessions back in the day."

London exhaled loudly and rolled her eyes. "I can see where this is going." She swallowed the last of her drink. "Meeting you here tonight was a mistake. I was hoping that we could be friends, but I see now that's not possible." She stepped down from the barstool.

"I've got a million friends, London. The last thing I need is another one."

"Well, then, I'm sorry I've wasted your time."

"You haven't wasted my time. You're only wasting yours playing wifey to that punk you call a husband." He tossed back another mouthful and set his glass down on the bar. "You know I saw him the other day."

London sucked her teeth. "Saw who where?"

"Your husband. He was at the bookstore with a nice little stallion hanging all over him, and he didn't seem to mind not one bit." He paused to gauge her reaction to his report. "But I guess he needs a few friends, too." He could see that she took the bait, so he went on. "It seems to me that you're having a hard time keeping your man's attention."

"Bernard and I are doing just fine and, if I ever have the urge to justify my relationship to someone, it certainly won't be you!"

"If your marriage is so great, London, then why are you here? The fact that you wanted me to meet you tonight tells me that you're either not wanted or not needed at your house. A man doesn't go out to eat when the cookin' is good at home, you know."

Not only was his assessment a blow to London's ego, but it was made worse by the fact that he, of all people, had said it.

"Forget you, Creighton!" she fired with hot tears stinging her eyes. She picked up his glass and lobbed the drink at him. "You are despicable and cruel, and I don't want you to ever call me again."

He was unfazed by her actions. "I won't have to." Creighton signaled for another refill as he blotted his blazer with a napkin. He smirked. "You're gonna call me."

When she dragged herself home around midnight, Bernard and Rayne were entangled in each other's arms, laughing and munching on popcorn. They didn't even know that she was in the room. She slinked into her bedroom and closed the door. She wanted to cry but wouldn't let herself do so. Instead, against her better judgment, she picked up the phone and, once again, called Creighton.

Chapter 26

"You really need to let me know when you're going to have company over," chided London the next morning when she stumbled into the kitchen.

Bernard folded his newspaper. "We were just watching TV. What's the big deal?"

"The big deal is that I don't like getting ambushed as soon as I come in from a long day at work," she contended.

"Ambushed?"

"Yes! Suppose I'd had a date with me."

Bernard shrugged. "Why would I have a problem with that? It's your house. You can have whoever you want over."

"What if I just wanted to have the house to myself?" she posed.

"Fine, next time we'll go to her place."

The thought of their being alone in Rayne's bedroom was more agonizing than having to watch them. "That won't be necessary," she added quickly.

"London, what is with you? You said that you were okay with this."

"I'm not okay with the possibility of walking into a room and catching the two of you going at it like a couple of mutts in heat. The couch isn't scotch-guarded."

"Come on now, you know I wouldn't disrespect your house like that. Besides, Rayne and I are just friends."

"Well, you should know that I've called Creighton over," she revealed, hoping that the news would hurt him as much as seeing him with Rayne hurt her. "He'll be here any minute. We're going out for breakfast."

"No shock there." He shook his head. "Why are you doing this, London? Didn't he do enough damage last time?"

"It's not like that anymore."

"Is he still married this time around, too?"

"No." She knew that he knew that she was lying. "They're separated. He's moved out."

"Or so he says," uttered Bernard.

"Creighton and I belong together. I've never gotten over him and as soon as this sham of a marriage is over, we can make it official."

"Has he told you that?"

"He doesn't have to."

"Of course he doesn't," Bernard replied sarcastically. "All he has to do is feed you a few lies after a roll in the sack, and you'll believe whatever comes out of his mouth."

"I wasn't asking for your advice or approval, Bernard. I was simply informing you. I didn't want you to hear about it in the streets."

"So this is your way of dealing with the issues in our marriage?"

"And running around with that little bookstore bunny is yours?" she hurled back at him.

"I've already told you that there is nothing going on between us. Plus, you were the one who said you didn't care if I hung out with her. Heck, you encouraged it!"

"You didn't require much convincing."

He blinked back. "Oh, so, now you care all of a sudden?"

"Just forget it!" she answered, flustered. "You can do whatever you want with your girlfriend. Just don't do it here."

"It's not like that with her."

"Are you kidding me? I saw the way she was looking at you, Bernard. She couldn't wait to get rid of me last night."

"But did you see me looking at her that way," he paused for a second, "the way I look at you?" He moved in closer.

She backed away. "Stop it. You're trying to get me all mixed up."

"I'm not trying to confuse you. I'm not the one who sits around playing mind games with you; that's what Creighton does."

"Don't start, Bernard." She tossed his newspaper into the recycling bin. "I get it, okay—you don't like him."

"No, I don't. I hate the way he treats you."

"I didn't think you noticed too much of anything outside of Rayne these days," she sniped, taking a banana out of the hammock.

"You almost sound jealous. Did it bother you to see me with Rayne last night?"

She rolled her eyes in disgust. "I'm not dignifying that with an answer."

He gave her a furtive glance. "Do you remember what we used to do when we wanted to force the other one to be honest?" he asked her.

"Bernard, if you try to tickle torture me, I swear I will punch you dead in your throat!" she threatened.

He pried the banana out of her hands and bit into it.

"That was one of our more effective tactics, but the one I'm thinking about was even better." He led her to the sofa.

"What?"

"Don't you remember what we used to do when we wanted to know the real dirt on each other? Truth or dare," he remembered with a smile.

"We haven't done that in years; not since you dared me to chew my own toe."

He laughed. "Yeah, that was a good one! All right, what's your pleasure—truth or dare?"

"I didn't agree to play," she pointed out.

"So, does that mean truth?"

"Bernard, this is so juvenile. We're not fourteen anymore."

"Maybe that's what we need. Things have been too serious around here. So what's it gonna be?"

She exhaled and shook her head. "Truth."

"Are you jealous of my friendship with Rayne?"

"I already told you that I wasn't answering that."

"All right, I'll drop it for now, but don't think we won't work our way back around to it." He paused to think. "I've got another question for you. Did you really go all the way with Chris Vining in the gym when we were in tenth grade?"

"*What?*"

"Everybody on the basketball team knew you two were messing around."

"No, we never went all the way, and I don't care what he told y'all in the locker room. We fooled around a little; that's all." Bernard laughed, and she loosened up. "Okay, your turn: truth or dare?"

He answered truth.

"Have you ever kissed Rayne?"

Bernard squirmed uneasily. "Girl, what are you talking about?"

"Your reaction just answered the question," she stated, a little disappointed.

He shrugged. "If you can dodge a question, so can I. Truth or dare?"

She grinned mischievously. "Dare."

"Get naked."

"Bernard!"

"All right—just let me see you do something naughty. You can keep your clothes on."

"I changed my mind. I pick truth."

"Do you honestly believe that Creighton is going to leave his wife for you?"

She sighed. "A part of me has doubts, but he says they've split and I choose to believe him. Your turn—truth or dare?"

"Truth."

"If you could have either me or Rayne as your wife, who would it be?"

He blushed. "Are you sure you want me to answer that one?"

"No, I'm not, so it's another forfeit."

"Then it's my turn—truth or dare?"

"Dare—a real one this time!"

He thought for a moment. "I dare you to kiss me."

"Very funny, Bernard—and I suppose you want me to stuff my toe in my mouth while I'm at it, huh?"

"Hey, that's your prerogative. I only dared you to kiss me."

"All right, Mr. Phillips, go for it."

"The dare was for you to kiss me."

She beckoned him with her finger, and he wrapped his arms around her waist. Each one moved in to kiss the other one and they both broke into laughter.

"Come on, now, we've done this before."

"You stopped first," he told her. "What's the matter, Lon? Are you scared?"

"Oh, I'll show you *scared*, mister!" She grabbed the back of his head and pulled him into a deep, amatory kiss. "That'll teach you to dare me, won't it?"

He caught his breath. "Well, it's definitely teaching me the necessity of a cold shower. I bet you don't kiss Creighton like that."

"Or you Rayne."

They hesitated for a second before falling back into another kiss. London climbed into his lap, and Bernard kissed on her neck as he dug his hands into her body. He seized her from behind and whispered in her ear. "Are you going to make me take that cold shower by myself?"

She didn't answer, but her lips found their way back to his, parting from him only long enough to slip his shirt over his head. Bernard had unfastened three buttons on her blouse when the doorbell rang.

"Let it ring," moaned London as he peeled back her shirt.

It rang again, followed by knocking. "London, you home? It's me."

They both stopped and sighed in frustration. "I guess I better get that," bemoaned London and dismounted him. She quickly buttoned up her blouse and greeted Creighton at the door.

"What took you so long?" he asked, then spotted Bernard on the sofa, who looked as flustered as London. "Did I just interrupt something?"

Bernard waited for London to respond and take a stand for their marriage. When she didn't, he knew that it was time to accept that she would never choose him over Creighton.

"Naw, man," answered Bernard. "She's been waiting for you. I was just leaving." Bernard and London exchanged wistful glances, then Bernard grumbled, "She's all yours," and left.

Creighton chuckled as he watched Bernard ease out. "You need to get rid of him; seriously, London."

London, half paying attention to Creighton, wondered if Bernard was headed to meet Rayne, was a little disappointed that he didn't insist that Creighton leave.

"Did I or did I not say this would happen," crowed a smug Creighton. "I knew you would call."

"Don't get cocky," she warned him, "I can always call security, too, and have you removed from the premises."

"No, I don't want you doing that." He let himself in and closed the door. "It took me this long to even get you to agree to talk to me again. Now, come over here and act like you're happy to see me."

She thwarted his attempt to embrace her. "We need to talk first. If we're going to do this, I have to set some ground rules." She pointed to the sofa for him to sit down. "Are you ready?"

"All right—shoot."

London stood over him. "Rule number one: no more lies! You have to be totally honest with me about everything, including your wife."

"You mean my soon-to-be-ex-wife, don't you?"

"Let's hope, at least, that much is true. I meant what I said, Creighton. I can't be involved with someone I can't trust or who lies to me. I can't forgive that, not again."

"London, I've learned from my mistakes. I won't lie to you anymore. You can trust me."

"Second, just because we're seeing each other doesn't mean we're sleeping together. I'm going to need some time on that one."

"Not too much time, I hope."

"Don't try to pressure me on this. I'm still married and so are you. We can take things further once we've taken care of all that."

He exhaled. "Any more rules?"

"Yeah, you can't come by my house without permission. The job is neutral territory, but at home, I have to think about Bernard's feelings, too."

"Was he thinking about yours when he brought his girl up in there?"

"Creighton, I told you that was a long, complicated story. Just don't drop by without calling first, all right?"

"Whatever. That better be it."

"That's it for now."

"And what do I get in return for my cooperation."

"What do you want?"

"I think you already know the answer to that one."

"Well, then, what do you think you deserve?"

He touched her lips. "You could—"

She cut him off, sensing what he was alluding to. "I don't think so."

He eyed her with suspicion. "Now, I've got a question for you. What did I walk in on earlier with you and Bernard?"

"What? Nothing," she alleged.

"Are you sure? That's not what it looked like to me."

"He left, didn't he? All that matters is that I'm here with you, which is right where I want to be."

"Then bring those luscious lips over here and act like it." She kissed him and looked up in time to see Bernard, who had returned to reclaim his wife, standing in the doorway. He didn't say a word, only shook his head and closed the door.

Chapter 27

"Today makes the fourth one," said Essie the moment London opened her front door. She was dressed in her Sunday best.

London rubbed her eyes. "The fourth what?"

"The fourth Sunday in a row that you haven't bothered to show your face in church!" London sighed as Essie barged into the house. "If you get dressed now, you can still make the afternoon service. Go on back there and put your clothes on. I'll wait."

"Nana, I can't. I have plans today."

"By the looks of it, you're already in the spirit." Essie picked up any empty bottle of wine and set it back down on the coffee table. "Girl, what kind of sin have you got yourself so caught up in that you can't even come to the Lord's house?"

"I've just been busy, Nana," she answered, disoriented from a nasty hangover.

"Too busy to praise the one who woke you up this morning? Too busy to give thanks to God for everything

He's given you? How can you say you're too busy for the Lord when He ain't never been too busy for you?"

"So I've missed a few Sundays in church. You're making a much bigger issue out of this than it is."

Essie shook her head. "I'm worried about you, Lonnie. I bet you don't even read your Bible anymore, do you?"

"When I can," she admitted. "Nana, I have a lot going on in my life right now. I can't get to everything like I want to."

"I bet you don't have any trouble carving out time for Creighton." London turned away from her. "We serve a jealous God, Lonnie. You better not be putting any man before Him, especially one that's not even your husband."

"He will be," she insisted.

Essie exhaled and started digging into her over-sized purse.

"What are you looking for?" asked London.

Essie pulled out her Bible. London groaned. "Well, Missy, if you won't go to the church, the church will just have to come to you, won't it?"

"Can't we do this some other time? My head really isn't in this today."

Essie sat on the sofa and yanked London down with her. "Where's Bernard? He needs to hear this, too." She removed her hat.

"He's at work."

"Since when did he start working on Sundays?"

She shrugged her shoulders. "Just recently, I think."

"It doesn't matter. I can go 'round there to him, too, but I'm going after your soul first." She slipped on her glasses and opened the Bible to John, chapter 15. "*Stay joined to me, and I will stay joined to you,*" she read. "*Just as a branch cannot produce unless it stays joined to the vine, you cannot produce fruit unless you stay joined to me. I am the vine, and you are the branches. If you stay*

*joined to me, I will stay joined to you, then you will pro-
duce lots of fruit. But you cannot do anything without
me. If you don't stay joined to me, you will be thrown
away. You will be like dry branches that are gathered up
and burned in a fire.*

*"Stay joined to me and let my teachings become part
of you. Then you can pray for whatever you want, and
your prayer will be answered. When you become fruitful
disciples of mine, my father will be honored. I have
loved you just as my father has loved me. So remain
faithful to my love for you. If you obey me, I will keep
loving you because I have obeyed him. I have told you
this to make you as completely happy as I am."* Essie
lowered her reading glasses.

"So are you trying to say that I'm a discarded branch
now because I've missed a couple of Sundays at church?"
London asked.

"No, I just don't want you to lose fellowship with the
Lord. You need Him more than you need anything else, including Creighton."

"Why are you acting like I've become an atheist or
something? I still love the Lord. I still believe in prayer. I
know that He's my everything."

"Then start acting like it! Give Him the time and the
worship that He deserves!" beseeched Essie.

"I will, but don't blame Creighton. If I'm not right with
the Lord, it's because of me, not him."

Essie shook her head. "You still don't know how the
devil operates, do you? If he can keep you bogged down
in this wrong relationship with Creighton, he can keep
you from developing the right one with your husband and
the Lord. This thing with Creighton has got you feeling so
shame-faced that you over here drinking and have just
about given up God altogether. I don't believe any man on
this earth is worth all that."

"I haven't given up on anything, Nana."

"Just know that there ain't room in your life for God and Creighton. Either you're going to do what's right or what's wrong. You're gonna either choose life or choose death."

London was still trying to convince herself that Essie was over-reacting when she met Creighton at her office the next day. It was almost Christmas, the first one that she and Creighton would spend together, and she wasn't about to let anyone, including Essie, spoil her joy. Creighton greeted her with a kiss and set a wrapped gift on the desk.

London reached into a shopping bag and pulled out a video game system. "I got this for the kids. I hear that this thing is all the rage this year. I had to stand in line for over an hour to get it."

Creighton seemed more uncomfortable than touched by the gesture. "That was sweet of you, London. You didn't have to do that."

"Well, they'll be my step-kids one day. I can't wait to meet them." She clasped her arms around his neck. "I think now would be a great time for an introduction. It's hard to hate someone who just spent a few hundred dollars on you."

His face soured. "Now's not a good time for that. They've been having a hard time with the separation. That's why Yolanda and I are working so hard to make Christmas special for them this year."

"I know how hard divorce can be, especially for the children. I think it's great that the two of you are setting aside your differences for their sake."

"I'd do anything for my kids; so would she."

London pursed her lips together and nodded. The

sooner the conversation veered from Yolanda, the better. "So, will I see you this weekend?" she asked hopefully.

"It's Christmas, London. You know that I have to be with my family."

Her heart sank. "I was just hoping that maybe Christmas Eve or for a couple of hours Christmas Day—"

"I can't. I'm sorry."

"Creighton, it's not like you're going to be with them all day and all night. You could make it happen if you wanted to."

"When I'm not with the kids, I'll be working. I already told you that I'm due back in court the first of January. Besides," he looked away from her, "I promised the kids that I'd be home for Christmas."

"Home?" London broke away from him. "What does that mean? It sounds like a lot more than dropping in on them for a few hours."

"It means that I'm moving back in. It's only temporary, though, just for the holidays."

"And your wife? Are you moving back into her bedroom, too?"

"We haven't discussed all that." She turned away. "Baby, all the kids asked Santa for this year was to have their parents back together for Christmas. I know you don't expect me to deny them that."

"I guess I shouldn't expect anything from you. That seems to be the only way I won't end up disappointed."

"It's just until the New Year, London."

"What if they want you to stay until Valentine's Day or until Easter or whatever, then what? You're letting them manipulate you. Staying now will only make it harder on them when the divorce is final."

"London, I don't need you telling me how to raise my kids, all right?"

"I wasn't trying to. I'm trying to protect them."

"Yolanda is their mother, not you. *We* will decide what is best for our children and right now, we've decided that it's best that I come home for the holidays, got it?"

She crossed her arms in front of her. "Don't talk to me like a child, Creighton."

"Then don't act like one!"

A deathlike silence filled the office, but London was not one to go down that easily. "Don't expect me to sit around waiting for you either. You see, I've got to do what's best for me, too."

"You've still got that clown laying up in your house, don't you? Until you handle your situation, don't tell me how to run mine."

"Fine." She held the door open for him. "Don't let the door knob hit you on the way out."

He grabbed her arm. "Wait . . . I can't leave you like this. Come here." She put up a brief fight but submitted to him, as always. "It'll only be for a week, and then things will go back to normal. You know that you're the one I want, right?"

She nodded and slid into his arms. "I can't believe that we're not going to spend Christmas together. It's our first one as a couple."

"It won't be the last one, baby, I promise you that." He released her. "I got you a present, you know."

She giggled, taking on the air of a giddy schoolgirl. "Let me see it!"

He handed her the sleekly-wrapped box. She sat down on top of her desk and ripped it open to find a lacy red negligee tucked inside. "Now is this for me or for you?" she asked, dangling it from her hands by the straps.

"It's for both of us. Why don't you run back there in the bathroom and try it on. Then you can let me take it back off."

"I think I'll save that for another time; it'll give you something to look forward to after the holidays." She neatly folded the negligee.

"I hope I don't have to tell you that it's for my eyes only."

"I know," she said, laying it in the box.

"I mean it, London," he issued sternly. "I don't want you prancing around with it on for that excuse you call a husband."

"You jealous?" she teased.

His tone was menacing. "I'm not playing with you. If I found out that you're still sleeping with him—"

"Creighton, it was only once. Besides, how are you going to question me about what I do with my husband when you're moving back in with your wife?"

"I don't want to argue with you, London. I'm just letting you know that I won't stand for you trying to play me."

She laced her arms around him. "Baby, I love you. No one's playing games here."

"Then I need for you to look me in the eyes and tell me that you're not going to sleep with him again."

She did as he asked. "I promise."

"While we're on the subject, I don't know how much longer you expect me to keep waiting around for it either. It drives me crazy that you won't let me touch you."

"It's hard for me, too, but it'll happen as soon as we start the divorce."

"I hope you plan on making that sooner rather than later."

"I could say the same to you." She laid her head on his chest. "Tell me something, what do you think about waiting until we're married to be together like that?"

He sprang back. "What?"

"Well, you know what the Bible says."

"London, I'm not trying to hear about the Bible right

now. The Bible says a lot of things that don't fit today's world and that whole no-sex-before-marriage thing is one of them. Besides, we've already crossed that bridge more than once. Ain't no need to try to repent for it now."

"There's always a need to repent."

"That's for the ones who are ready to stop sinning, and I'm not if it means having to wait months to hold you in my arms again."

"Don't you think I'm worth waiting for?"

"Of course you are, but we've waited long enough. Aren't my needs important, too?"

"Yes, but do you ever feel guilty about what we're doing? Like it or not, we're both married. We shouldn't be sneaking around like this."

Creighton shook his head. "When did you get all religious on me?"

"I've always been a Christian, Creighton. I just think—"

"I think you should give me a call when the real London returns, the one who's a wildcat in bed and doesn't mind putting on a little lingerie and leaves dissecting the Bible to the old ladies at church." He touched her cheek. "Give me a call when you've gotten all this spirituality out of your system, and you're ready to be the woman I fell in love with."

Chapter 28

"What's going on in here?" asked Bernard, walking into the townhouse that evening. London was squatting on the floor decorating the Christmas tree.

She smiled in his direction. "I was in the spirit. It's Christmas Eve. This place could use a little holiday cheer, don't you think?"

"Yes, it can. Better late than never, I suppose." He hooked an angel ornament onto the tree. "You want me to plug in the lights?"

"Not yet." She hung a silver bell on one of the limbs. "Okay, now." When the tree illuminated, London sighed and stepped back to admire their work. "Christmas has always been my favorite time of year."

"I know."

She grinned. "I guess you would." A mixture of intensity and excitement lingered in the air for a moment as their eyes met. "So do you and Rayne have plans for tonight?"

He tossed icicles on the tree. "Nope, she flew to Charlotte to see her folks for the holidays. What about you and Creighton?"

She shook her head. "He's spending time with the kids, and he has a big case coming up. I don't expect to see him again before the New Year."

"How are things going between the two of you?"

"Okay, I guess," she answered cautiously. "We're still trying to figure each other out. What about you and Rayne?"

"We're still getting to know each other, too. She's a good girl."

London spotted a new gold watch around his wrist. "I'd say she's a *very* good girl and a rich one, too, if she's responsible for that new timepiece you're sporting."

Bernard was embarrassed. "It's no big deal, just a Christmas thing."

"So, did you buy her a *Christmas thing*, too?" She could tell that he didn't want to answer. "Fess up, B. I'm not going to get mad," she lied, attaching a miniature angel on the tree.

"She saw some boots in the mall she wanted, so I surprised her with them."

"And I'm sure she thanked you over and over again," mumbled London.

"No, it wasn't like that at all. I told you, we're just friends."

"Friends who buy each other expensive gifts," added London. "It's kind of ironic, really."

"How so?"

"You bought her shoes; she bought you a watch. According to superstition, that means that she's going to walk out of your life, and her time with you is going to run out."

He suspended a ceramic Santa from the tree. "Thankfully, I don't put much stock in superstitions."

London scrounged her Christmas box for more ornaments. "Ohh, look, B! Do you remember this one?" She held up a weathered reindeer made out of pipe-cleaners and popsicle sticks.

"Yep, fourth grade, Mrs. Lowell's class," he recalled with a laugh. "You had dropped your book bag, and everything fell out of it and your reindeer broke."

"And you gave me yours," finished London. "I knew then that we would always be friends."

Bernard watched her clip the reindeer to the tree. "We haven't been doing too well in that arena lately."

London shook her head. "No, we haven't, and I know that I'm to blame for most of it."

"Hey, there's enough blame to go around. Don't be so hard on yourself." He hung another ornament on the tree. "So, I guess you'll be going to your grandmother's tonight?"

"You know our tradition—Christmas Eve worship service, then a big dinner at Nana's with all of my cousins and aunts and uncles." She tightened one of the tiny red bows that had been tied to the tree. "It would be nice to have you there. It could be Pop-Pop's last Christmas."

Bernard thought about it but declined. "Christmas should be a happy time with your family. My being there would only make things uncomfortable."

"Well, you're my family too, aren't you? Plus, you already know everybody who's going to be there. It'll be fun. Anyway, what are you going to do if you stick around here?"

"I don't know; watch *A Christmas Story* for the billionth time."

"That's what I figured. You should come," she urged. "You know Nana wants you there."

"And what about you?"

She let down her guard. "I want you there, too."

* * *

"Merry Christmas," sang London's perpetually perky aunt, Crystal, draped in her familiar reindeer sweater and green Christmas pants. She welcomed them in with outstretched arms. Contemporary Christmas music rang out over all of the myriad of conversations and laughter around them from at least four generations of the Harris family, all packed into Essie's living room.

London gave her a quick squeeze and a kiss on the cheek. "Merry Christmas."

"Now, is this that handsome husband of yours I keep hearing about?"

London grinned. "Yes, ma'am."

"Well, come here and give me a hug; we're family now." Bernard complied. "And he smells as good as he looks," remarked Crystal after releasing him.

"Thank you," said Bernard.

Crystal stood back watching them, beaming. "You two sure make a pretty couple. It does my heart good knowing that you're doing so well, especially on a day like today. I know your parents are looking down on us and are as happy as I am."

"She seems nice," noted Bernard as they watched Crystal sail off to greet other family members.

"She is. She's Nana's youngest sister. I don't get to see her much because she lives in Texas, but she definitely makes her presence felt when she's here."

"Lonnie? Lonnie, girl, is that you?" called London's raspy-voiced uncle, Stokey, as he flashed her a toothless grin. As always, he reeked of whiskey. "Come here, girl!"

"Uncle Stokey, it's good to see you again." London embraced him in such a way that pushed him away as he held her. She turned her head to avoid the dizzying aroma of alcohol.

"Girl, you sho' is pretty; lookin' just like your mama!"

"Thanks."

"This here's your husband, Benjil, right?" he asked, spilling some of the liquor inside of his cup.

"His name's Bernard."

"That's what I said, ain't it? Aye, Lula, come over here and meet ol' Lonnie's husband . . . uh . . . uh . . . Benjil—Bernard." He waved his equally intoxicated wife in their direction.

"Hey, Lonnie, how you?" Lula slurred, drink in hand.

"Good. I see you're doing well," London threw in sarcastically. "This is Bernard. You remember him, don't you?"

Lula nodded and smiled up at Bernard. "Yeah, I know you!" she exclaimed. "You're Sam's boy, right?"

"No, ma'am," answered Bernard.

"Child, I know your daddy. He used to be sweet on me back in high school. How's old Sammy now?"

"My father's name is Donald."

"Yeah, that Sam could dance just like them folks on TV. When he got to movin' them feet like this," she began stumbling through a James Brown impression, "it was something to see! You tell him Miss Lula asked about him, you hear?"

Bernard smiled and nodded, and Lula and Stokey went off in another direction.

"I'm so embarrassed," said London, shaking her head. "You must think that you've married into a family of alcoholic rejects."

"I love your family, London. They've got a lot of character and spunk. I see where you get it from."

"If I in any way remind you of my drunk Aunt Lula or even drunker Uncle Stokey, then I need to stop and re-examine whatever it is that I'm doing wrong." They both laughed.

"London, darling, over here," called London's aunt,

Camille, drawling out each word in her pseudo-accent. She snaked her way through the crowd and greeted London with a kiss on the cheek. "London, you absolutely must go over there and taste my poached pears. I marinated them in this exquisite raspberry sauce that is to die for. It's too bad that no one else will touch them. But look how they all swarm around Mama's Red-Velvet cake and banana pudding like a pack of angry bees! I guess they're more chitterlings than champagne, if you know what I mean."

London smiled politely. "Camille, this is my husband, Bernard. You remember him, don't you? He catered Nana's birthday party a couple of years ago."

Camille offered Bernard her fingertips in an awkward handshake. "That's right! You're a restaurateur aren't you, darling?"

"Yes, I am," he replied. "And it's good to see you again."

"That's fascinating. Our little London here always knew how to pick 'em. Except, of course, that awful June Bug person that you insisted on dragging home from college that year. Honestly, London, I don't know where you found him. He couldn't have been a student at the university."

"I can't believe you're bringing that up. That was like, ten years ago."

"We must never forget our mistakes, London; otherwise, we're apt to repeat them," she lectured before shifting the conversation. "So, are you two procreating or what?"

London nearly choked, and Bernard patted her on the back. "We haven't thought about it too much," he stated.

"Oh, but you must! And start saving now. With the way college tuition is going up every year, I just don't know how we're going to be able to send Jay-Wesley to an Ivy League school."

London patted Camille on the back. "He's three, Camille."

"You have to start saving the second they come out of the womb, London." She shook her head in pity. "You know, I think I'm going to go help myself to some of cousin Grace's potato salad. It's not really my cup of tea, but it does have a certain zest to it. I guess living in the country all these years has taught her something; it certainly didn't teach her how to dress, though. Don't forget, the pears are in the back," she reminded them as she jetted off.

"Wow!" replied Bernard.

"Yeah, she's something all right."

"Talk about somebody needing some vitamin D in her life!"

"Oh, she has that if the D you mean stands for dollars. She and her husband are loaded. You should see their house."

"A bunch of money doesn't necessarily translate to happiness. I mean, look at us, not exactly my idea of ballin', but we're happy."

His observation surprised her. "Are we?"

"At this moment, I'm happier than I've been in a long time, just hanging out with you and your crazy-behind family."

"Shut-up," she retorted playfully, "They're *your* crazy-behind family members now." London looked up in time to see her cousin approaching them and muttered, "Look at what the cat dragged in."

"Who's that?" Bernard asked as the woman sashayed through the crowd in a skimpy red dress that left very little to the imagination.

"That's Cherelle. She's like the slutty cousin off of *Soul Food*."

"Do I know her?"

"Probably not, seeing as how you've made something

of yourself. Then again, she's probably treated you to a lap dance at some strip club or another. Can you believe she made a play for June Bug that year I brought him home for Christmas? Worse than that, she ended up sleeping with him, too. I was devastated."

"Yeah, I remember. That's when you were going through your thug phase."

"She never lets me forget it either; always finding some way or another to rub it in my face that she took my man." London stopped short as she and Cherelle faced off.

Cherelle eyed her suspiciously before speaking. "Hey, London."

"Hey, Cherelle," hissed London.

Cherelle chomped down on her chewing gum a few more seconds before speaking again. "I heard you went and got yourself all married."

"That's right," she answered curtly.

Cherelle's gaze drifted over to Bernard, a sight that immediately brought a smile to her face. "It looks like my cousin has lost her manners and forgot to introduce us. I'm Cherelle." Bernard extended his hand, but Cherelle shook her head. "You better come over here and hug me; we're family, baby." He stiffly leaned into her as she groped his frame. "I must say, London, you've good taste. I almost wish I had grabbed him first."

"But you didn't," snapped London.

"That never stopped me before." Cherelle lifted her arms and began to sway as The Temptation's rendition of *This Christmas* poured in. "Ohh, this is my jam. You wanna dance, sexy?"

"I think I'll just chill out here with my wife right now," declined Bernard.

Cherelle pulled him toward her. "She don't mind, do you Lonnie?"

"*I* mind," he corrected her, standing firmly. "She's the only woman I want to have in my arms tonight."

Cherelle looked the two of them up and down. "Funny, that ain't what I heard," she retorted spitefully. "The word on the street is that the two of you are having problems, that this ain't even a real marriage."

Bernard stepped in before London tried to form a defense. "Lady, the only problem we're having is trying to figure out if it's possible to be more in love tomorrow than we are right now. Now if you'll excuse us, I'm going to take my beautiful wife out here to the dance floor." He slipped his arm around London's waist and led her to the floor. London smirked and waved at Cherelle over her shoulder.

She broke into laughter as soon as she and Bernard started dancing. "You are so crazy! Did you see the look on her face?"

"Serves her right," said Bernard. He drew London to him and held her as close as he could. "Besides, haven't I always come to your rescue?"

"You're my hero." She laid her head on his chest and circled her arms around his neck. They danced, lost in the music and each other.

"Look who's standing under the mistletoe," exclaimed Crystal over the music. Bernard and London looked up to discover that they were the guilty party. "Kiss, kiss, kiss," cheered Crystal.

"Go on and kiss that man, Lonnie," pushed Essie.

"Well," urged Bernard with a grin, "better do as the lady says." He lifted her chin, leaned down, and kissed her. The room applauded.

Crystal took down the mistletoe and handed it to Bernard. "Maybe you better take it with you so y'all can finish up at home." They smiled bashfully as they became the target of playful jeers. Holding hands, they scurried from the dance floor.

"I bet you didn't think I had the nerve to French kiss you in front of your grandmother," touted Bernard.

"I can't believe she let you!"

Bernard gestured his head toward the door. "When did your cousin get out?"

London turned to see who he was referring to. It was the black sheep of the family, Whip. "Whip is in and out of jail so much that we don't bother keeping track anymore." The baggy-pants, diamond pendant-wearing figure limped toward them. London greeted him with a quick hug. "Hey, Whip, you remember Bernard, right?"

"Yeah, what's up, man?" He gave him a pound. "Look at y'all, all married!" London and Bernard couldn't help blushing. "Y'all enjoying this marriage thang or what?"

"We're getting there," answered Bernard. "It's one day at a time."

"I heard that! My old lady's been talking about getting married and having babies and all that, but I ain't trying to hear that, man. Too much work out there, you know what I'm saying?"

"Whip, maybe you should have thought about that before you and Kenyatta had three kids together," suggested London.

"Hey, you know what they say—first comes the baby carriage, then the marriage."

"I believe it's first comes love, then marriage, then Kenyatta with the baby carriage, or in your case, three of them," joked London.

"Well, this is the remix! Babies come first." London laughed and shook her head. "Aye, yo, it was good to run into y'all again. I gotta jet. Honey over there in the black is looking all right!"

"Whip, that's our cousin, Kira!"

"After second cousins, it don't matter. 'Xcuse me.'"

"There's one in every family," muttered Bernard after Whip left. "Your cousin is cool, though, when he's not pushing up on family members. Did she just give him her phone number?" Bernard asked after watching the paper exchange.

"I don't know. Scratch that, I don't *want* to know!"

Bernard scratched his head and shuddered at the sight. "London, does your family know about our, um, marriage arrangement? Cherelle sure seemed like she knew something was up."

"That was just Cherelle on a fishing expedition. No one knows the details except Nana. As far as everyone else is concerned, I married my best friend and couldn't be happier."

"Look, there's your granddad," said Bernard as Essie escorted Frank into the living room. "How's he been?" The family began crowding him with hugs and kisses.

"Some days are better than others. Come on, I want you to speak to him." London grabbed Bernard's hand and slinked her way through to him. "Hey, Pop-Pop." She bent down to kiss him on the cheek. "Merry Christmas."

"Merry Christmas, baby girl." His frail hand squeezed hers as best he could.

"You remember Bernard, don't you?" Bernard stood at London's side.

He studied Bernard's face for a few seconds. "This here's your husband, right?"

She nodded. "Yes, Pop-Pop."

His wide, glassy eyes locked onto Bernard. "You be good to her, you hear?"

"I'm trying, sir."

"This is my baby," he went on. "Been taking care of her since she was seven years old. Now, it's your turn."

"I'll do my best," answered Bernard, humbled.

"Bernard's a good boy," confirmed Essie. "We can trust him with our baby." Essie stood in the midst of the crowd, with everyone camped out around her and Frank. She cleared her throat to speak. "Y'all don't know what it means to me and my husband to stand here, seeing my whole family around us celebrating the birth of our Lord and Savior, Jesus Christ. In Genesis 17, the Lord tells us that if we obey Him and do what's right, He'll give us more descendants than we can count. I look out at all of y'all, and I know that everything the Word says is true.

"Like all families, we have our troubles and our victories. We celebrate birth just like we grieve when one of us passes. Through it all, though, we remain steadfast and strong. We're a family, and we gon' always be a family. I thank God everyday for each and every one of you who's in this room right now. Let's join hands, touch, and agree as we go to the Lord in prayer."

They formed a circle, holding hands, as Essie led them into prayer. As London gripped Bernard's hand and bowed her head, she wondered if this was a scene she'd ever share with Creighton or if she was destined to remain locked out of his family's circle forever.

Chapter 29

"Well, I guess you're officially a part of the family now," proclaimed London as they entered their house after leaving Essie's home.

"Yeah, that was fun. I'm glad I went."

She smiled and hung the mistletoe in the entryway. "I'm glad you came, too. It wouldn't have been the same without you. And sticking it to Cherelle was probably the best gift you could have given me."

"It was my pleasure," he replied. "Are you ready to turn in?"

London checked her watch. "It's a little after ten, still kind of early for me. What about you?"

Bernard stretched across the sofa. "I think I'm going to stay up awhile and listen out for sleigh bells on the roof."

"In that case," London squeezed in next to him, "I better join you. You're gonna want witnesses."

He rubbed the small of her back. "It's our first Christmas together as an old married couple. Can you believe it?"

"I guess it really is the season for miracles."

"Well, we haven't fought in the past six hours. I think that definitely qualifies as one."

"Fighting seemed like it was the last thing on your mind at the party tonight." She sat up and looked him in the eyes. "What was up with that kiss?"

"What about it?"

"You seemed to be really feeling yourself for a minute there."

"I don't remember you shying away from it."

"Only because we're supposed to be this ideal couple, and I didn't want to destroy the illusion. Not at Christmas."

"So when you kissed back, that was just to perpetuate the myth, right?"

"Exactly."

"What about when you slipped me the tongue?"

"I did not!" she denied.

He laughed. "It's okay, London. Everybody likes a little chocolate at Christmas."

"You are so full of yourself."

"Yeah, but you wouldn't have me any other way, would you?"

"I didn't say all that."

"The legions of my devoted groupies deem otherwise," he boasted.

She wrapped the sofa throw around her shoulders. "I guess we both know who the leader of that club is, huh?" He didn't answer her. "Do you miss her?"

"Who?"

"Rayne, who else? I mean, with it being the holidays and everything, I'm sure you'd much rather have her sitting here than me, wouldn't you?"

He dodged the question. "Do you miss Creighton?"

"It doesn't matter whether I do or not. His kids have to

come first. It wouldn't be a real Christmas for them without him."

"So I take it that he's spending the holidays with his wife, too." She nodded, too ashamed to look up. "London, you're better than that. Why do you keep letting him do this to you?"

"I don't want to talk about him with you, okay? You and I will never see eye-to-eye on this, so let's drop it and enjoy what's left of the evening."

"That's fine with me." He grabbed the remote control. "You up for that *Christmas Story* marathon?"

She rolled her eyes. "Do I have a choice?"

He nuzzled up to her, "Nope, not unless you really want to give me something I need instead."

"You are so nasty—and on the Lord's birthday! Shame on you."

"Hey, I'm just trying to get you in the spirit of things. Don't forget what they say about it being better to give than receive."

"I'm not even going to ask what it is you're implying." She stood in front of him. "I do have something to give you, though."

"Not another bill, I hope."

"No, I . . . I know that we said that we weren't going to exchange gifts," she stooped down and reached underneath the sofa and pulled out a long white box, "but I got you something anyway. It's not much, just something I thought you needed." She handed it to him.

He rotated the box to find a place to open it. "What's in here, a car? This box is huge."

"Hardly! Open it."

He lifted the lid and held up a brown leather jacket. "Wow, Lon, this is nice!" He slid his arms into the sleeves. "This is real nice!"

"Well, I noticed that your other one was getting a little Orphan Annie-ish. Besides, it was on sale."

He posed in a mirror. "Check me out. I'm in my Tyson Beckford—Denzel Washington—Jay-Z mode right here."

She stood behind him and brushed lent off of his shoulders. "I wouldn't put you in the same category as those men on your *best* day! But, you do look good."

He faced her, grinning. "You know I, uh, got something for you, too."

"For real?"

"Don't move." He dashed into his bedroom and returned holding a slender, gold box in one hand. "I hope you like it. I saw it in the jewelry store the other day, and it looked like you."

London quickly unwrapped the box and gasped. "Bernard, it's beautiful!" He slid the diamond eternity necklace from the box and clasped it around her neck. She watched their reflection in the mirror, fingering the jewelry as she did. "It's perfect!"

"It looks as good on you as I thought it would," he replied softly. "It matches the wedding band. It really brings out your eyes, too."

She blushed. "Thank you."

"You know, it's too bad we're not a real couple. We look pretty good together."

She squint her eyes. "Yeah, in a sexless, dysfunctional kind of way, I guess."

"I'll take some of the blame for the dysfunctional part, but the *sexless* part, that's all you."

She cracked a smile. "Well, there *was* that one exception."

His hands coasted down to her waist. "I vaguely remember something like that."

"Why haven't we ever talked about it?"

"What's there to talk about? You were scared and you

leaned on me . . . and on top of me . . . and underneath me . . ." She shoved him. "I was just glad that I could be there to comfort you."

London placed her hand on his. "Do you ever think about it?"

"Do you?"

"Can you not answer my question with a question?"

"Can you?" he asked and grinned.

She hit him. "If I ask you a question, would you tell me the truth no matter how embarrassing the answer is?"

"The embarrassing answers are the ones I live for."

"Bernard, I'm serious!" she squawked.

"All right, what's your question?"

She chewed on her fingernails and asked, "How was I?"

His forehead creased. "How were you what?"

"You know . . . how was I in bed?"

He roared with laughter. "Do you really want me to answer that?"

"Yes! Every girl wants to know how she is, but is too embarrassed to ask her man."

"Then why are you asking me?"

"You're not as much a man as you are like some weird cousin who keeps hanging around! Now, tell me . . . how was I?"

"Am I ranking you on a scale from one to ten?"

She sighed, "If you must."

"Can I add or subtract points for creativity and stamina?"

"Bernard . . ."

"All right, let me think . . . . Do something to refresh my memory."

London threw up her hand and shook her head. "You know what—never mind. I should have known better than to ask a five-year-old."

"Okay, okay, I'll tell you." He leaned down and whispered in her ear. "You broke the scale, how about that?"

She smiled. "Thank you. You weren't so bad yourself; not the best, but not the worst either."

"Gee, thanks," he said dryly.

"Well, what do you want—a medal or something?"

"It wouldn't be the first time." Bernard peered up. "Don't look now, but I believe we're standing under the mistletoe again."

She glanced up, too. "You know, I believe you're right."

His eyes locked with hers. "It could spell bad luck in the New Year if we don't comply with the rules."

"I thought you weren't superstitious."

"Just to be on the safe side; otherwise, one of us could leave out of here and run smack into a bus."

She inched closer to him. "We couldn't let that happen, could we?"

He shook his head, and they gazed at each other a moment before their lips met in a kiss that led to several kisses that left them both wanting more.

Despite the fact that his hormones were in overdrive, Bernard forced himself to give her an out. "London, if you're planning on stopping me, I would really appreciate it if you did it now."

"Do you want me to stop you?" she asked breathlessly between kisses.

"Is that a trick question?" He stopped and pulled away from her. "On second thought, maybe we should chill out for a second and get our heads together."

"Yeah, you're right," she conceded, "right after we finish." She yanked him back into her arms. He crushed his lips against hers, and she eagerly returned his kisses. She wanted to be consumed wholly by his presence, his body, his love.

He glided his hand along the small of her back, pressing his cheek on hers. She didn't know what he said, only that whatever it was, it caused her clothes and resistance to melt away with each stroke of his hand. Within minutes of that fateful kiss under the mistletoe, he had whisked her off and confined her into a world of unimaginable passion and ecstasy, and there was no other place on earth that she'd rather be.

She lay in his arms indulging in the after-glow as the blazing fire crackled in front of them. "I guess you got what you wanted for Christmas."

"Yeah, and I didn't need a fat man in a red suit to get it either." He kissed her hand.

She sighed. "So what does this mean?"

"It means that I'm having a *very* good Christmas."

"I'm serious. We can write the first time off as extenuating circumstances, but this was premeditated and intentional."

"So what? We're married. We've had sex twice in four months. By most standards, that sucks."

"We're not your typical married couple."

"Yeah, most wives don't have a husband and a boyfriend," he added snidely.

"And most husbands don't have girlfriends."

"You better double-check your research on that one. And just so we're clear, she's my friend, not my girlfriend."

"You might want to tell her that."

"She knows."

"Are you going to tell her about tonight?"

"Are you going to tell Creighton?"

"I don't know," she admitted. "Sometimes I wonder if Creighton really is the man for me. Between Nana and her Bible belt, and his wife and kids, I don't know if he's even worth it. Sometimes I wonder if you and I—" Bernard's ringing cell phone cut her off.

"Who in the world is calling me this late?" he wondered aloud.

"Only one way to find out," replied London, furious about the call's timing.

He reached over into his pants' pocket and pulled out his phone. "Hey, what's up? Merry Christmas." A smile sneaked across his face as he listened to the voice on the other end of the phone. "Yeah, I can't wait either. I've missed you, too." He nodded and smiled again. London was hurt. She wanted to be the reason that he smiled like that. "I'll see you on Tuesday. Good night."

"So I suppose that was Rayne," she surmised.

"She told me to wish you a Merry Christmas." London nodded, covering her naked body with one hand and reaching for her shirt with the other.

"Is something wrong?" he asked as she turned her back to him to slip into her shirt.

"No, I'm tired. I'm going to bed."

"Why don't you sleep out here with me?" He extended his hand, inviting her back to their makeshift bed on the floor. Resisting it was almost more than she could bear.

"It's better this way," she answered, shaking her head. "We don't need to complicate things."

"Lon, we're married. It's not like we're doing anything wrong."

"Then why does it feel like we are?" She didn't wait for an answer but disappeared into her room and locked the door. She hadn't been alone for a minute before she already missed being in Bernard's arms, wondering if he was feeling the same way about her or if those feelings were now reserved for Rayne.

Chapter 30

Bernard looked up from his account balance sheet at work and smiled. "So, did Santa Claus bring you everything you wanted?"

"Not yet," replied Rayne, bouncing into the restaurant. She leaned over the counter and kissed him on the cheek. "Now, he has."

"How was Charlotte?"

She plopped down on a barstool. "Cold and lonely. I missed you."

"The ATL wasn't the same without you either."

"Did you get everything what you wanted for Christmas?"

His mind flashed back to his romp with London. "I made out okay."

"You must've been on the 'nice' list then, but I intend to have you on the 'naughty' one before the year is out."

He refilled the napkin holder. "Just what are you trying to get into tonight, young lady?"

"Everything—I love New Year's Eve. With all the parties and celebrations going on, you can't help but get caught up in the excitement. So, what party do you want to hit up first?"

"The one between the pews on Shannon Drive. I've been going to Watch Night every New Year's Eve since I was a kid."

She frowned. "Church?"

"Yeah, why not? Might as well start the year off right."

"Church isn't really my scene, Bernard. I don't agree with any kind of organized religion."

"Don't you believe in God?"

"I didn't say that I'm the anti-Christ. I just think that a lot of that stuff is a bunch of bologna."

"Like what?"

"All this jazz about commandments and sins, for one. It's an impossible standard to live up to."

"Difficult, but not impossible. Anyway, God doesn't expect us to be perfect. It's a process. That's why He gives us grace and mercy and forgiveness."

"That's just the thing," she cut in. "If it doesn't feel wrong to me, why is it a sin? Why would I need to ask for forgiveness?"

"Are you denouncing the existence of sin?"

She squirmed in her seat. "No, I didn't say that. I just think that there are a lot of gray areas. Take, for instance, murder. The Bible says that killing is a sin, right?"

"Right."

"But what if it's self-defense? What about lying? What if you inadvertently tell a lie thinking that it's the truth?" She shook her head. "There's too much room for conjecture."

"If you come to church with me, I guarantee that you'll find the answers to at least some of those questions."

She hesitated. "Is London going to be there?"

"Probably. Her family is really into the church and all that."

"Then I think I'll pass on this one. Church is the last place I'm trying to be tonight of all nights."

"You sure I can't change your mind?"

"How about a compromise? Why don't you come back to my place after church and spend the night. That way, you can fill me in on everything I missed."

He blushed. "You know I can't do that."

"See what I mean about all this religion stuff? It totally wreaks havoc on any kind of fun; especially a sex life."

Bernard shook his head. "You're crazy, you know that?"

"Yeah, crazy about you. I think this coming year is going to be the best one yet for us. A lot of wonderful things are going to come our way," she predicted.

"Do you have a crystal ball stashed in your purse that I don't know about?"

Rayne's lips curled into a smile. "Among other things."

"You sure I can't talk you into going to church with me?" he asked again, not ready to give up on her. "There ain't no party like a First Creek Baptist party!"

"I'm positive. But since you're being such a good boy now, doesn't that entitle you to a little sinning with me later on?"

He chuckled. "I'm afraid it doesn't work that way."

"You know, I wasn't kidding about all the things I have in my purse." She reached down into her bag and pulled out something that she concealed in her hand. She slipped it into his hand. "Think of this as part two of your Christmas gift. Bring it when you swing by tonight." She kissed him on the cheek and left.

He opened his hand to see what she'd given him. To his surprise, it was a key to her apartment along with a condom.

"I don't know why I let you drag me out here tonight," bemoaned London as she and Essie settled into the second pew twenty minutes before the New Year's Eve church service was set to start. "I told you that I had decided to spend a quiet night at home this year."

"Well, I can't promise you it'll be quiet, but you are at home. You're in the Lord's house, which is right where you need to be." Essie smiled and waved at two women sitting down behind them. "Besides, I know what this is all about. You want to sit at home by that phone waiting for that old snake to call you like some common Jezebel, and I won't stand for it. First Creek Baptist is the only place you need to be tonight, and Jesus is the only man you need to be waiting for."

"Shouldn't Bernard be getting this same lecture? I'm sure he's somewhere breaking a few commandments with Rayne while I'm sitting here in church."

"Didn't you ask him to come tonight?"

"I didn't think I had to. He knows we're having Watch Night."

"Don't you think it would have meant something to him if you had invited him to come with you? He wants to feel like you want him here. I bet that Rayne girl asked him to go out with her instead of sitting around wishing for it to happen. She may be a conniving little home-wrecker, but you've got to give her credit for having enough sense to go after what she wants."

"So you want me to be like her, chasing down another woman's husband?"

"Isn't that what you're doing anyway? If you're going to chase a man, it might as well be your own."

Essie's comment brought a scowl to London's face. "What are you talking about?"

"Lonnie, don't lie to me. Creighton is married, isn't he?" London didn't say anything, disinclined to lie in church. "Tell the truth, Lonnie. Tell the truth and shame the devil."

London didn't have it in her to lie to her grandmother's

face. "Nana, I didn't know, not at first. You have to believe that."

"But you know now and you're still seeing him."

"He's getting a divorce."

"That devil is liable to tell you anything, and you're sitting over here fool-headed enough to believe him! I know you know better than to be carrying on like this. You act like me and your granddaddy didn't teach you nothing about having some morals and respect for marriage—respect for yourself, for that matter!"

"This isn't about you and Pop-Pop, Nana, or anything you've taught me. It's about me and my happiness, and Creighton makes me happy. He says he's going to leave his wife, and I believe him."

"Lonnie, a man does not respect you if he'll carry on with you knowing that he has a wife at home. That's like him saying that he knows that you're low enough to jump in the bed with anybody, married or not. Does he have any kids?"

"Three," she answered.

"And how are you going to feel, Lonnie, knowing that you played a part in his marriage breaking up? You know what it feels like to lose a family because you lost your own. How can you do that to those babies? How are you gon' live with yourself?"

"I'm not the one breaking up that family. I never told Creighton to divorce his wife for me; that was his decision. Even if I wasn't in the picture, their split was bound to happen sooner or later. That marriage has been over for a while now. The kids are just having a hard time accepting it."

"And what about your own marriage?"

"I think you need to be asking my husband that. He's the one out with another woman," London said, sulking.

"The Lord ain't holding you accountable for what Bernard

does; He's holding you accountable for what *you* do." Essie
shook her head and quoted scriptures to herself. Reciting
them put her at peace. "I sure enjoyed having y'all over for
Christmas. Your granddaddy enjoyed it, too. I really wanted
it to be special for him because . . . well, you just never
know. It could be the last Christmas for any of us."

"Yeah, seeing the family and everyone gathered around
the tree singing and happy was beautiful."

"Sure was," agreed Essie, nodding. "I noticed that you
and your husband seemed to be getting along better."

"The holidays bring out the best in everybody, I guess;
even me and Bernard."

"You just gotta keep working at it, honey. It might take
some time, but you'll be glad you did in the end. And leave
that married man alone! He's bad news, Lonnie."

"I'll leave Creighton alone when Bernard leaves Rayne
alone. I can just imagine what they must be doing right
now."

Essie's eyes widened. "I can't speak for what she's
doing, but there Bernard is right there." Essie waved
Bernard in their direction. A part of London wanted to
float up out of the pew to meet him halfway.

He weaved through the pews and members to make his
way to them. "Sorry I'm late. The restaurant was crazy
busy today," he explained.

"Child, you haven't missed nothing. They're just getting
started. Sit on down next to Lonnie."

"I'm kind of surprised to see you here," said London as
Bernard settled in next to her. "I thought you'd be somewhere else tonight."

"Like where? When have you ever known me to miss
Watch Night?"

"Well, with Rayne coming back in town, I thought you'd
want to be with her."

"This isn't her kind of crowd. She's planning on bring-

ing in the New Year with a drink in one hand and who
knows what in the other."

"That's the kind of person you want to associate with?"
questioned Essie.

"No, ma'am. I'm starting to wonder if we have as much
in common as I thought." London was secretly pleased. "I
don't suppose you were keeping this seat warm for ol'
Creighton, were you?"

London shook her head. "New Year's is a family night
for them."

"You'll never be a part of that, Lon; not with him,"
Bernard reminded her.

"Bernard, we're in church for God's sake!" She rose
with the rest of the congregation for prayer. "I don't want
to argue about this right now." Without thinking, Bernard
reached over and grabbed London's hand as they bowed
their heads for prayer. He held on even after the prayer
was over.

"I'm glad you're here with me tonight," he confided to
her during the choir's performance. "Maybe the New Year
can signal a new start for us."

She gazed lovingly at him. "I hope so. Happy New Year,
Bernard."

"To you, too, London." He kissed her hand. Essie smiled
to herself, pleased.

The love-fest continued throughout the service until an
usher came and tapped Bernard on the shoulder. Rayne
was standing at the usher's side.

Bernard looked up and smiled. "What are you doing here?"

Rayne squeezed into their pew. "Well, conventional wisdom says that whoever you're with at midnight on New
Year's Eve is who you're going to spend the rest of the
year with, and I couldn't think of anyone else I wanted to
spend the next 365 days with more than you." She peeked
over his shoulder. "Hi, London, Happy New Year."

London nodded, willing herself to look happy. "This is my grandmother, Essie." Essie nodded with her lips pressed tightly together.

"Nice to meet you. I'm Rayne Hollis."

The pastor called for everyone to get on bended knees to pray before the clock struck midnight.

London kneeled in front of the pew. Through her peripheral vision, she spotted Bernard and Rayne kneeling together, hand-in-hand.

"I don't know much about this praying stuff," Rayne admitted to them.

"Just talk to God and tell Him what's in your heart," instructed Bernard. London looked on as they prayed silently, thinking that if Rayne's theory proved to be true, Rayne would be spending the next year with Bernard; Creighton would be spending it with his wife and kids, and she would be spending hers alone.

Chapter 31

Once again, London found herself staring up at the ceiling, wondering what had happened to her life. She was just as confused as she was the morning she awoke as Bernard's wife. Only now, there was a new woman in Bernard's life to contend with and the guilt of aligning herself with Creighton once again.

"You can't blame him for moving on," supposed Cassandra, setting down a plate of cookies and handing London a cup of coffee. "How long did you expect him to wait for you?" she asked after London landed on her doorstep after church let out.

London bit into a cookie and abruptly spit it out. "Not as long as you've had these cookies in the cupboard—yuck!"

"Maybe if you'd held on to *your* cookies a little longer, you wouldn't be in this mess."

"Holding on to them is not the problem; it's when I give them away that all hell breaks loose! And by the way, Bernard is the only one who's nibbled them in months."

"Try keeping it that way."

"You know, I can understand Bernard going on with his life, but did he have to have her all up in my face like that at church of all places?"

Cassandra flung her son's iPod onto the adjacent settee. "Church is a public place, and from the way you talk, she needs to be up in there more than anybody. Besides, you said he didn't know that she was going to come, so you can't fault him for her just showing up like that. Who knows—maybe it did her some good."

"I'm sure it's going to take more than a few 'hallelujahs' and praise songs to make that happen. The girl didn't even know how to pray."

"Don't be so hard on her, London. You were raised in the church, and it hasn't done much to curb your heathen ways." Cassandra sipped her coffee. "Where are they now?"

"I don't know. They claimed they were going to get something to eat, but with her, you never know. *Getting something to eat* is probably code for something nasty." Cassandra laughed. "You know, it wouldn't have been so bad if they didn't look so happy together," London groaned.

"Or if Creighton had been available," Cassandra concluded. "That's what this is really all about."

London sulked and crossed her arms over her chest. "Here it is, another holiday, and I'm all alone while he's off being the family man. Why can't he just leave and let it go?"

"They have kids together, London. He's not going to abandon them to appease you. You shouldn't even want a man who'd do that."

"I know, and I wouldn't mind including them in our lives. He won't even let me meet them, though."

"And just what do you think is going to happen when you do meet them, huh? Those kids are never going to accept you. You will always be the reason that their parents aren't together. Kareem and I haven't been a couple in years, but do you think Isaiah will have anything to do with his new wife? He resents her because, in his mind, she took his daddy away from him. I doubt if Creighton's kids will see it any differently."

London bit into another cookie. "Then what should I do? You make it sound like a no-win situation."

"You need to drop Creighton and focus on your husband while you still have one! It's obvious that this Rayne person is going for broke, and he's getting all of the attention from her that he should be getting from you. It's not too late to change things around, London, but if you keep going the way you're headed, it's going to reach that point of no return very soon."

"I'm not even sure that I want Bernard."

"Then why does it bother you so much that he's seeing this other woman? Why haven't you filed for a divorce?" Cassandra dunked a cookie into her coffee. "Why did you sleep with him yet again?"

"I asked you not to bring that up." London buried her face in her hands. "Why does it have to be this hard? I'm so confused." She lifted her head. "I do love Bernard, but it's not strong enough to sustain a marriage. And deep down, I know if Creighton asked me to marry him, I'd drop Bernard in a second. After everything we've been through together, I owe Bernard more than that."

"Then let him go. Let him find happiness with Rayne or whoever can love him in the way you can't."

"I can't do that either."

"Why not?"

"Because I promised him that I'd try. I promised Nana, too."

"But you're not trying," Cassandra pointed out. "You're both involved with other people."

"Therein lies the problem. I can't go back, and I can't move forward."

"You can move forward whenever you get ready, London. But it will require some growing up on your part."

"Are you trying to insinuate that I'm not taking this seriously?"

"I'm saying that you have to make a choice and that you need to be prepared to live with the decision once and for all. You can't have them both. If it's Creighton, then stop holding Bernard back and let him go. If it's Bernard, you need to give ol' Creighton the boot." Cassandra looked London squarely in the eyes. "So, my dear, who's it gonna be?"

Chapter 32

London defiantly turned her cheek, averting contact with Creighton's lips.

He leaned against the doorframe. "Oh, it's like that?" he asked. "A brother can't get a little affection from his main girl?"

"*Main girl*? The phrase denotes that there are others in addition to me."

He groaned. "London, it's been a long two weeks. Please don't start that, not today."

"Where have you been?" she fired. "The holidays officially ended four days ago."

"And?"

She sucked her teeth and marched back to her desk. "And you haven't bothered to check in with me once since we were last in this office."

He closed her door and waltzed in. "I'm here now. Doesn't that count for something?"

"Not when I wind up having to spend Christmas and New Year's alone."

"Baby, it's not like you didn't know where I was. I was with my family."

"And just how is knowing that you've spent the last two weeks with your wife supposed to make me feel better?"

He stepped back. "Whoa, what's with the attitude?"

"I don't like feeling like I'm the other woman, Creighton," she griped, stacking file folders on her desk. "You promised me that things would be different this time. They're not. If anything, they're worse."

"London, I've told you time after time that you're the woman I want to be with. I don't know how to make that any clearer to you. You need to stop being so paranoid about Yolanda. I chose you, remember?"

"How can you accuse me of being paranoid when you're living with her?" London asked, her voice, rising to a shrill. "I'm not imagining that; those are the facts."

"Temporarily and it's for the kids. You already know that."

She rolled her eyes, still fuming. "You said that it would just be through the holidays. Check your calendar, Creighton. The holidays are gone, but you're still there."

"I know. As soon as the kids get back in school and things settle down, I'll move back out." London shook her head and swirled her chair around. "You don't believe me?"

She faced him again. "No, I don't."

He shook a finger at her. "You see, that's what's wrong with this relationship. You never believe in me or have faith in us. I told you that I was through lying to you, but, apparently, my word isn't good enough. You still don't trust me. Well, you know what, London? I'm done."

"What?"

"I'm sick of trying to prove myself to you. No matter what I do or what I say, you're going to hold the past against me, so I'm out. It's been fun."

She sat silently for a second as he advanced toward the

door, then leapt out of her seat and called out, "Creighton, wait!"

He doused the smile that had crept across his lips before turning around.

"I'm sorry, all right? I've missed you, and I was starting to feel unappreciated. I do believe in us, and I know that you're telling me the truth."

He walked over to her and cupped her face in his hands. "I don't need for you to keep questioning the way I'm handling things with my family. The divorce is going to be hard enough on the kids as it is. I can't let them think that I've abandoned them, so if this is what it's going to take to make them feel secure, then so be it."

"I understand all of that, Creighton—"

"Just trust me." He kissed her forehead. "I've got this, so don't worry your pretty little head about anything. I'm right where I want to be."

London smiled up at him. "Is that so?"

"Now, if you just have to fret about something, it should be over when and where you plan to model that Christmas present I got you."

"I'll think about it, how about that?"

He leaned in for a kiss, but they were interrupted by Cassandra. "Ahem," she coughed, cracking the door open. "London, I found that file you were looking for." Cassandra held up a manila folder.

"Thanks," replied London, embarrassed. She slid out of Creighton's embrace.

"Well, I guess I better let you ladies get back to work," said Creighton as he caught sight of Cassandra's disapproving scowl. "I'll see you later, sexy," he told London.

"You don't have to leave," said London.

He checked the time. "I've got a deposition in about an hour. I've gotta go, but I will call you." He gave her a peck on the cheek and nodded his head, "Cassandra."

"Creighton." Cassandra's eyes followed him out of the door.

"Don't say it, okay?" began London once he was out of range.

"Say what, London? That what you're doing is wrong? That you're cheating on your husband? That you have no business flaunting your affair with Creighton at work of all places?"

"Take your pick."

Cassandra narrowed her eyes at London. "Didn't our talk the other night mean anything to you?"

"Yes, but you have to see it from Creighton's point of view. He's doing everything in his power to protect those kids, and I can't condemn him for that."

Cassandra shook her head. "You know, it takes a sorry excuse for a man to blame his infidelity on his children and a simple-minded woman to accept it."

"I resent that, Cassandra. Creighton chose me. I'm the one he wants."

Cassandra slung the folder onto London's desk. "You should take a cue from him and start choosing you, too. You need to do what's right and what's best for London."

"I am."

"Not by being his doormat! Bernard would never treat you this way."

"What do you call his seeing another woman?"

"London, all you have to do is say the word, and Bernard would drop her just like that." Cassandra snapped her fingers. "A man is always going to choose his wife over some tart he can pick up and put down whenever he gets ready."

"What makes you so sure about that?"

"You don't have to take my word for it. Just ask Creighton."

Chapter 33

"Yeah, right there . . . that's perfect," moaned Rayne, breathing heavily while she lay back on her sofa. She closed her eyes. "I needed that."

"You had quite a workout, didn't you?" asked Bernard, caressing the balls of her feet. "I knew that last lap was going to do you in."

"Yeah, yeah, yeah."

He closed the lid of the massage oil and set her aching feet back on the ground. "The next foot massage is on you, all right?"

Rayne opened her eyes and pinned her arms behind her head with a sigh. "Bernard, what are we doing?"

He shrugged his shoulders. "I was giving you a massage, and you were thoroughly enjoying it."

"No," she sat up and touched his hand, *"What are we doing?"*

He placed his hand on top of hers. "I don't know," he admitted, understanding her now. "Telling you that it's *complicated* seems like such a cowardly move, you know?"

She nodded. "What is it that *you* want, Bernard?"

"World peace," he joked.

"I'm for real. I know that by law, and in your mind, you are obligated to London. But emotionally, I think you're bonded to me."

"Of course I am. We're friends."

She brought his hand to her lips and kissed it. "We're a lot more than that, and you know it."

He took his hand away. "The question is whether or not we should be," he replied solemnly, his eyes downcast.

Rayne exhaled. "You're so loyal to her. Strangely enough, it's one of the things I love about you. I admire the way you want to honor your friendship and your vows."

"Uh-oh, I feel a *but* coming on."

"But," she drawled, "at some point, you have to do what makes you happy. You can't live your life trying to please everybody, including London."

He stretched his lips into an exaggerated smile. "Don't I look like a happy guy to you?"

"Yes, when we're together, but I think that's the only time you truly are. She doesn't make you happy, Bernard. She's not worth you giving up your peace of mind . . . nothing is."

"It just seems so selfish, you know? I made a commitment to her, and it seems wrong to bail out on her now because it's convenient."

"Don't you think you're committing an even greater wrong by being here with me?"

He lowered his head. "Maybe. Trust me, I wrestle with my conscience and my God everyday about it, but I can say that I've been very upfront with London about the two of us and where things stand. She's fine with it. She has her own stuff to sort out."

"So you've told her everything?"

"Yeah, she knows we hang out, that I spend time at your place. What else is there for her to know?"

"I can think of one thing you haven't told her, probably because you haven't told yourself."

"And what's that?"

"Isn't it obvious, Bernard? This is more than you just enjoying my company or us hanging out and being friends." She took a deep breath. "You've fallen in love with me just as hard as I've fallen in love with you."

Bernard emerged from his bedroom, where he had been holed up all afternoon thinking about what Rayne had said, wondering if it was true. He found London stretched across the sofa reading a book.

"What's up?"

She sat up. "Hey." She closed her book and stood.

"You leaving?"

"The light in my room is better," she stated.

"Why do I get the feeling that the light in here only got bad the second I walked into the room?" She couldn't answer him. "Have we gotten to the point where we can't even be in the same space together at the same time?"

"You stay gone all the time or locked in your room so much that I just assumed that you wanted to be left alone," said London.

"I don't do that any more than you do. I mean, lately, the only time I see you is when you're running out of here in the morning or coming in late at night. I've all but given up hope of us spending time together or catching a movie together like we used to do." His gaze held her. "I miss that. I miss all the stuff we used to do before."

She laughed a little. "You mean before we screwed everything up by getting married, don't you?" He nodded. "I miss the old times, too, Bernard. I do. I'm just . . . ."

"What?"

She stared at the floor. "After what happened Christmas Eve, I'm almost afraid to be alone with you," she revealed.

"London, I know that I can be persistent at times, but I'd never force myself on you. You've got to believe that. If I've done anything to make you think—"

She vigorously shook her head. "I wasn't implying that you would. I didn't mean it like that. I know that you'd never do anything to hurt me." He exhaled, relieved. "It's just made things sort of awkward between us, you know?"

He agreed. "But why do we have to keep punishing ourselves for giving in to our emotions that one time?"

"Twice," she interjected.

"All right, twice; but we're both consenting adults. Shoot, we're married! There's no sin in making love to my wife."

"Then why does it feel that way?" she asked softly.

"It shouldn't. London, we live together; we're both fairly attractively, heterosexual people. It was bound to happen sooner or later."

"See, that's the thing," she said, gesturing with her hands, "I don't think we need to put ourselves in the position of it happening again. Talks in front of the fireplace, staying up late at night watching movies, and having candlelit dinners," London shook her head, "Way too much temptation."

He curved his hand around her waist. "Then why are you resisting it?"

"Whenever we sleep together, it only confuses things. Besides, they're other people involved now. It's not fair."

"You mean to Creighton," he clarified.

She moved away from him. "I mean to *us*."

"Look, I don't buy any of this garbage about us not being able to hang out because we might end up in the bed together. We have more self-control than that, or at least we should. Then again, I don't see the harm in us hitting the sheets every once in awhile either," he kidded.

"That right there—that attitude—is the problem," charged London. "Obviously, I don't treat sex as casually as you do."

"And I don't take everything as seriously as you do. Lighten up, will you, Lon? All I want is to take my wife—correction, my best friend—out somewhere to just chill and have fun like we used to."

"Like where, Bernard, the bedroom?" she added sarcastically.

"Hey, you said it, I didn't." She rolled her eyes and smacked her lips at him. "Just name the venue. I'll take you anywhere you want to go."

"You don't have to do that," she stated graciously to allow him to bow out.

"No, I want to do it. I miss you, London. I want to spend some time alone with you, away from this house and all of the tension that's been between us lately."

London paced the floor as she contemplated his proposition. "And I get to choose the place?"

"You're not going to take me to your grandmother's house, are you?" he asked wearily.

"No, actually, Cassandra is having a get-together at her house tonight. She's banned Creighton from the premises so I wasn't going to go, but I'm game if you are."

"What's the occasion?"

"She's celebrating how fabulous she is."

"I ain't mad at that," replied Bernard with a chuckle. "What time does it start?"

London glanced at her watch. "About thirty minutes ago."

"Are we classifying this as a date?" ventured Bernard, smiling mischievously.

"Sure we are," answered London, standing to her feet. "Classify it as February fourth."

When Bernard and London arrived at Cassandra's house, the party was already in progress, and a lively debate was sparring among the crowd of about twenty seated on the floor from the overflow of the sofa.

"Well, come on in," invited Cassandra, handing the two of them iced drinks. "I didn't think you were going to show."

"And miss out on all this free food?" asked Bernard, snapping up a Swedish meatball as they grazed by the abundant spread Cassandra had laid out on the buffet.

"Sounds like we interrupted something," remarked London as a bawl of laughter erupted from the great room as they entered into it.

"Is there anywhere to sit?" Cassandra asked the guests.

"Hey, there's room over here," called one of them to London and Bernard, motioning them to a spot on the floor.

"Everybody, this is my friend London and her husband, Bernard. London and Bernard, this is everybody!" announced Cassandra and squeezed onto the sofa to reclaim her spot next to her date de jour. "So, what did I miss?"

"Darren just added having a threesome to the list," answered a woman with a thick Caribbean accent.

"Sounds like my kind of list," piped in Bernard, lowering himself onto the floor. London held his hand as she squatted down beside him.

"Kim's brother is writing an article for this magazine," explained Cassandra. "He has to come up with thirty things that everyone should have done by the time they hit 30 years old. We're up to number . . . nine?"

"Eleven," informed a fair-skinned female, who London presumed was Kim. "More like eight if we're going by serious ones. By the way, Shateik, I'm not considering the threesome as a serious one."

"You're right," Shateik agreed, "By the time I turned thirty, I had upgraded to foursomes." He and a few other males in the room slapped hands, concurring.

"You see what we single women have to choose from?" asked a woman in black-rimmed glasses and her hair covered with Kinte cloth. She turned to Bernard and London and extended her hand. "Hi, I'm Trish."

"Pleased to meet you," replied London, shaking her hand.

"Okay," resumed Kim, "back to business. Who else has a suggestion?"

Cassandra raised her hand. "What about having a checking account? Better yet, a savings account."

"How much in savings?" asked Kim, jotting it down.

"The experts say three months' salary," chimed in Trish.

"Yeah," said Kim, nodding. "You'd be surprised at how many grown men and women are still hiding cash in the mattress and Crown Royal bags. What else?"

"Know your credit score and have a current copy of your credit report," replied an attractive bald man seated next to Kim.

"What about community service and giving back?" asked Kim, looking up from her notebook.

"How about being out of your mama's house?" asked London.

"Amen!" exclaimed Cassandra.

"You need to have a car, too," weighed in the bald man.

"In your own name," added Kim.

Bernard swallowed his drink and added, "Every man should own at least one suit by the time they hit 30."

"And taken an AIDS test," said Cassandra.

Trish nodded. "Good one."

"All right, that's 13 . . . 14 . . . 15," said Kim, counting them off on her list. "What else?"

"Be able to enjoy your own company. You know, it took me the longest time to be able to go sit down in a restaurant and have dinner by myself," admitted Trish.

"Read the Bible from cover to cover," suggested Cassandra.

Bernard shook his head. "You can't assume that everybody who reads this is going to be a Christian."

"What about: have a relationship with God?"

"Learned from your mistakes," added London, looking at Bernard.

"Treated yourself to some big, extravagant, unnecessary gift," weighed in Kim.

"By 30, everyone should have one really nice pair of shoes," added the woman with the accent.

"I think you should have had at least one hot, mind-blowing affair. It doesn't have to be in love, just extremely good sex," replied another female.

"I disagree. I think celibacy is the way to go until you get married," said Trish.

"Obviously, you haven't had the kind of hot, mind-blowing affair she's talking about," stated Shateik.

"Visited another country," suggested London.

"Fallen in love," said Cassandra.

"In that case, we're going to have to add had your heart broken, too," said Kim and looked over at London and Bernard. "Well, London, you seem to have a nice, normal, mature husband. Tell the rest of us the secret."

"It's no secret, really," London replied nervously. "We had been best friends since forever, then just decided to get married."

"How Clair and Cliff Huxtable of you," teased Kim.

"Not even close," inserted Bernard, which was met by a score of jeering "oohhs."

"What is that supposed to mean?" questioned London, a little offended.

"Uh-oh, trouble in paradise," taunted Cassandra's date.

"Shut up, Tommy. London and Bernard act like this all the time."

"See, that's what happens once you tie that knot," proclaimed a dred-locked man seated next to Trish. He raised his glass. "Once they get that ring, the good times stop and the nagging starts."

"Well, Bryce, if we start nagging, it's because y'all start trippin'!" fired off Kim.

"Thank you," agreed a female whom London had heard referred to as "Dee." They clinked their glasses together.

Another man stood up and cleared his throat. "Now, I've got something to say."

"Sit down, Raymond," ordered Kim. "Don't nobody want to hear what your pseudo-preaching, tight-shirt wearing, five-times married behind has got to say."

"Ignore her," Raymond advised to London and Bernard. "She hasn't had a man since we were in eleventh grade."

"It hasn't been for your lack of trying, Negro," Kim replied testily.

Raymond continued. "Now what I was about to say before I was interrupted by Sister Souljah over here was that marriage ain't for everybody. Shoot, it ain't for nobody who wants to stay sane and happy. Now, I've just celebrated my third divorce, so I can tell you from experience that it ain't gon' get no better than what it is." He took a swig from his glass. "That's why Paul said that it's best not to marry."

"Who's Paul?" asked Shateik.

Trish tossed a sofa pillow at him. "From the Bible, stupid! He wrote most of the New Testament."

Shateik rolled his eyes. "You know your club-hopping behind don't know nothing 'bout the Bible."

"Paul said that it's best not to marry if you have the gift of celibacy," explained a woman named Kira. "Now, I don't know about none of you, but I haven't had that gift since I was sixteen!"

"Obviously, a gift you can't stop giving," mumbled Kim.

"My man likes it," rebutted Kira in jest, "and your does, too!"

"See, that's what I'm talking about. Once you get married, all that stops." stated Bryce. "Ain't that right, Bernard?"

Bernard glanced over at London and muttered, "No comment." London's jaw dropped.

"That just proved my pointed!" exclaimed Bryce.

"No, you've got it all wrong," cleared up Bernard. "Marriage is so much more than just sex, man. Yeah, it's important, but it's not the end-all, be-all."

"Go on, Bernard," encouraged Trish. "And the rest of you no-counts need to hear this."

"First of all, you can't go into marriage with any preconceived notions about what it should be. If your girl was shy when you were dating, don't expect her to just become a freak overnight. If your man left his drawers on the floor when you were single, chances are that he's going to do that after you're married. You can't marry anyone for the person you want him or her to be, but for the person that they are."

"Yeah, y'all females are always trying to change somebody," weighed in Shateik.

"If you knew how to treat us, we wouldn't have to," added Kim.

Bernard shook his head. "See, that's another thing, and it was probably the hardest thing I had to learn. The way you treat your spouse shouldn't be based on the way they treat you. It needs to be based on the way you want to be treated. Ladies, if you want your man to be considerate and send you flowers and all that stuff, then you do it for him. Even for the dudes, if you want your girl to loosen up in the bedroom, you've got to be willing to go the distance for her. That's why the Bible tells us to have that Christ-like love for one another. You have to come out of self and what you want. It's got to be about that other person. It's the only way a marriage is going to work."

"I heard that!" sang Kira.

"But, ladies, you can't do that for every man," cautioned Cassandra. "You see, Bernard is talking about what saved folks do. You try that with some of these fools out here, and you'll end up out in the cold, looking stupid, ain't that right, London?" London knew that it was a crack at her and Creighton.

"London, you're mighty quiet over there," observed Kim. "If Bernard is backing up all this talk at home, you must be a very happy woman."

London cleared her throat. "Bernard has ideas about marriage, and I've got mine."

"Do tell," pressed Trish.

"Well, I have to side with the fellas on this one," began London. "I just think that the marriage is nothing if you don't have that pizzazz, that fire. Words and good intention alone don't make a marriage."

"Now, that's what I'm talking about!" put in Shateik. "London, I think you and I would make very good friends."

"Boy, stop trying to push up on her like that," scolded Trish. "You know she's married."

"Married folks can have friends," replied Raymond.

"That is such bull," said Kim. "Friends are just people you haven't slept with yet; therefore, married folks don't need them."

"If you're secure in your marriage and in yourself as a woman, why would it matter?" asked Greg.

"Baby, if you ever come home talking about you've got a friend, both of y'all are getting cut, for real," promised Angie.

"So, Bernard, what's your theory on having friends of the opposite sex?" posed Trish.

The question made Bernard and London uncomfortable. "Well, how realistic is it to think that you're never going to have friends outside of your spouse?" asked Bernard nervously.

"So, you're okay with it if London has male friends?" asked Kim.

He swallowed hard. "Sure."

"How do you know they aren't sleeping together?"

His eyes shifted to London. "I don't. I just have to trust my wife."

"What about you, London?" struck up Cassandra. "Does it bother you if Bernard has friends?"

"It's cool until he has them all up in my face," she answered.

"I've never had anyone up in your face," corrected Bernard.

"Oh, so you weren't all hugged up with Rayne on the couch and parading her around at church?" accused London, forgetting that they were amongst strangers.

"Who's Rayne?" asked Trish.

"Rayne is my friend. That's all she is, and that's all she'll ever be. And, no, we weren't hugged up on the couch."

"I think it's disrespectful to have her at your house, period," said Kim.

"London said she could come over," maintained Bernard.

"Oh, are you two into swinging?" asked Shateik, amused.

"No," replied London. "But I'm not going to sit here and pretend like Bernard and I have this great marriage when we don't."

"So, you just want to air our dirty laundry right here and now?" asked Bernard, looking around at the crowd, who was entranced by the spiraling argument.

"I'm not going to back down just because we're in a room full of people," retorted London. "You sat right here and talked all that junk about what a good marriage and what a good husband is supposed to be when you don't practice any of it. You're a hypocrite!"

"London, I tried to be a good husband to you, and you know it. But for the past year, you'd been so blinded by that punk, Creighton, that you can't see what's right in front of you!" he charged.

"Who's Creighton?" whispered Kira.

London pointed a finger at him. "I didn't start seeing Creighton until you started fooling around with Rayne."

"That's bull, London!" bellowed Bernard. "You might not have been sleeping with him, but he was always there, on your mind and in your heart. Now, tell me I'm lying!"

"When we got married, you still had feelings for Vanessa, too."

"Dang, how many people are in this marriage?" asked Raymond.

"I never denied still feeling something for Vanessa, but I put those feeling aside to try to make it work with you. You were my wife, not Vanessa. You were the one I wanted to be with."

"Why?" London asked in a huff.

Bernard calmed down, "Because you're my best friend, London. You know me, inside and out. I've never had to front with you or lie to you. My friendship with you has been the one constant thing in my life." He stared at the ground. "I don't know what I'd do if I didn't have you."

"Awww," gushed Cassandra.

London rolled her eyes. "What about Rayne?" she asked, still upset.

"Rayne is not the one holding us back. Creighton is."

"If this is what I have to look forward to when we get married, we might want to end this right now," Greg said to Angie.

"Your marriage doesn't have to be this way," explained Bernard. "London and I both have made some huge mistakes in our relationship."

"You can say that again!" mumbled Kim and downed her drink.

Bernard gazed at London. "But through all the fights and arguments and drama, she's still my best friend. She's a big reason that I am the man I am today. I love you, London."

London's eyes boiled over with tears. "I love you, too, B." They hugged, and everyone else clapped for them.

"So, what's up with that foursome?" asked Shateik. "London, I'm thinking you, me, Rayne, and Vanessa!"

After having their fill of conversation and the buffet table, London and Bernard left the party. "The next time we go to one of Cassandra's parties, remind me to bring my muzzle," teased Bernard as he and London drove home. "With you and those loose lips of yours, I thought you were about to tell them my social security number, drawer size, and account number."

"My mouth wasn't the only one running a mile a minute. Was there any detail about our marriage that you left out?"

"I didn't tell them how you make those little cooing noises when I—"

Embarrassed by what he was about to say, London slapped Bernard on the arm with more force than she had intended. Her hitting him caught him off guard and caused him to tilt the steering and swerve into the next lane. They jumped out in front of an 18-wheeler that was behind them. The driver slammed on the brakes and blared the horn to get Bernard's attention.

Startled by the horn, London looked up and saw that they were in route to crash into the car in front of them.

She screamed, and to avoid both hitting the car in front of them and being rear-ended by the truck behind them, Bernard swerved onto the shoulder. The car shook as it tumbled over the rocks and debris on the side of the road.

He put the car in park and looked over at London, who was hyperventilating. "You all right?" he asked, gently rubbing her back.

She clutched her chest. "Oh, my God!" she gasped. "I thought we were dead." Bernard could feel her body trembling. "Hey, it's okay." He unbuckled his seatbelt and slid over next to her. He drew her into his arms and stroked her hair. She closed her eyes and allowed herself to be comforted. They sat quietly for awhile.

"Are you feeling better now?" asked Bernard once London stopped shaking.

She nodded. "I'm sorry, Bernard. I shouldn't have hit you. I almost got us killed."

"It wasn't your fault. I should've been paying closer attention to the road. If anything ever happened to you because of something I did, I don't know what I'd do." He looked over and realized that she was still in his arms. Remembering his promise to keep a respectable distance, he quickly pulled away from her.

"What's wrong?" she asked.

"Nothing, I just didn't want you to think that I was trying to take advantage of the situation. Touching you is what got us into this weird place in our marriage."

"I was just thinking about that. In light of what just happened, I think I over-reacted. I like it when you hold me like this. I just don't want things to get out of hand. I like how we are right now, and I don't want to complicate matters."

"So does that mean that the occasional touch is permitted?"

She smiled and nodded. "Only under special circumstances, of course—scary movies, the Hawks going to the play-offs, near-death experiences . . ."

"Fair enough. Do you want to go grab something to eat?"

"I don't think I could keep anything down right now."

Bernard cranked up the car. "So, have you reconsidered your stance?" he asked.

"My stance on what?"

"On whether or not we can kick it without somebody ending up naked," he reminded her.

"Well, Mr. Phillips, after careful consideration, the court finds that we are capable of being friends, benefits excluded," she answered didactically. "Actually, it would be nice to have you around to talk to again. I think I miss that part of our friendship more than anything."

"And it would be nice to have someone around who can irritate the heck out of me every once in awhile. It keeps me humble. None of my other friends have mastered the art of aggravation the way you have." She playfully nudged him. "See? That's how you almost got us killed ten minutes ago," teased Bernard. "We can't go this long without talking again. It shouldn't take an accident or a tell-all party to bring us together."

"You're right. We've been too close for too long to let our friendship fall by the wayside."

"London, like I said before, you're still my girl, my best friend, no matter what. You don't have to worry about me pressuring you for anything. Simply being in your company is enough. Always has been." He kissed her forehead.

Their conversation and make-up session continued the duration of the ride home. London started feeling like herself again until she opened the door and stopped suddenly.

"What's wrong?" asked Bernard, seeing her face change.

"I don't know." She held her stomach. "I started feeling nauseous all of a sudden." She flopped down on the couch.

"Are you still shaken up from the accident?"

"Must be." She took in a few deep breaths. "It's passing now, I think."

"You look a little green."

"I feel a little—" London belched and promptly vomited all over the sofa.

"You had the meatballs at the party, didn't you?" concluded Bernard, drawing back her hair as she hauled up anything left in her system.

"I think I'm okay now," she said, inhaling deeply.

"You go on and lie down," issued Bernard. "I'll clean all this if the sight and the smell don't make me throw-up first."

London thanked him and settled into bed with the gnawing feeling that whatever was wrong with her was a lot more serious than nerves and meatballs.

Chapter 34

"I hope that was the last of it," prayed London, coming back into her office. "There's nothing left for me to throw up except air and the last strands of my dignity."

Cassandra looked on sympathetically. "Did you really throw up in that couple's living room?"

"Yes, and the family that I was showing the house to was not impressed with having to witness what I ate for breakfast this morning. Now, on top of losing the sell, guess who's got to pick up the carpet shampooing bill, too?" She eased into her desk chair, rubbing her stomach.

"Including what you just did in the bathroom, this makes about the fifth time this week," noted Cassandra.

"I know. I'm making an appointment with my doctor next week. Between the nausea and no energy, I don't know what's going on. John says he thinks I have a touch of that virus that's been going around. Three people have been out all week with it."

Cassandra wasn't convinced. "You're sure that's all it is?"

"What else could it be?"

"Well, I'm no doctor, but I am a mother, and by the looks of it, so are you."

London tried to read her facial expression. "I'm not following."

"London, girl, get a clue." Cassandra poked her stomach. "You're pregnant!"

"Pregnant?" London laughed. "*Pregnant?* Unless we're in the midst of another immaculate conception, I don't think so."

"Well, you and Creighton have been pretty hot and heavy lately."

"Creighton and I aren't sleeping together. I don't know how many times I have to tell you that."

"As many times as it takes for me to stop walking in on you with your tongues down each other's throats," replied Cassandra then paused. "What about Bernard?"

"He's not sleeping with Creighton either."

"But he has slept with you," she pointed out.

"Do you know how long ago Christmas was? Besides, this is Bernard we're talking about. He can't even make his bed, much less a baby!"

"I don't remember you telling me that you put a condom in Bernard's stocking, and you stopped taking the pill after you broke up with Creighton. How can you be so sure that you're not pregnant?"

"I know my body, San. Anyway, I just had my period . . . ," she picked up her desk calendar and began counting back, ". . . six weeks ago." She gulped.

"Need any more proof?"

London paused reflexively. "It's just stress, that's all. Everybody knows how tense it's been at work with the housing boom slowing down. And just this morning, Bernard and I got into a huge fight about which one of us ate the last Pop-Tart. Plus, with everything going on with Creighton and that skank, Rayne, it's no wonder that the stress is causing me to be late. Frankly, I'm surprised that I'm still getting a period at all."

Cassandra was still skeptical. "Are you saying that the possibility of being pregnant has never crossed your mind?"

"Why would it? At this point, I think my sex life qualifies me for nunnery."

"It only takes one time, missy."

London still rejected the odds of it being true. "No, I refuse to listen to this. You're getting me all riled up and for what—because I'm a couple of days late? Everybody skips a period at least once."

"I don't think you're being realistic."

"My life is almost perfect right now, San. I love my job, Creighton and I are back together, and things between Bernard and me are cool again. Things are finally starting to go my way, and I don't need any major drama or problems to deal with. I'm not about to let anything mess this harmonious balance I've got going on here, especially a baby that I don't want and didn't ask for."

"Are you saying that you'd have an abortion?"

"I told you that I'm not pregnant, San."

"But if you are? What if there really is a baby growing inside of that belly?"

London took in a deep breath. "I don't want any problems in my life right now. If it turns out that there is a problem . . ."

"What?" prompted Cassandra after London's words trailed off.

London looked her in the eye. "Then I guess I'd have to get rid of the problem."

Chapter 35

After another day and another round of purging, Cassandra decided to take matters into her own hands.

"Here." She dropped a plastic bag onto London's desk.

"What's this?"

"London, you've been moody and tired and throwing up all over the place. Either you're dying or you're pregnant. It's time to rule out one or the other."

London looked into the sack. "I asked you for salt-and-vinegar chips and you bought me a pregnancy test?"

Cassandra closed the door and sat down. "Don't you want to know?"

"San, I'm not pregnant . . . I can't be."

"Unless you had a hysterectomy while I was at the drugstore, I believe you can."

"I've slept with Creighton about a thousand times, and I never got pregnant, and believe me, we were not always careful. I seriously doubt that I'm going to be pregnant after one time with Bernard."

"How many times do you think it takes, little girl?"

"I'm not stupid, San, but I'm not pregnant either."

"Then humor me and take the test."

London pulled out the box and stared at it, "Maybe later, just to prove you wrong." She put it back in the bag.

"London, would it be so bad if you are pregnant?"

"Well, let me see. I'm married to Bernard, but I'm in love with Creighton. What do you think?"

"I think you need to wake up and face the facts." London groaned and pounded her head onto her desk. "I know how you feel. I was just sixteen when I found out I was pregnant with Isaiah. The last thing I wanted to see was that stick turn blue, but everything worked out fine. It will for you, too."

London lifted her head. "Do you think I might be pregnant—*me*?"

"There's only one way to find out."

London picked up the bag again just as Creighton barged into her office. "You ready?" he asked her. Cassandra excused herself.

"Ready for what?"

"You said you wanted to go to dinner. You didn't forget, did you?"

"No, um, let me get my coat," London replied dryly, standing up.

Creighton watched her tread across the room. "What's with you? You sick or something?"

"It's just some stomach virus, I think. I'll be okay."

He spotted the pregnancy test on her desk and held it up. "What is this, London?"

She didn't even bother to explain herself. "What does it look like?"

"Don't you need to call your girl back in here and tell her she forgot something?"

"No."

"Is it yours?"

"Yes, now can we get out of here? I don't want to get into this right now."

"It looks like you've been 'getting into' something, or rather something's been getting into you!"

"Don't act like that," pleaded London in a hushed voice.

"So all this time that you've been putting me on hold, you've been letting Bernard hit it whenever he got ready."

"He's my husband, Creighton. What did you expect?"

He narrowed his eyes. "I can't believe you've been playing me."

"You mean like you played me?" she shot back

"So you call yourself trying to get revenge?"

"No, it's not like that. Bernard and I were only together once . . . twice."

"And you expect me to believe that?"

"It's the truth, Creighton. Why are we arguing about this anyway? I'm probably not even pregnant."

"If you didn't think you were, you wouldn't have bought the test."

"Cassandra bought it, just to be sure. Can we just go to dinner?"

He tossed the test onto her desk. "Let that fool feed his own baby." He stormed out, leaving London alone, heartbroken, and facing the biggest decision of her life.

Bernard unlocked the door to a darkened apartment when he returned home from work. The neon light pouring in from the outside cast a dim beam on everything in the living room. He saw the faint outline of London's body against the sofa when he walked through the door.

"Why are you sitting here in the dark?" he asked. She didn't answer him, only sniffed and wiped a fallen tear from her cheek. Bernard flipped on the light-switch. He immediately became alarmed when he saw that she had been crying. "Babe, what's wrong? Did something happen to Pop-Pop?" She shook her head. "Your grandmother?"

"No," she murmured.

"Is it," he took a deep breath, "is it Creighton?"

"No, it's you!" she cried.

"What did I do?"

"It's what *we* did on Christmas Eve." She blew her nose. "Bernard, I think I'm pregnant." Bernard's whole body froze, trying to process the news. "Did you hear me?" she asked after a few seconds.

"Yeah . . . yeah," he replied, still reeling from the shock.

"Don't look so surprised, B. Nana always said that if you're having sex, don't be surprised when you get pregnant; be surprised if you get pregnant when you're not." She waited for him to respond or to at least look at her. "Don't you have anything to say?"

He faced her. "Are—are you all right? Is the baby okay?"

"I don't even know for sure that there *is* a baby. I just know that I'm late."

"How late?"

"Two weeks. Plus I've been throwing up and tired and irritable." She placed her hand on her stomach. "It looks like that necklace might not have been the only thing you gave me for Christmas."

"Wow," he uttered, "a baby!"

"Could the timing and circumstances be any worse?"

"The timing?" He thought for a moment. "Is there a chance that this could be Creighton's baby?"

She glared at him. "I can't believe you just asked me that."

Bernard shook his head. "I'm sorry. Please don't take it the wrong way."

"Is there a *right* way to take you thinking I don't know who my child's father is?"

"Calm down, I don't want you getting upset. Stress isn't good for the baby."

"You mean the baby that could either be yours or Creighton's." London pulled away when he reached out for her. "Tell me, Bernard, whose baby do you want it to be?"

She couldn't read his face, and he was taking longer than she thought he should have to answer. Just as panic began to set in, he took her hand and peered into her eyes. "Mine . . . I want it to be our baby."

London was relieved. "Well, you're in luck," she answered. "Creighton and I haven't been together since before the two of us got married."

"That's good to know, not because of the baby's paternity but because—"

"What?"

"Because I can't stand the thought of another man touching you," he admitted.

"I don't think you have to worry about that once I'm waddling around at two hundred pounds trying to remember what my feet look like."

"I can't believe it," he said, lightly touching her belly. "We're going to have a baby!" He hugged her.

"Nothing's official," she reminded him. "I haven't even taken a pregnancy test."

"What are we waiting on?"

She shrugged. "Scared, I guess."

"Look, I can run down the street right now and get a test. What else do you need? Pickles? Ice cream? Pickled ice cream?"

She laughed. "The store runs can wait until the midnight cravings hit. Anyway, I already have a test. I've just been too chicken to take it."

He looked around the room. "Where is it?"

She pointed to a bag on the counter top. "You know that if it says that I'm pregnant, it's going to change our lives forever," she cautioned him, opening the box after Bernard brought it to her.

"It'll be a blessing, though, right?"

"Hope so. Well, I'm going to go on to the bathroom and . . . you know."

He rose. "I'll come with you."

"Bernard, sweetie, I'm going into the bathroom to pee on a stick. It's not really the kind of thing you bring friends along to do."

"London, if you're pregnant, I want to be there for every minute of our baby's life, including this one. Don't worry—I won't try to help or anything; I just want to be there when you find out." It was pointless to stop him, and a part of her didn't want to.

"What's it doing?" she asked Bernard fifteen minutes later as he leaned over the sink to read the test results.

"What is it *supposed* to be doing?"

"It says here that one line means you're not pregnant, two lines mean you are." He brought the test to her. "Does this look like a second line to you?"

She squint her eyes. "It looks faded."

"But there's definitely something there, right?" He was already beaming.

"I think so."

"You know what this means, don't you?" he asked, ready to burst from excitement.

She tossed the test into the wastebasket. "I'm pregnant," she mouthed sadly.

"You're pregnant!" He folded her into his arms. "We're having a baby!"

"Yeah, it's . . . terrible." She collapsed into a crying heap on the floor. Bernard kneeled down to comfort her.

"Baby, what's wrong?"

"It's more like *what's right?*" she sobbed. "Our marriage is a mess, we're both dating other people, and I . . . I'm going to make a terrible mother."

He squeezed her hand and kissed her forehead. "You'll be a wonderful, sexy, intelligent mother, you hear me? You might as well stop all this crying."

She shook her head. "My life wasn't supposed to be like this."

He kissed her tears. "I know that you're feeling overwhelmed right now with the marriage and the baby, but you'll be fine. We're going to have a great life."

"You do know it's not you, right? I couldn't ask for a better father for my baby," sobbed London. "It's me. I'm just so afraid that I'm going to screw this child up like I do everything else."

"Don't talk like that. You haven't screwed anything up and you won't. I don't want you worrying about anything either. Just concentrate on taking care of yourself and taking care of our baby. All of the other stuff will have to work itself out, okay?" He lifted her off the floor. "Just trust me."

She leaned on his shoulder. "Bern, do you think that God is punishing us?"

"I think that God is *blessing* us. I mean, we're having a *baby*, London. We created a new life—me and you—on Jesus' birthday, no less. Maybe this is God's way of waking us up and showing us what's really important."

"I'm scared, Bern," she admitted. "I've never been so scared in my whole life."

"Don't be. We're a family now. You never have to be afraid again."

"What does this mean for us? A baby won't fix everything wrong in our marriage. It might even make things worse. It's still very early in the pregnancy. We still have options."

"London, the only option I'm considering is whether to name the baby after you or after me," he stated firmly. "I don't care how bad things may be between us, there are no other options as far as this baby is concerned."

She knew then that Bernard would never forgive her for aborting their child, and chances were that she wouldn't be able to forgive herself if she did. "I just don't want this pregnancy to make matters worse."

He smiled at her. "London, I started loving this baby the second you told me you were pregnant, and I probably started loving his mother the first time I laid eyes on her. It doesn't get any better than that."

"What are you saying, Bernard?"

"I'm saying that you are my wife, and this is my child. Nothing and nobody means more to me than that."

"What about you and Ray—"

"Shhh." He laid his fingers on lips. "I said nobody." He moved his finger and put his lips there instead.

Chapter 36

"You're pregnant!" exclaimed Essie the second London stepped into her kitchen.

"Dang," whispered London, "and in under five seconds!"

"Well, it's written all over your face. You're about to put the sun out of business with all that glowing," rejoiced Essie, taking London's coat.

"Be honest, Nana—did Bernard tell you?"

"He didn't have to. A mother knows these things. In fact, I knew that day you came over after Christmas; it just wasn't time for me to say anything. Now, come here and let me look at you and that baby." London stood helplessly as Essie inspected and prodded her. "I sho' hope it's a boy. We need some more men in the family."

"I'm just hoping for an easy pregnancy and a healthy baby." She broke into a grin. "Can you picture me being a mother?"

"Sure, I can!" Essie beamed at London. "You and Bernard are going to be wonderful parents."

"You know, the only thing that could make this moment more perfect is if my mother was here to see it."

"She is here, baby," Essie assured her. "I see her every time I look at you, and her spirit will be in this baby, too."

"Thank you, Nana."

"And even though your real mama's gone, I want you to know I've never seen you as anything other than my own daughter. Your granddaddy and me couldn't love you more if you were our own."

"Where is Pop-Pop, by the way?"

"He's sleeping; he needs his rest."

"Do you think it'll be okay to tell him?"

Essie nodded. "I think it'll give him something to look forward to, something to live for."

"Wouldn't it be great to see Pop-Pop chasing the baby around the backyard and playing hide-and-seek like he used to do with me?"

"That would be a blessing. But even if he can't, you've got Bernard to fill in. How's he handling the prospect of being a daddy?"

"Nana, he's been great. I love seeing him so excited about the baby. Yesterday, he dragged me all over town looking for cribs and strollers. He even bought a rocking chair for nursing the baby."

"I'm not surprised one bit. Bernard's a good man, Lonnie. I just hope that this means that the two of you have come to your senses about this marriage. It's not just about the two of you anymore. There's a child involved now."

"I know. The baby has changed everything for us. I think we're both committed to making our marriage the best it can be and creating a loving home for our baby."

"I'm so happy to hear you talking like this. Lord knows it took long enough, but I never stopped praying for y'all. I never gave up."

"By all means, don't stop now," implored London. "I'm going to need all the prayers you can muster."

"Now what are you going to do about Mr. Creighton?"

London flung her hand. "Creighton who?"

"That's my girl!" Essie patted her on the back. "So you been to the doctor yet?"

"Just to confirm the pregnancy. He says the baby'll be here in October."

"Same as your mama," noted Essie.

"Yep."

London winced as a sharp pain cut across her body, drawing immediate concern from her grandmother. "Lonnie, you okay?"

She nodded. "I'm fine, just a little flutter or something."

"You want me to call the doctor for you?"

"Don't be silly, Nana; it was nothing, really."

"You're pregnant now, Lonnie. There's no such thing as too careful."

"We're *fine*—trust me. I have to go. I'm meeting that handsome husband of mine for lunch." She leaned over and kissed Essie on the cheek. "I'll call you later."

Essie looked on as London pulled out of the driveway and into the street. She had a grave vision as her granddaughter sped off carrying her great-grandchild and prayed that her premonition was wrong.

Chapter 37

"See that right there? That's gon' be you!" envisioned Rod as he and Bernard watched a frustrated young father strapping a baby into a car seat outside of the restaurant. "You and London with a kid; I'm still trippin' off that one."

"Yeah, it's crazy," Bernard concurred, wiping down the counter. "But I can't wait." He waved at the last customers as they filed out.

"I'm praying that it's not a girl. I don't know if the world is ready for another smart-mouthed, neurotic London to be running around in it."

Bernard laughed. "You're right about that one! If it is a little girl, let's just hope that she bypasses that part of my wife."

"Which gene?"

"The *witch* gene!"

Rod cracked a smile and shook his head. "So, have you told Rayne yet?"

"Told Rayne what?" she asked. Neither brother had heard or seen Rayne come in.

"Hey, I wasn't expecting to see you today," said Bernard.

"Obviously. I just stopped by for a cup of coffee on my way to work." She noticed their guilt-ridden faces. "What did I miss?"

"I'm going to take care of some things in the back. I'll check you out later," said Rod and left the two of them alone.

"Bernard, what's going on? What is it that you haven't told me?"

He poured her a cup of coffee. "Do you want something to eat?"

"No. Answers would be nice, though."

He took a deep breath. "I have news."

"Good or bad?" she asked cautiously.

"I guess that depends on how you look at it." He paused. "London is pregnant."

Rayne blinked and raised her cup. "My, that girl is full of surprises, isn't she? Well, at least you have legitimate grounds for a divorce now. I mean, not even her grandmother can blame you for leaving now that she's carrying another man's child."

He raised his eyes. "Rayne, the baby is mine."

She froze. "*Yours*?" He nodded, confirming it. "How is that possible? You said that you weren't even sleeping her."

"It was one night, but apparently, it was the right one for her to get pregnant."

Rayne set the cup down. "Bernard, I don't mean to sound crass, but how can she be sure *who* the daddy is? She hasn't made it a secret that she's seeing another guy."

"It's my baby, Rayne," he stated firmly.

"How can you be so sure when—"

"I know it's mine. Let's just leave it at that."

Rayne didn't press further and drank her coffee in silence. They looked everywhere except at each other.

Everything had changed with those three words: *London is pregnant.*

"I suppose I should congratulate you," said Rayne at last.

"You don't have to. I understand if you can't right now."

"No, it's okay. If you're happy, I'm happy for you. I know you'll make a great dad. I was just hoping that it would be with me," she added with a half-hearted laugh.

Bernard looked down at her. "Rayne, being a good father is very important to me . . . so is being a good husband."

Rayne tightened her lips. "Does this mean that you don't . . . you don't want to see me anymore?" She wiped her nose, trying to hold back her tears.

"Rayne, the last thing I want to do is hurt you, but my marriage and my family have to be my priority, now more than ever."

She shook her head. "You don't have to explain. I knew that you were married and that there was a chance that this day would come." She dropped her head. "I just didn't think it would hurt this much."

He lifted her chin. "It's hard for me, too."

Rayne was hopeful for a moment. "You know, nothing really has to change between us. You don't have to stay married to her to be a father to your child."

"I made a commitment to her and to this baby. I have to honor it. Besides, this is a very stressful time for London. I couldn't live with myself if I walked out on her knowing everything she's going through."

"What about us? Are you just going to pretend like we never happened?"

Bernard exhaled. "I couldn't do that if I tried. But the fact of the matter is that there isn't room in my life for both of you. London's my wife, Rayne. She comes first."

Rayne opened her mouth to say something then closed

it. Finally, she blurted out, "It's not fair! We could've been so happy together."

"We will be, just not with each other. We can make all the plans we want, but sometimes God has a different plan."

"Who cares about God and His so-called plans," she raged. "You remember that night in church? I prayed. I prayed and asked God to let you get out of this marriage with London so that we could be together. I was stupid enough to believe that since I prayed, it might actually happen." Rayne shook her head. "I won't be making that mistake any time soon."

"Rayne, God doesn't operate like that. Your prayers have to line up with the scriptures. You can't pray and ask God to give you someone else's husband, which is what you did."

"Bernard, please don't give me a sermon about the Bible and scriptures or the mysteries behind the way God operates. I tried Him, and He failed me. Worse than that, now I've lost you, too."

"Sometimes we've just got to accept His will."

"Why do we have to do that?" she demanded to know. "London is not a good person, Bernard. She doesn't even love you. Why does she deserve to win?"

"This isn't a contest, and you're wrong about London. She does love me. We love each other. We just lost our way for a minute. We let our anger and being selfish blind us from what was important."

"Are you saying that I didn't mean anything to you? That you never cared about me?" she asked him.

"I care about you a lot. Rayne, it's just as hard and hurts just as much for me, but I know what I've got to do now."

"And that's staying and working things out with London," summed up Rayne as tears ran down her cheeks.

"It's for the best."

She nodded her head and clutched her purse. "I hope that isn't goodbye for good and that you'll call every now and then."

"Let's just see what happens." He hugged her, and she cried softly in his arms. "I'll never forget you, Rayne Hollis."

"This feels an awful lot like goodbye for good."

"Sometimes making a clean break is the best thing."

Rayne pulled away and kissed him on the cheek. "She better make you happy."

"I want you to be happy, too. And don't give up on prayer, Rayne. It really does work."

"I'll think about it." She gently laughed and reached up to touch his face. He kissed her hand as it rested on his cheek. "I better go," she whispered and scurried out, having held back the tears as long as she could.

Once safely out of the diner, she looked in at him one last time. "It's not over yet, Bernard," Rayne said to herself. "Not even close."

Chapter 38

"I think it's a girl," concluded Bernard after a long silence as he and London lay on the sofa watching a movie on television.

"I hope not! You know I can't do hair."

"Yeah, we can look at your own head and tell that." She scowled at him. "Don't worry. I had four sisters, remember? I learned a thing or two during that time. So when's your next doctor's appointment?"

"The receptionist said to come by on Thursday around two. They're just going to be running tests and making me fill out a bunch of forms. I'm about two months now, so they may check the baby's heartbeat. You don't have to come if you don't want to."

"Are you kidding? This is my kid's first doctor's appointment. I'm going to be there with my little notebook asking questions, snapping pictures and taking notes— the whole nine."

London sighed and rested her head on his chest. "I was sort of hoping you'd say that."

"London, we're in this together. Despite whatever we

may go through as a couple, I will always be there for our child . . . and for you." He kissed her softly. She smiled. "So, have you told your grandmother yet?"

"I didn't have to. I wasn't going to say anything until after we talked to the doctor and made sure everything was all right with the baby, but she knew the second I walked through the door. I told you she's psychic. Have you told anybody?"

He swallowed hard. "I told Rayne."

London didn't know if she was relieved or worried. "What did she say?"

"I did most of the talking. I told her that you and the baby are the most important people to me and that I don't have room for anyone else."

Every part of London's body wanted to smile. "Did you tell anyone else?"

"Rod knows. He's already talking about taking junior out for his first drink and to his first strip club when he turns twenty-one."

"Over my dead—ouch!" London sat up, gripping her stomach.

Bernard sat up. "Baby, what's wrong?"

It pained her to talk. "I don't know; I just felt an— ouch—there it is again!"

Bernard rushed to the telephone. "I'm calling the doctor."

She shook her head and took a deep breath. "I'm okay, just a little twinge, that's all. It's gone now."

"Are you sure you're feeling all right?" he asked, rubbing her back.

She exhaled. "I'm fine, B."

"Why don't you go in the bedroom and lie down just to be on the safe side."

"I am a little tired," confessed London.

"Can I do anything for you? You want some tea or some milk?"

"Hmmm . . . a bubble bath would be nice."

Bernard kissed her on the jaw. "Whatever my baby's mama wants."

"I can't get over you spoiling me like this."

"Don't get used to it; it's just until the baby's born. Come October, you're on your own." He grinned and disappeared into the bathroom and returned ten minutes later. "Your bath is ready."

"Thanks." She leaned on his strong arms as he helped her off of the couch.

"So, do you need me to wash your back or help you get undressed?" he teased.

She smiled. "I think I can handle it, Bernard. That's how we got here in the first place."

"I was just trying to be helpful," he claimed.

"Yeah, I bet," she called back, strolling down the hallway that led into the bathroom.

She stripped and looked at her naked body in the mirror, trying to imagine what she'd look like in a few months. She turned to the side, protruded what she could of her lean, flat stomach, and squint her eyes. She touched her belly and giggled. It was official: she was going to be a mother.

As London stepped into the tub, she noticed a crimson stream trickling down her legs. She touched it, and her hands began to shake. She screamed for Bernard, but she didn't need him to confirm what it was. She was bleeding, and her baby was in trouble.

Chapter 39

"Will you stop trying to get up?" ordered Bernard, seeing London out of bed and folding laundry. "Don't you remember what the doctor said?"

"He said to take it easy. He didn't confine me to the bed," she told him.

"Well, I am," replied Bernard, taking the towel out of her hand and ushering her back to bed.

"Dr. Carlton said that a little spotting is nothing to worry about as long as it doesn't happen again," she reminded him. "It's been two days, and nothing else has happened. I'm going to go out of my mind if I stay in this bed another minute!"

"That's too bad, London. I don't want you up until we go back to the doctor on Wednesday, you hear me?"

"I'm closing on a house tomorrow, and I have to be there." He frowned. "Will you stop looking at me like that? I'm fine, and the baby's fine. It was just a scare, that's all."

"At least let me make you something to eat."

"I thought we were trying to keep the baby healthy," she kidded.

"Oh, you've got jokes, huh?" Bernard sat down next to her on the edge of the bed. "We'll see what happens to your comedy routine when you're in labor seven months from now."

"And we'll see how many jokes *you* have when you're up changing diapers at three in the morning."

"Naw, Lindsey wouldn't do that to her daddy."

London blinked. "Who's Lindsey?"

Bernard reached over and cupped her hand. "I've been thinking about Lindsey Berniece if it's a girl—if that's all right with you."

She smiled. "Yeah, I like it," she answered softly. "Lindsey Berniece Phillips."

"Has a nice ring doesn't it? Bernard, London, and Lindsey—who would've thought?"

London looked down at her stomach. "You hear that, Lindsey? You've got a name." She looked up at Bernard. "And a family."

"Now that we've gotten the name settled, you better not try to pop out a little boy. We'll save that one for next year."

"And where is he going to sleep? This place is already going to be tight with the three of us living here."

"Yeah, I've been thinking about that. We really need to start looking for a new place."

"I know. A beautiful four bedroom just came on the market a few days ago. The owners are Cassandra's clients, and they're really desperate to sell."

"Maybe we can take a look at it when you're up to it." He looked down at her stomach. "You know, I haven't stopped smiling since we found out about the baby."

"It's like we have this wonderful secret that the rest of the world hasn't been let on to yet. I already feel like she's a part me even though I'm not really showing it yet. I can't wait to hold her. October can't come quick enough."

Bernard kissed her hand. "It's so weird, too, because at first, I wasn't even sure if I wanted this baby. Now, I can't imagine my life without her."

"I know how you feel. When we heard her heart beating for the first time, the feeling of pride and love was indescribable. I've never experienced anything like that."

"I was just relieved to know that she was okay. I don't know what I would have done if we'd lost her that night."

Bernard rubbed his hand over London's stomach. "People try to tell you how special being a parent is, but you can't really have an appreciation for it until you have a child of your own."

"You're not going to start crying again on me, are you?"

"Hey, what can I say? I'm a sucker for the ladies."

London laughed, but her smile quickly morphed into agony as she leaned forward, clinging to her stomach. She cried out in pain.

"Baby, what is it?"

"Something's wrong with the baby—I can feel it!"

Bernard leapt from the bed. "I'm calling 911."

London seized his arm. "Please don't leave me, Bernard." She closed her eyes, doubling over.

He could feel her body trembling as she clung to his sleeve. "Baby, I'm just going to the kitchen to get the phone. I'll be right back." He pried himself out of her clutch.

"Hurry—it hurts!" she whimpered, pushing back against the pillow. She looked down and saw that she was sitting in a pool of blood. "Bernard, look!" she cried. He charged back into the bedroom. Both of their eyes were wide with fright. "Why is this happening? Oh, God, don't let my baby be dead!" she prayed. "Please don't let her die!"

London awoke in a fog to her grandmother and her husband hovering over her hospital bed. She couldn't remember how she'd gotten there or the reason that she was there, but the look on everyone's face let her know that the prognosis wasn't good.

"It wasn't anyone's fault," explained Essie to London after Bernard broke the news that she'd had a miscarriage and subsequent D & C. "These things just happen sometimes."

"But why did it have to be *my* baby?" she wailed.

Bernard squeezed London's hand. "The doctor said that this probably means that something was wrong with the baby, kind of like your body's way of telling you that."

A pudgy, red-haired nurse stepped in. "How are you feeling, Mrs. Phillips?"

"Empty," answered London.

"That's normal and you may feel that way for a while. Just know that you didn't do anything wrong, okay?" London nodded. "Are you in any pain—physical pain, I mean?" London shook her head. The nurse came to London's bedside. "Mrs. Phillips, I can't imagine what it must feel like to lose a child, but there are a lot of people who do know. I'm going to give you the names and numbers of some support groups and grief counselors. We even have a memory garden here at the hospital if you and your husband want to plant some flowers in your baby's honor."

"We'd like that. Thank you," said Bernard.

"The doctor is going to come in and give you a few instructions, then you'll be free to go. Again, I'm so sorry about your loss . . . to all of you," the nurse added, looking around the room. "And the important thing is that nothing is wrong with you, Mrs. Phillips, and you can conceive again as soon as you're ready and the doctor okays it."

"Thank you," London replied weakly. The nurse left the room.

"Turn to the Lord, and He'll comfort you. *My kindness is all you need,*" quoted Essie from Matthew. "*My power is strongest when you are weak.*"

Bernard brushed back London's hair. "We have to lean on that, babe, now more than ever."

Essie stood next to her granddaughter. "Baby, I'm going out in the hall to call and check on your grandfather. Some women from the church are at the house with him now. Plus, I'm sure you need a minute alone with your husband."

"Okay, Nana." Essie leaned down and kissed London's forehead before leaving.

London sat up in the bed as much as the pain would allow her. "You know why this happened, don't you?"

"The doctor said—"

"I'm not talking about what the doctor said. I'm talking about you and me."

Bernard was confused. "What about us?"

"Nana always says that God speaks to you in a whisper. When you don't listen to that, He has to speak to you a little louder. God's not happy with us, Bern. That's why He did this."

"God didn't kill our baby, London."

"We've sinned against Him with this farce of a marriage. Now, He's punishing us through our baby."

Bernard sat at the edge the bed and took her hand. "London, you're tired and you've been through probably the worst thing a woman can ever go through. It's understandable that you might be a little confused and stressed out right now."

"Why are you treating me like I'm crazy?" she asked defiantly.

"I'm treating you like a woman who's just lost her child," reasoned Bernard.

"You can sit here in denial all you want to, but I can't. What we've been doing is wrong and now an innocent baby has had to pay for it. This is something that I'm going to have to live with for the rest of my life."

"Baby, let's just hear what the doctor has to say and figure it all out when we get home."

"I've already figured it out, Bernard." She looked up at him. "It's time that we faced the truth and admitted that this just isn't working. I want a divorce."

Chapter 40

They moved about the house in silence, grieving over both the deaths of their child and their marriage. Essie did her best to lighten the mood, but it was apparent even to her that they'd reached the point of no return.

"I'm going out," murmured Bernard, grabbing his keys and heading toward the door. London's eyes followed him out, but her lips were silent as she lay stretched out on the sofa.

"I just don't understand it," said Essie after he left. "Something like this ought to bring you together, not drive you further apart."

"Bernard and I are a lost cause, Nana. I don't even think we can be friends anymore."

"Baby, don't say that. You know, I watched him in the hospital, the way he stayed by your side and made sure that the doctor took care of you even though he was scared out of his mind worrying about his baby. The one thing he kept asking the doctor was if you were okay.

That boy loves you something powerful, girl. You remember that before you're so quick to throw him away."

"I know that he loves me, and I love him. That's not the issue. We just have no business being married."

"Lonnie, now, you know that your granddaddy is sick. He can't take care of himself, he can't feed himself, he can't even go to the bathroom by himself. Half the time, he don't even know who I am. Now, some people would say that I was crazy for loving a man like that. Even *you* said I ought to put him in a home."

"Nana—"

"But, child, don't none of that matter because I made a promise to my Jesus that I was going to love that man and take care of him as long as there's breath in my body. And I do it with pleasure, not just because I know he'd do the same thing for me, but because it's an honor to live with him and to be his wife. I thank God everyday for Frank Walter Harris."

"Nana, what you and Pop-Pop have is magical, more like a miracle. My marriage to Bernard is nothing remotely like yours."

"Child, don't you know that you and that boy ain't the first couple to have problems? Didn't I tell you about the time I packed up all my stuff and moved back into my mama's house for two months? Or when I caught your granddaddy in the woods behind the house with that ol' good-time gal, Sarah Brantley? I grabbed his shotgun and tried to kill 'em both!" Essie laughed to herself. "But we never gave up on each other. See, that's what's wrong with you young folks. Nobody wants to have to try no more. You ain't got no fight in you. The least little thing happen and y'all running off to divorce court. In my day, you stayed together and you worked it out. Wasn't no such thing as giving in, not as long as you had the Lord."

"I'm not so sure that I do have Him."

"Now, why would you go and say a fool thing like that for?"

"What kind of God takes away a sweet, innocent baby before that baby even has a chance?" London asked.

"The same Lord that gave you life and blessed you with so much already. He will be the same God that'll help you and Bernard get through this if you let Him. It could have been much worse, Lonnie. We could've lost you, too. But you're strong and healthy, and you can have more babies. You and Bernard—"

"There is no me and Bernard," interjected London.

"Baby girl, you ain't in no condition to be making these kinds of decisions. You better listen to your old grandmother."

"I listened to you when you told me to give this marriage a chance. I listened to Cassandra when she told me what a blessing having this baby would be. I listened to Bernard when he sat right here on this sofa making plans for our baby and the kind of life we were going to have. I even listened to the doctor when he told me that everything was going to be okay if I just took it easy and took care of myself and the baby." London wiped the tears from her face. "Well, Nana, I'm through listening to everybody, including you. I said from the beginning that this marriage was wrong, and I knew from the moment that I found out I was pregnant that it was a mistake. Funny, nobody listened to me, and you see what happened."

"Child—"

London interrupted her, which was something she'd never done before. "No, Nana, I don't want to hear it! My baby is dead, and no amount of listening is going to bring her back."

"My son is dead, too, Lonnie, so is my daughter-in-law.

But I didn't let it make me bitter. I didn't let it cause me to turn my back on Jesus or my family."

"I'm not like you," London said coldly. She gathered the blanket around her. "You can let yourself out." Essie watched as London walked down the hallway and shut the bedroom door behind her, not once looking back.

Chapter 41

Bernard hovered around London's bed, unable to force himself to walk out of their home and out of her life. Finally, he sighed and asked her, "How do you want to do this?"

"I don't know. You should get a lawyer, I guess." He nodded. "Creighton said it should be simple enough. It's not like we have anything to fight over like property or child—" She caught herself before saying *children.* "You know what I mean."

"Yeah. Listen, Creighton is not your attorney for this, is he?"

"Creighton specializes in corporate law; this isn't his field. Besides, I wouldn't do that to you. My lawyer is Cassandra's attorney. I doubt if you even know him."

"I don't suppose I have anything you want, do I?"

London shook her head. "Just my freedom."

Bernard started to say something, but stopped. Instead, he threw his bag over his shoulder and ambled toward the door. She watched him in silence. "I really didn't want it to end this way. To be honest with you, a part of me still wants to stay and try to work it out," he said and slowly turned to her. "But the main thing is that I want you to find the peace that you're searching for."

"I want that for you, too," she said softly. "I just don't think we can find it with each other."

He looked around at the room—the ornate vanity table, her robe crumpled up on the floor and heels strewn across the carpet, the patterned wallpaper and faded curtains—one last time. His heart broke all over again when he spotted the empty oak rocking chair in the corner of the room. "So, this is it?"

She forced a weak smile. "It'll be all right."

"You have my number if you need anything."

"Thanks, but Nana's just a phone call away if I run into any trouble. I need to stop calling and running to you whenever there's a problem."

"No, you don't!" he insisted. "Don't ever stop calling, and I don't just mean when you're in trouble either. If you're sick or lonely or want a laugh or sell a house, even meet a guy, I want you to call me, you hear?"

Her smile wasn't faked this time. "Okay."

Bernard stared at the floor. "This seems so final, you know? Leaving is a lot harder than I thought it'd be."

"It's all right," she assured him. "We'll be all right. This is just the hard part, that's all."

He looked at her and let his bag fall to the floor. "What are we doing, Lon?" he asked her, exasperated. "We just lost the baby two weeks ago. This is no time to be making a decision like this. You're still grieving, for God's sake, and I know that because I still am."

"Of course we're still grieving, Bernard. Our baby died, and it's going to hurt for a long time. But this . . . this is something that I've got to deal with on my own if I'm ever going to get through it."

"It's too soon," he argued.

"We need to do this before it's too late, before we start hating each other and hurting one another more than we already have."

"And Creighton?"

Her eyes drifted away from him. "I don't know. I can't even think about him right now."

When Bernard knew that there was nothing more to say and no fight left in him, he reached into his coat pocket and, with his hand shaking, pulled out a long white envelope that held the separation papers she'd given to him earlier in the week. He handed it to her.

"I signed it. Not because I don't love you." He paused and her eyes met his. "But because I do."

Chapter 42

"I'm so sorry, Bernard." Rayne opened her arms to him and he gratefully received her comfort. "Come on in. Make yourself at home."

"Thank you for letting me come over."

She closed the door. "You sounded so sad on the phone. When you told me about the baby, I could almost feel how much you were hurting. I wouldn't want you to be alone right now."

"You have no idea how much this means to me."

"How's London? I can't imagine what she must be going through."

"She's depressed, hurt and confused, I think. She blames herself for what happened to the baby. She thinks that God is punishing us for getting married the way we did."

"Is that what you think, too?"

Bernard shook his head. "I don't believe God works that way. Yes, He allowed this to happen, but I don't think it was to hurt us. He loves us too much."

"It can't be healthy for your marriage if London is blaming the baby's death on your relationship."

"That's what I meant about her being confused." He raised his eyes. "She asked me for a divorce, for real this time. I think she finally feels justified in giving up on our marriage."

"Bernard, I'm sorry. I never wished anything like this for you. This isn't what I prayed for, I swear. Yes, I wanted us to be together, but not like this. I hope you believe me."

"I do. Maybe a divorce is for this best. At least now we can honestly say that we tried. It just wasn't meant to be. I have to accept it. This is what London wants. If this is what's going to bring her some peace and help her deal with the loss, then it's the least I can do."

"What about you—how are you dealing with it? Your baby died, too, you know."

"A part of me died in that hospital with her," he confessed. "I can't let myself feel it, you know? I can't even let myself cry about it because I'm afraid I won't be able to stop."

"You can't keep it bottled in, Bernard."

He began pacing the floors. "I can't get it out of my mind . . . seeing all that blood and hearing London screaming like that." He shook his head. "She was so scared, and I couldn't do anything for her, and I couldn't save my baby. I let them down, Rayne. I failed them in the worst possible way." His repressed hurt, confusion, and anger all erupted at that moment. He was too overcome with emotion to speak or do anything except cry. Empathizing with him and seeing Bernard in such pain made Rayne cry, too, and she held him tightly her arms.

He lay in her grasp for what seemed like an eternity as she cradled his head in her lap and stroked his face. She wiped his tears and whispered, "It's all right" to him over and over again until she felt him calming down. "Are you okay?" she asked.

"Yeah," he said rising, a little embarrassed. "I'm sorry for breaking down like that."

She shook her head. "Don't apologize, Bernard. You've been holding this in for far too long. When a woman loses a child, everyone fusses over her to make sure she's all right—and they should—but you can't forget that the man is suffering, too. That baby was just as much yours and it was London's. You had dreams and hopes of your own for the baby. You need support and someone to lean on just like she does."

"You're right. I've been trying to hold it together so I could be strong for London."

"You don't have to do that anymore. Let me be strong for you now."

"I already loved her. The doctor confirmed that it was a little girl, but I already knew. In my heart, I was already her father. I could picture her birthday parties and play dates, taking her on her first date so she'd know how a man was supposed to treat her, pulling my pistol out on any young thug who tried to touch her." Rayne laughed a little. "I'll never get to have that with her."

"Bernard, you're going to have that life one day and with a woman who can appreciate it and appreciate you, and I want you to stop blaming yourself. It was out of your hands."

He closed his eyes and reached out for her. "I really don't want to be alone, Rayne, not tonight."

"Then you'll stay with me, and we'll get through this together. We can talk or we can just sit here quiet all night long. Tell me what you need."

"I want to forget. I need the pain to stop for a little while."

She held his face. "Let me help you." She kissed him lightly on the lips and stroked his head. "Let me take the pain away. I love you so much, Bernard. Just let me show you how much."

She kissed him again. He gave into her for a moment then stopped. "Rayne, we shouldn't be doing this, not now."

"We've waited so long, baby," she whispered. "Let me lavish some of what I feel onto you, and you can share all of your pain with me. I can make the hurt and the loneliness stop if you let me."

"What about London?"

"London made her choice, and I've made mine. This is our time, Bernard." He took her in him arms, hugging her. "Let me give you the child she couldn't."

"Rayne, I'm nowhere near ready for anything like that. I just need. . . ." He dropped his head, realizing that he had no idea what it was he needed.

"I'll take care of you," promised Rayne. "All you have to do is let me."

Then she took him by the hand and led him into her bedroom.

Chapter 43

"Look who's back," announced London, stepping into Cassandra's office.

Cassandra shrieked and ran over to hug her. "I didn't expect to see you back at work for two more weeks."

London sat down. "I didn't need the whole six weeks. Besides, I was about to go crazy being in that house with all those broken dreams and disappointments."

"How are you holding up?"

"It gets easier everyday. Your flowers helped and so did your calls."

"Well, it's not like you returned any of them."

"I know. I needed some space and the time to be by myself. Hearing your messages uplifted me, though, in some of my saddest moments."

"I'm glad I could help. I've been praying for you, we all have. The entire staff was worried sick about you."

"I can tell. I've got more cards and flowers and covered dishes than I know what to do with."

"A lot of people love you, London, especially your husband." London dropped her head. "He's been calling me, asking about you. He says you won't talk to him."

"He's called to check on me, but I'm not ready to deal with Bernard yet."

"So, I guess he hasn't told you about the house then?"

London's eyes widened. "What house?"

"You remember that four bedroom that you were interested in awhile back? Bernard closed on it last week."

"He did? I had no idea." It was then that it dawned on London that she really wasn't included in his life anymore. "I'm glad he finally has somewhere to live."

"Yes, *they* were very happy about it," played up Cassandra, leaning back in her chair.

"They?"

Cassandra leaned forward. "I don't know if I should be telling you this with everything you've been through and all."

"I'm fine, just spit it out," pushed London.

"That girl Rayne was with him at closing."

It was a bitter pill, but not one she wasn't expecting sooner or later. "Did they purchase the house together?"

"No, she waited outside of the lawyer's office, but she did come with him when I showed him the house. You should have seen the way she was hanging all over him, acting like she's already the wife. I see what you meant about her being possessive."

"They must be getting close," concluded London.

"She certainly thinks so but if you ask me, I think he's still in love with you."

"Yeah, so in love that he signed the separation papers and has practically moved in with another woman."

"London, you didn't give him a whole lot of hope, or choice, for that matter."

London shrugged her shoulders and exhaled. "He's moving on . . . that's what he's supposed to do."

"And you?"

"I'm moving on, too," she professed with confidence.

"With Creighton?"

"There's nothing holding us back this time."

"Not unless you include his wife," said Cassandra. "I saw the two of them out to dinner last week."

"I wouldn't read too much into that if I were you. If he's gone back to her, it's only because he thought I wanted to be with Bernard."

"*You do*," asserted Cassandra.

"No, I wanted to be with Bernard and our child. The baby was the only thing holding us together."

"London, I don't believe that any more than you do. Like it or not, you fell in love with your husband."

London shook her head. "I fell in love with the idea of having a family. It's not the same thing."

Cassandra crossed her arms in front of her. "So it's not going to bother you in the least if Bernard up and marries this chick?"

"No. In fact, I'd come to the wedding and wish them well."

"You may have to eat those words."

"Why? Did they say something to you about getting married? Are they engaged? Was she wearing a ring," London catechized.

"My, my, aren't we curious for someone who couldn't care less?" taunted Cassandra.

"You don't suppose that they're sleeping together, do you?"

"Let's just say she definitely didn't seem like the type to play hard-to-get."

London looked down at her ring, which had remained locked around her finger since the day he had given it to her. "Then I guess it really is over, huh?"

Cassandra rubbed her back. "I'm sorry, kiddo."

"It's fine," she replied, sniffing. "If it wasn't meant to be, it wasn't meant to be." With that, she slid off her ring for the first and last time.

London looked up from the piles of folders on her desk and into the face of Creighton Graham.

"I heard about the baby," he said solemnly. "You must've been devastated."

"How'd you find out?"

"I called up here looking for you, and the secretary let it slip. Why didn't you tell me?" He walked into the office, closing the door behind him.

"Creighton, you made your feelings about my baby and me painfully clear the last time you were in this office. I didn't see the point in calling you after that."

"All right, I'll admit that I could have dealt with your pregnancy with a little more tact, but when I saw that pregnancy test and I knew it couldn't have been my baby, I felt betrayed. You can understand that, can't you?"

She thought of Bernard and Rayne. "More than you know."

"So, how are you doing?"

"I'm fine. Some days are better than others, but I manage."

"I suppose it's only right that I ask how your husband is doing."

"From what I hear, he's doing great—a new house, a new girlfriend, and a pending divorce."

"Have you finally decided to put this faux marriage out to pasture?"

"I filed for a legal separation. The divorce is only a matter of time."

Creighton smiled. "Would it be considered insensitive if I did a 'happy dance' right now?"

"At this moment, it would. Why don't you try again next week?"

"Where does this leave us, London? I've been losing my mind thinking about you."

"Oh, really?" she asked incredulously.

"Why do you have to say it like that? Do you have any idea how much I've missed you? What I feel for you is the real deal. I'm not playing games here."

"What about your wife?"

He sighed. "If you want me to lie and act like she doesn't mean anything to me, I could do that, but the bottom line is that we were married for eight years, and she's the mother of my children. I will always be connected to her, but it's nothing like what I feel for you."

"Are you still at the house?" He didn't say anything. "Creighton, answer me. Have you moved back in with Yolanda?"

"Look, it's not what you're thinking," he stated. London closed her eyes and exhaled, bracing for the fallible explanation to follow. "What was I supposed to do? You were pregnant with Bernard's baby; you decided you wanted to do the family thing with him. I know I'm a lot of things, but I'm not one to chase after a lost cause. So I said, 'heck, if they can make it work, so can me and Yolanda.' "

"Then why are you here?"

"Because it's *not* working. How can it when I'm in love with you?"

At that moment, it didn't matter to London whether or not he meant it. It only mattered that he said it and that he was a pair of open arms to run to for solace. "Every time I start to believe in you, I always get hurt. What's so different about now?"

"Everything is different. I know now that I never want to come that close to losing you ever again."

"And you're willing to show and prove, to put some action behind all this talk?" she challenged.

He smiled seductively. "That can be arranged if you let me take you out to dinner."

"Creighton—"

"What's one dinner?"

"You know, they say that the definition of insanity is doing the same thing over and over again and expecting a different result. Do we really want to go down this road another time?"

"No matter how much we try to avoid it, we always end up back on this road. Face it, London—we're addicted to each other."

"Addictions are usually unhealthy and self-destructive."

"Yeah, but any addict will tell you that it's worth the high." He gently kissed her. "I'll call you next week about that dinner."

Chapter 44

"Wow, you're really making yourself at home, I see," noted Bernard, coming home and finding a paint-splattered Rayne applying an olive green faux finish to his living room walls.

"Is it too much?" she asked timidly.

"It's perfect. I love what you've done in here, not to mention the thousands you're saving me in hiring an interior designer."

"I can't wait to show you my ideas for the bedroom. I was thinking of a whole safari themed-room with mosquito netting over the bed, maybe a black comforter with animal-print accents, and a nice spice color to warm up the walls. I've got some swatches right here." She crossed the room and handed him the fabric samples. "What do you think?"

"I think that somebody has OD'd on the *Home and Garden* channel."

"I can't help it!" she gushed. "This house is amazing, and I have about a million ideas running through my head to spruce up the place. Once I get through with the bathroom and get our room out of the way—" She bit her bottom lip, realizing that she'd said *our* instead of *your* bedroom.

Bernard set the mail down on the ottoman. "So, it's *our* room now, huh?"

"No," she answered quickly. "I mean, if you want it to be . . ." She exhaled. "I know that I've rushed things between us before. Like I did that night you came over after you and London broke up. I knew that the time wasn't right for us to have sex, and I shouldn't have tried to pressure you in to it."

"No harm was done. I mean, we both realized that it would've been a mistake, and we stopped before things went too far. I'm not mad at you for that," Bernard assured her.

"I know, but that was weeks ago. Since then, we've gotten a lot closer, and we spend almost everyday together any way. Why not just make it official?"

"What are you trying to say, Rayne? Do you think we should move in together?"

She smiled apprehensively. "Would that be such a bad thing?"

"No, but I promised myself to stop doing the whole cohabitation thing. If I'm living with a woman, she has to be my wife."

"Well, there's a first time for everything."

"It wouldn't be a first. I've lived with a woman before, two actually."

"No, I meant living here with me . . . as your wife."

"Ray—" he began.

"Don't say anything. Not right now, at least. It's just a thought. I know your situation, and I'm sure that the last thing on your mind is rushing into another marriage. But, Bernard, we click, you know? We get each other, and I believe we have what it takes to build a marriage and a family. Baby, I can give you that daughter you lost; I can make this place a real home. Promise me you'll think about it."

"I will, Rayne; I promise."

She dropped her hands to her sides. "Well, that wall isn't going to paint itself," she replied. "You mind grabbing a sponge and helping me out?"

"Sure, just give me a minute to change." He wandered into the bedroom, visualizing Rayne's concept for the space. Then he tried to imagine how London would have decorated it.

"She'd probably have it looking like a garden exploded in here," he said to himself, thinking about London's affinity for pink and flowers. It was then that he realized how much he missed his life with her. He missed the way she would sing to herself as she washed dishes and the way it took her thirty minutes to give a five minute summation about her day. He missed smelling her coconut shampoo and their fights over whose turn it was to do laundry or buy the groceries. More than anything, he missed going to bed and waking up happy in the knowledge that she was his wife.

"Hey, baby, you coming?" called Rayne from the living room.

"Yeah, I'll be there in a second." Like everyday since their split, Bernard pushed thoughts of London out of his head and tried to convince himself that he could build a new life without her.

Chapter 45

"Well, long time, no see," shrieked Essie after spotting London in her doorway. "Come on in, but watch out for where I'm sweeping."

"Hi, Nana. I'm sorry I haven't called."

"Or come by or sent word or did anything to let us know you were okay," reproved Essie.

"I just needed some time to think and to sort things out."

"Did you do that?"

She nodded. "Bernard finally consented to a divorce. He's moved out. It's for the best."

"You're the biggest fool in the world, you know that?" Essie declared, shaking her head as she swept dirt into her dustpan.

"But you said to listen to my heart, and I did that," countered London. "I thought long and hard before I made that decision."

"And that's the best you could come up with? I tell you, neither of you has got the brains you were born with!"

"I think I did the right thing," London said with conviction. "Bernard and I never should have gotten married, and it's time that we stopped fooling ourselves and trying to force something that isn't going to happen. In time, you will see that I'm telling the truth."

"Child, all I see is a woman who just let a good man get away. Now, Lonnie, that boy loves you, and it must be something strong, too, for him to let you up and divorce him like that because he thinks that that's what's gon' make you happy. But as much as I can see the nobility in what he tried to do, he shouldn't have done that. Marriage is about staying in there and making it work no matter what."

"Nana, Bernard has accepted that I will always love Creighton. I think it's about time that you did the same. I will never feel for Bernard what I do for him."

"And I thank God for that!" Essie exclaimed. "Honey, you don't love Creighton any more than the chicken does the fox. He's just convenient and easy and looks good to you, but that ain't love. What you have with Bernard, that's real love, child." Essie began humming to herself as she continued her sweeping.

"Nana, it's not that simple. I feel alive when I'm with Creighton," she dished. "The heat between us is unreal."

"You think you're feeling hot now; wait 'til you're burning in hell."

"Nana, I'm saved, remember? You can't scare me into thinking that I'm going to burn in hell if I keep seeing Creighton."

"Saved folks are supposed to know better than to be living any old kind of raggedy life. You certainly can't say you got this kind of behavior from me."

"Being strong, trusting my instincts, doing what I feel is right for me—I got all of that from you, Nana."

"Ain't you got no respect for the Lord? What you're doing ain't right, Lonnie. I already told you that you're blocking your blessings."

"What are my choices, Nana? To be single and lonely and hope that the blessings will flow? Or take my chances on having them blocked to be with the man I love?"

"You could have it all if you stayed with your husband."

"Bernard has a new house and a woman and has made it perfectly clear that he does not want me."

Essie touched London's shoulder. "He's your soul mate, baby. Are you really ready to give that up?"

"I'm ready for peace, Nana, and these days, I'm grabbing it wherever I can find it. And right now, where I've found it is in Creighton's arms."

"What you've found with Creighton is safety. I don't mean security, just safe because of everything you've been through. To you, it probably seems like you end up losing everybody you love, so you're holding on to who's going to hurt you the least if he leaves, too. But that ain't love, sugar, and it ain't gon' bring you no real peace either."

London shook her head. "You're wrong. I do love Creighton, and it has nothing to do with losing my parents or the baby or Bernard."

"Search your soul, honey. Search your heart, and ask God to lead you. And watch—when He does, He's going to lead you right back to your husband."

Chapter 46

Bernard knocked on the door of Rayne's apartment, apprehensive about the mysterious dinner she had alluded to over the phone. She opened it with a smile as bright as the red Mandarin-inspired dress she was wearing. Her long hair was pulled back and secured with chopsticks.

"Welcome to the Orient," she said, leading him into her dining area.

"Is today the Chinese New Year?"

Rayne pulled out a chair for him. "Please sit."

"What's all this?" he asked, sitting down at the table. There was a massive spread consisting of an array of colorful, vibrant delights.

"This is an authentic Chinese dinner. We have some egg drop soup to start us off, a little Crab Rangoon, shrimp fried rice, lo mein, snow peas with mushrooms, Mongolian beef, and glazed bananas for desert."

"Wow, everything looks good. Did you cook all of this yourself?"

"I had a little help from our neighborhood carry-out, but I did glaze the bananas myself."

Bernard was overwhelmed. "Rayne, this is great, but what's the occasion? I hope today isn't some off-the-wall anniversary that you females keep locked up in your memory bank that you expect men to remember, too. If that's the case, you'll have to forgive me for coming empty-handed."

"Relax, you don't have to run out and buy something, but tonight *is* a special occasion."

"Enlighten me," he said, dipping a spoon into the rice platter.

"I know you don't get to travel much, so I'm bringing the rest of the world to you. Tonight's stop is China."

"Come here." He pulled her onto his lap. "You really are something, you know that? I've never met anyone like you. A man would have to be crazy not to make an honest woman out of you."

"Then I suggest you don't do anything crazy." She pecked him on the lips.

"Aren't you going to sit down and join me for dinner?" he asked.

"In a minute." She slid a CD into the stereo, which sent a soothing, melodic Chinese instrumental flowing through the room. "What's dinner without a little music? And look," she handed him a photo album, "these are some of the most beautiful and exotic places in China."

He opened the book. "Hey, is this you?"

"Yeah, that was about three years ago when I spent the summer backpacking through Asia when I was an undergrad."

He flipped through the pages. "Look at all the culture and architecture here. I've got to get out of the country more often," noted Bernard. He pointed to a picture at the top of the page. "That's a really good shot of you."

"Thanks; but do you know what's missing from this picture—from all of these pictures?"

"What?"

"You." She closed the album. "Today, I was offered a really good opportunity for a co-op in Beijing. I want you to come with me."

He was floored. "You're moving to China?"

"It'll only be for a year, but it's a once-in-a-lifetime deal. I was one of six chosen from a pool of three hundred applicants. I couldn't pass it up."

"When are you leaving?"

"In a few weeks, at the end of the semester."

"China . . . wow," he managed, blown away. "It sounds incredible, Rayne. I can see why you would want to take advantage of it."

"And so should you. Let me take you to see the mountains and China's rich history. I want you to experience China through my eyes and create lots of beautiful memories and pictures for ourselves. What do you say?"

"You want an answer right now?"

She circled her arms around his neck. "I want you to at least think about it."

"Rayne, you know that I'm still married."

"And I also know that you're one signature away from being free. You have nothing keeping you here. Your family is spread out all over, and Rod can run the restaurant until we get back. Just say yes, say that you'll come. A fresh start in a new place would be great for us. Imagine waking up every morning in paradise with a woman who loves you and wants nothing more than to be with you. London can't offer you that. I can."

"And just what would I do in China while you're interning in class all day?"

"You could live out your dreams. Haven't you ever wanted to write for a year or paint or join a band or just be able to sleep until noon every day? You can do whatever you want and forget all the things that have hurt and disappointed you over the last year."

"You might be right. I could use the break and the distance from the restaurant and losing the baby."

"And from London," put in Rayne. "Don't forget her."

"That's exactly why I should go—so that I can."

Chapter 47

"How did I let you talk me into this?" asked London when she found herself in a hotel room with Creighton following their dinner date.

He wrapped his arms around her waist. "I didn't have to do much convincing. You know you want this as badly as I do." He planted a kiss on her lips. "You can't stay away any more than I can."

"You said that I always come back to you, and here I am. I guess you were dead-on with that one."

"Well, don't say it like that," he snapped, still holding her. "My arms ain't a bad place to be. Neither is my bed."

"No, it's not. I'm just not sure if it's the *right* place to be."

"Not sure, huh? Let me see if I can convince you." He kissed her. "You convinced yet?"

She smiled. "I'm getting there."

He kissed her again, sliding his hand underneath her shirt and gently unsnapping the buttons that held it together. She pulled back from him. "This isn't right, Creighton. You know that."

"What's not right is us both being stuck in marriages that don't do for us what we do for each other. Nobody's gonna get caught, and nobody's gonna get hurt. You trust me, don't you?" He buried his head in her neck.

"Stop it, Creighton; I can't," she whispered.

"Yes, you can. Stop fighting it."

"No, I can't." She thrust him off of her. "You're married and so am I."

"That's never mattered before." He drew her back into his arms. "Besides, it's just a piece of paper."

"It's a piece of paper that says you belong to Yolanda and that I belong to Bernard."

"Baby, what we have is so much more than that."

"Then why won't you leave her?" she demanded. He groaned and turned away from her. "Leave her and be with me for real this time. I'll walk away from my marriage, I swear, but I can't be with you like this."

"You know I can't leave right now, London. The girls are just getting used to having me back home, and Craig is only eleven months old. It wouldn't be fair to leave him before he's even turned one. Just give me six months, no more than a year."

"To do what, Creighton? To shoot me the same bull that you're shoveling at me now? Do you really think that I'm stupid enough to believe that you'd leave your wife and new baby to be with me?"

"Now, don't get all self-righteous on me. I don't see you rushing out the door to sign divorce papers from Bernard either."

"I would if it meant that we wouldn't have to keep sneaking around and if you'd make a real commitment to me."

"You're the one worried about sneaking—that was never my idea. I don't care who sees us together."

"Well, I do, Creighton! I have a reputation to protect. I

have family and church members and a husband that I don't want to think I'm some two-bit home-wrecker."

"Why do you even care what he thinks? He has a sideline chick, remember?"

"This isn't just about what Bernard thinks or anyone else; it's about right and wrong. And he's only seeing that woman because he thinks I don't love him."

"Well, you don't, do you?"

"No." She thought for a moment. "I don't know . . . maybe."

"What do you mean, *I don't know—maybe*?" he fired. "I thought we had an agreement, London, an understanding."

"I'm just really confused right now. Yes, a part of me does love you and wouldn't hesitate to run away with you and never look back. But there's another part, too, that's having a hard time pretending like me and Bernard never happened."

"Look, I forgave you when you went behind my back and slept with him. I even let it go that you messed around and got pregnant even though that hurt me to my soul. But I've got to know that you're in this for real, London. Don't have me walking away from my family if you're not."

"You want honesty, Creighton? Well, so do I. I want to know where you stand with Yolanda. I need to know if you still love her."

"She's the mother of my children; I will always love her."

"But can you walk away from her for good? Can you promise me forever?"

"Nobody can make that promise to anyone."

"Bernard wanted to, and he tried. And I believe if I hadn't pushed him away, he would've gone through with it."

"London, if you want him so bad, then why are you here with me? Why do you keep coming back to me?"

"Because it's easy," London said at last.

"What?"

"It's like my grandmother said: you're safe. You see, Creighton, deep down, I've always known that you're never going to leave your wife, so there was no real pressure to make things work with you. I was in no danger of having to follow through on any commitments because I knew you wouldn't. It's not like that with Bernard. He wanted that commitment from me, and I couldn't handle it. I got scared because I've lost so many people that I love, and I was afraid of losing him, too. I pushed him away."

"Baby, you're just confused with the baby and the divorce . . . You don't know what you're saying."

"Yes, I do, Creighton. My spirit has been restless about this for a long time. I tried to ignore it, but I can't do that anymore. I can't be with you and still feel good about myself. Everything about our relationship is wrong, and I can't go around calling myself a Christian and live this way."

"London, where is all of this coming from? Who's been brainwashing you?"

"Most people would say you have. I don't blame you, though. Any bad decisions I've made regarding you have been of my own choosing."

"What does all this mean for us, London?"

"It means that there is no us. I don't belong to you anymore than you belong to me. I have a husband who I've denied for way too long. I should be with him, not in some seedy hotel room with you."

"You're acting like all of this is beneath you now. Where was all this talk when we got together a year ago?"

"A year ago, I was searching for something with you that I already had with Bernard. You and I may have been good together, but we were never right for each other."

Creighton held her hands and whispered in her ear. "Come on, baby, it's me. I know that you can't walk away from us just like that."

"It's not about walking away from you; I'm walking toward where my life is supposed to be." She caressed his face. "I'm sorry, Creighton, but I can't be with you anymore."

He nodded and sucked his teeth. "I guess there's nothing left to say." He picked up his blazer. "I better get on back to Yolanda and the children."

"You should. They need you a lot more than I do."

Creighton got a last look at London and walked to the door. "I do love you, London."

"It's just not the way you love your wife. Or the way I love Bernard."

The door shut quietly behind him, and London knew that Creighton's chapter in her life was finally closed.

Chapter 48

Essie's eyes lit up when she answered the knock at the door. "Well, look who the wind blew this way! It's so good to see you!" She pulled Bernard into a warm embrace.

"I'm sorry I haven't come by sooner. Everything's been sort of . . ." His words faded out as his mind wandered to London and their shattered marriage.

Essie nodded. "Yeah, I understand." He knew that she did. "Come in and sit down for a spell."

"Have you talked to my estranged wife lately?" he asked, taking a seat.

"She just left here about an hour ago."

"How is she?"

"She was real quiet like she's got a lot on her mind, but you could call and ask her yourself."

"Believe me, I've tried. She won't take my calls."

Essie offered him a slice of pecan pie. "She's still raw, baby; give her some time."

"I'm trying."

"Just be patient with her. You know, I haven't given up hope on the two of you."

"Don't waste your time, Miss Essie. There are much more worthy causes to believe in."

Essie raised an eyebrow. "And I don't believe you've given up hope either, Bernard." He grinned bashfully. "So tell me about this new girlfriend of yours."

"She's not my girlfriend; she's a friend."

"I hear that it's a little more than that."

He shrugged his shoulders. "I mean, we're cool, but that's about it. She's been there for me at a very difficult point in my life. To be honest, I don't know how I would've gotten through it without her."

"Oh, *she's* the reason you made it through. Funny, I thought it was the Lord."

"Miss Essie, you know what I mean. Rayne has been great during all of this. She's been a real friend at a time when I needed one."

"I'm sure she's expecting a lot more than friendship from you, though."

"I'll admit she's dropped a few hints here and there. And I'd be lying if I said I never have been tempted to take things further with her, but she knows I still have unresolved issues with London. She understands."

"So you're saying that she knows you're still in love with Lonnie—and don't bother denying it either, because you know I can read you and Lonnie like a book. Besides, you can see it in your face whenever I mention her name."

He grinned sheepishly. "Can we talk about something else *please*?"

"I don't know what for. Isn't that why you came over here?"

"I didn't come just to talk about London. I came to see you. I wanted to know how you were doing."

"I'm fine, and I could've told you that much over the phone. My guessing is that you want to know where you stand with Lonnie, maybe you were even hoping to run into her while you were here."

"I never was any good at hiding things from you, whether it was hickies on my neck, F's on my report card, or my deep, dark secrets," he conceded, sliding his fork into the pie. "So, what's the verdict? Where *do* I stand with London?"

"Baby, Lonnie's so confused right now that she doesn't know if she's coming or going. I don't think she knows what she wants, and her mind is all twisted over this Creighton fellow." Essie shook her head. "She doesn't love him. I know my baby."

"He's in her blood, Miss Essie. I can't compete with that."

"Sure you can, honey. You're in her heart, and he can't compete with *that*! Lust brought her to him, but God brought you two together."

"I used to believe that," he lowered his head, "but not anymore."

"You're going to regret leaving her, you know that, don't you?"

"I love London; always have. But I can't make her love me. Frankly, I'm tired of trying."

"And I suppose this girl Moon . . . Clouds, or whatever her name is, makes it easy, huh?"

"It's *Rayne*. And at least I know she wants to be with me and only me. I can't say the same for my wife."

"So everything y'all have been through means nothing? I swear, y'all ain't got no fight in you."

Bernard swallowed a piece of the pie. "This is what she wants."

"I'm talking about you, Bernard. What do *you* want? You don't want a divorce, but you're too sorry to get off your butt and fight for your wife. You're just like London—want everything to be easy and handed to you. Don't y'all realize that anything worth having is worth fighting for?"

"Why should I keep putting myself through that, especially when there's Rayne, who appreciates everything I have to offer? I'm through chasing London, Miss Essie— *finished*!"

He composed himself. "Do you have any idea of how much I needed her after our baby died? I needed my wife; we needed each other. She was the only other person in the world who knew exactly what I was going through, and I needed to grieve with her. More than anything, I wanted her to need me, to reach out and let me comfort her, but what did she do? She shut me out and asked for a divorce."

"Proverbs tells us that we must trust the Lord and not our own judgment. I know you're frustrated and all that right now, but you've got to listen out for the Lord's voice. Let Him be your guide, not your emotions."

"I just wish He'd speak loud enough for me to hear Him."

She laughed. "He will, baby, just keep listening." Seeing his empty saucer, she cut him another slice of pie. "So, I hear you done went out and bought yourself a big, pretty house."

"You find out everything, don't you?"

She winked her eye at him. "When you gon' invite me out there to see it?"

"Soon. We're—I mean, *I'm* still working on it."

"Uh-huh. Boy, you got that gal living with you?"

"No, ma'am. Rayne has her own apartment, and I intend to keep it that way. She's just helping me out with the decorating. The irony of it all is that I bought the house for London. I wanted to surprise her. I was going to buy all new furniture, set up the baby's room, and bring her home to our new house. I never intended for it to be a bachelor's pad."

"You and my granddaughter trouble me. Y'all so full of hurt that you can't even think straight no more. You ain't thinking about getting serious with that gal, are you?"

"I don't know, Miss Essie. She wants me to go away with her to China for a year."

"Are you gon' do it?" Essie asked anxiously.

"I haven't decided yet."

"What about your house and your restaurant?"

"Rod can run things until I get back, and I'm sure he'll be all too happy to house-sit. He's always looking for a safe haven from his women."

"What about your marriage?" Before he could answer, they heard a groan coming from the back followed by a low thud.

"Frank!" cried Esssie and raced to the bedroom. She found him on the floor on the side of the bed unconscious. Bernard whipped out his cell home and dialed 911. Essie cradled Frank's head in her lap. "Frank—Frank, honey, can you hear me? Frank?"

"The ambulance is on the way," announced Bernard breathlessly. "He doesn't look like he's breathing—better let me try CPR until they get here." Essie turned Frank over to Bernard, staying far enough to keep out of Bernard's way and close enough to have an eye on what was going on.

"Hello? Is anybody home?" called London from the living room. "Where is everybody?" She walked into the room and clutched her chest at the sight of her seemingly lifeless grandfather. "No!" she screamed. Tears started streaming down her face. "What happened?"

Essie squeezed her hand and led her into the room. "The doctor's on his way—they're on the way."

"Is he breathing?" she asked Bernard. He shook his head and continued.

"I want to talk to him." Essie tried to hold her back, but London was stronger. She crawled over to Frank's body and grabbed his hand. "Pop-Pop, you're going to make it, you hear me? Just hold on a little longer."

"London, you're in my way!" screeched Bernard, trying to maneuver around her.

"Lonnie, move!" ordered Essie.

"Pop-Pop, I love you," she whispered, her tears resting on his arm. "Please hold on."

Essie gathered the strength to yank London off of him. "Pray, child, just pray."

"Bernard, can you hear a heartbeat, anything?" asked London.

"Not yet . . . I'm trying," he replied.

They heard sirens blaring in front of the house. London leapt up to let the paramedics in.

"He's back here," she directed them. "He's not breathing, and he doesn't have a heartbeat."

London and Essie clung to each other as the paramedics worked to save Frank's life. Time seemed to be moving in slow-motion. London was only cognizant of hearing phases like, "There's not much time" and "Get him to the hospital quick" being uttered by the medical team moments before they raised him up on the stretcher and carted him out to the ambulance.

"Miss Essie, you ride with them. I'll drive London," said Bernard, shepherding London outside and into his car. "He's still alive—that means there's hope," assured Bernard as they rushed to the hospital in his car. "Don't give up."

London couldn't stop the tears from flowing out of her eyes. "I've lost my parents and my baby," she wailed, staring out of the window. "I don't think my heart can take another loss, Bernard. I don't think I could live through that, not again."

"Just try to relax, okay? We'll be there in a minute."

"What if that's not fast enough?" She looked over at him. "What if it's already too late?"

Chapter 49

"Do you need a little more time with his body?" asked a soft-spoken orderly as Essie, London, and Bernard clustered around Frank's bed after all attempts to resuscitate him had failed.

"No, I said my peace. Frank isn't here anymore. This is just his shell. His soul, the part I loved, is gone to heaven," droned Essie. "You all can go on and do what you need to do." Essie rose and Bernard and London followed her out into the hallway. "I'm going to call the family and let them know what happened," she said sadly.

"Nana, let us do that. Why don't you just sit out here awhile and try to pull yourself together."

"I can do it," she insisted. "I want to be the one to tell Elmer and Rosa. His brother and baby sister ought to hear this from me. I suppose you all can call the cousins and whatnot." Essie left to use the phone.

London collapsed into one of the waiting room chairs. "He's gone, Bern, just like that. I didn't even have a chance to tell him goodbye or how much I loved him."

He held her as she cried on his shoulder. "He knows that." He kissed her forehead. "I'm sure he heard you."

"I keep seeing him, you know, lying there on the floor. I keep thinking that I should have done more. If I had gotten there sooner or if I hadn't been in your way—"

"London, you did all you could do. The doctor said that it was a stroke; there's nothing you could have done to prevent that."

"But what if Nana blames me?" London shook her head. "I couldn't live with that, Bernard. I just couldn't."

"Why would she?"

"She told me to move, to get out of the way, and to let you work. Maybe if I had, he'd still be here"

"London, we're only humans. Only God has that kind of power. He's the one in control over who lives or dies."

She lifted her head. "You know, I almost didn't come over today. I just came because I left my cell phone there earlier. If I hadn't come when I did . . ." She succumbed to her grief again.

"God must've led you back there. At least you were able to see him and talk to him before he died."

"I guess I should be grateful for that much, huh? We didn't even get a chance to hold our baby before she was taken away from us."

"We hold her in our hearts."

She managed a faint smile. "You're the only one who understands how I feel, Bernard. You've always been there for me, even when I didn't deserve it."

"I will always be there for you, London, never doubt that." He hugged her.

As he held her, she felt like the time had come to finally be honest with Bernard and herself. She tore away from him. "There's something I have to tell you, B."

"Go ahead."

London took a deep breath. "I think I made a mistake. I never should have let you go."

"London—"

"No, I mean it. I'm totally and completely in love you. I know that now."

Bernard looked on with sympathy. "London, you're grieving. You're in shock, and you want to reach out to someone, which is understandable. But don't mistake that for something it's not."

She clung to his sleeve. "No, Bernard, I see everything so clearly now. You're the one I want. You're the one I belong with."

"Yes, you feel that way now because you're in pain, but what about tomorrow or next week or next month when losing your grandfather doesn't hurt as much? What happens if, by some miracle, Creighton actually leaves his wife to be with you, then what?"

"I'd still want you. Baby, it's the truth this time. I love you; I've always loved you. Nana could see it; even Pop-Pop. I was so blinded by what I thought I wanted that I couldn't see what it was that I really needed."

His body stiffened. "London, I think you made the right choice the first time. I don't think we can go back now. Too much has happened."

"I know, and I know that I hurt you with my relationship with Creighton, but we can get past all that."

He sighed. "I'm not so sure that I can. I went through this with Vanessa, and I can't do it again with you. I told you, I can't be runner-up. It's all or nothing."

"But what about us?" she asked, her voice trembling.

Bernard stood up. "What about me, London? For months, I tried. I tried to be a good husband to you, but nothing I did was ever good enough. You took advantage of every opportunity to let me know that it was never going to work between us and that you loved Creighton. No matter how many times he lied to you, no matter how badly he dogged you out, you always went crawling back to him. Don't you know how much that hurt me?"

"You had Rayne," she replied sadly.

"You're right. I *do* have Rayne. London, I'm tired of riding this roller coaster with you. And now that I have something good in my life, I'm not going to be as quick as you were to give it up."

"I was scared. I was afraid of my feelings for you, but I'm not anymore. I need you, Bernard. I can't let you give up on us."

"And I can't keep putting myself through this. I won't be anyone's second choice, London, not even yours. And I won't settle for less than my first choice. I'm sorry, London, but that's no longer you."

"How can you do this?" she shrilled. "How can you say this to me after I've just lost the man who raised me? Am I not hurting enough for you?"

"I know you're hurting, and I loved him, too. We have to keep things in perspective, though. His passing has nothing to do with our marriage. Don't get me wrong—I will be here for you and do whatever it takes to get you through this as your friend. But that's all I can be, London. I've made my decision. My past was with you, but my future is with Rayne."

Chapter 50

"**D**o you ever feel like God has stopped listening to you?" London asked her grandmother. They sat on Essie's back porch drinking tea and watching the sun set behind a weather-beaten oak tree set a week after they buried her grandfather.

"The Lord is always listening," affirmed Essie.

London lifted her eyes toward the sky. "Sometimes I feel like He doesn't care. That's how I'm feeling now."

"Why would you say something crazy like that?"

"Look at my life, Nana. I lost both of my parents at the same time. I lost Creighton at a time when I thought I loved him more than anything. I lost Bernard right when I realized that I do love him. I lost my baby, now I've lost Pop-Pop. If he's such a merciful God, how could He do this to me?"

"God didn't do anything to you. A drunk driver killed your folks, not the Lord, just like a stroke killed your granddaddy. As far Bernard, you messed that up all by yourself."

"What about the baby?"

"Something was wrong with her, child. The Lord was trying to let you know that."

"How can you be so calm about it when you've lost just as much as I have? Yes, my marriage is over, but at least I can still talk to Bernard. You'll never see Pop-Pop again. Aren't you angry about that?"

"Angry for what? The Lord let us have forty-seven wonderful years together. We raised our babies and our grandbaby right here in this house. I was blessed to wake up next to the man I loved every morning for almost fifty years. Do you know what we did that morning he had the stroke? We ate breakfast together and sat out here on the porch just enjoying God's glory. Now, you tell me what I have to complain about?"

"Nana, Pop-Pop was your whole life. How can you face the future without him? Why would you even want to?"

"I loved him, yes, and I'm gon' miss him something awful. But he was never my whole life. You can't give another human being that kind of power. No, God is my life, child, and He hasn't gone nowhere. And believe me, it's a lot of life left in this old bird. I intend to keep praying, keep reading my Bible, and to keep on living. That's what Frank would want me to do. Anything less would be a dishonor to his memory."

"How do you even find the strength?"

"The Lord gives me all the strength I need."

"Well, maybe He's just forsaken me then."

"Lonnie, it's you who's strayed away, not Him. Child, it doesn't matter how saved and sanctified you are, you're going to have some heartbreaks and disappointments, but you never stop praising Him from what He's done and thanking Him in advance for bringing you out. Here you are sitting around, wondering what it is you got to be grateful for—plenty! You've got your health and a bunch of people who love you. You've got a good job and a little money in the bank. You're young, you're beautiful, and you're smart. If the Lord never did another thing for you, you ought to get down on your knees and thank Him for everything He's already done."

"I don't have love," whined London.

"You're surrounded by love. And you have God, and God is love. If you'd just start putting Him first, everything else will fall into place."

London sighed and sipped her tea, pouring over Essie's words in her mind.

"What are you over there thinking about, Lonnie?"

"What you said." She nodded slowly. "You're right, Nana, as usual. Sometimes we get so caught up in the minuses that we forget all the pluses." She reached for her grandmother's hand. "Thank you."

"So what are you going to do about Bernard?"

London stood up and toddled to the edge of the porch. "I don't know. I've put him through enough. I should probably just leave well enough alone."

"He's still your husband, Lonnie. You can still fight for your marriage if you want to. I saw the way he was with you at the funeral. He stayed by your side the whole time. Anybody can see how much he cares about you."

"Bernard was there for me that day because he's a good man. He knows how much I loved Pop-Pop and that it would be a difficult day for me, but that's about it. He went running back to Rayne as soon as the funeral was over."

"He probably didn't want to intrude."

London shook her head. "It's more than that. The night Pop-Pop died, I told him that I loved him, that I'd made a huge mistake in letting him go. I told him that I wanted us to try again."

Essie sat up. "What did he say?"

"He said it was too late and that he wanted a future with Rayne."

"Baby, I'm so sorry," commiserated Essie.

London shrugged her shoulders. "It's not your fault. I can't even blame Rayne, really. This was all my doing. I drove him away, and now he's afraid to trust me with his heart again."

"Lonnie, you know these things have a way of working themselves out for the best. If you haven't learned anything else from me and your granddaddy, I hope that you learned to never give up hope."

"I'm not giving up, Nana; just moving on. I blew it with Bernard, and I have to accept that, no matter how much it hurts." Then she cried—for her grandfather, for her parents, for her baby, for her marriage but most of all, for Bernard.

Chapter 51

"London, is that you?" London turned around in time to see Rayne emerging from Teddy's, a lingerie store, clutching a black shopping bag.

"Rayne, hi," London replied with a forced smile.

Rayne raced to catch up with her and gave her a quick hug. "How are you? I haven't seen you in a while. Bernard told me about your grandfather and the baby. I was really very sad to hear that."

"Thanks. I'm dealing with it. I try to stay busy. You know, work and all."

"That's not what I heard!" Rayne hedged.

London's defenses were up. She wondered if Bernard had told Rayne about her confession. The thought mortified her. "What are you talking about?"

"Creighton, silly! Bernard told me all about him. So you've snagged yourself a lawyer, huh?"

London smiled, relieved. "Yes, Creighton, of course. Wow, you and Bernard really do talk about everything, I see."

"He worries about you a lot. He really wants you to be happy, London."

"I want the same thing for him," she answered somberly.

"And we're both so glad that you've found someone who makes you smile. My only hope is that Creighton makes you as happy as Bernard makes me."

London looked at her, really seeing Rayne for the first time, not as her adversary, but as the woman who made her best friend happy. "You really love him, don't you?"

"I do," revealed Rayne. "He's wonderful, but I guess you already know that."

"Bernard's great, Rayne. You are lucky to have found each other. I think that he feels the same way about you. In fact, I know he does."

Touched by London's words, Rayne gave her another squeeze. "It's so nice to have your support, London. Maybe you can use some of your influence to sway him about China."

London was confused. "China?"

"Yeah, didn't Bernard tell you? I'm going there to study for a year. I leave in two weeks. I've been trying to convince him to come with me. I even got this to give him an extra incentive." Rayne held up a slinky black negligee.

"China," muttered London, still in shock.

Rayne dropped the gown back into the bag. "Wouldn't it be great? Traveling and exploring a new culture together. Who knows—we might even get married while we're out there," she added dreamily. Rayne looked down at her watch. "Oh, look at the time! I'm supposed to meet Bernard in twenty minutes; I've got to run. Keep your fingers crossed about China and good luck with Creighton!" Rayne waved and scurried away in the opposite direction.

If the building had fallen on London at that moment, the impact wouldn't have been nearly as crushing as the thought of Bernard going to China with Rayne. His departure would kill all hope of their ever having a marriage. The fact that he hadn't even mentioned the prospect of going attested to how emotionally detached he really was from her.

She loved him and would have given anything to be his wife, but it was too late. And there was no one to blame but herself.

London raced into the restroom at Teddy's and locked herself inside of a stall and cried. She didn't care who heard her or who thought that she was crazy. She once thought that marrying Bernard was the biggest mistake of her life, but now she knew that losing him was.

Mid-sob, it occurred to London that she still had options. She could contest the divorce, forcing Bernard to stay in Atlanta.

"But what would that get me?" she wondered aloud. "His resentment? His hatred? Certainly not his love!" She knew that if she wanted to retain any semblance of their friendship, the best thing she could do for Bernard was to give him his freedom.

London checked the messages on her cell phone and discovered a message from Bernard saying that he would be stopping by the townhouse to pick up the last of his things and to leave his set of house-keys. Her heart sped up when she spotted his car in the parking lot. She was anxious to see him, if only to tell him good-bye and what a fool she'd been.

London slowly turned the key to unlock the front door. She wanted to prolong the inevitable for as long as possible. Every second that she remained Mrs. Phillips was now precious to her, and she knew that once she entered her home, things would never be the same again.

"Hi," she spoke quietly.

"Hey." Bernard zipped his suitcase and propped it up against the couch. "What's up?"

She edged closer to him. "Can we talk for a minute?"

"Sure. There are a couple of things I've been meaning to discuss with you."

"I think I have a pretty good idea about what you want to talk about," she stated, settling down on the sofa. "I, um, bumped into Rayne today."

"Oh, you did?"

London nodded. "She told me about China, but what I can't figure out is why you never said a word about it to me. We used to talk about everything, even the little stuff. Now, you can't even tell something as major as moving to China." She whispered, "What's happened to us?"

"I didn't want to say anything until I made up my mind about the trip . . . and about you and me," he answered.

"Well, that's really what I wanted to talk to you about. I don't want to be the reason that you don't go to China with Rayne. I love you, Bernard, and I want you to be happy."

He sat down next to her. "So, you're giving me your blessing to go?"

"It all became clear to me today when I saw her. She was so happy. Anybody can see how much she loves you." London lowered her head, choking back tears. "I couldn't live with myself if I kept the two of you apart."

He was shocked. "Wow, I didn't see that one coming. That's mighty big of you to want to put Rayne's feelings first."

"That's a part of it, I guess, but it's mostly about the two of us. I'm no good at this marriage thing. And please don't blame yourself. You really tried to be a loving husband to me, but I couldn't handle it. I think that deep down I knew that I wasn't worthy."

"Wasn't worthy of what?"

"Someone like you. You're a good man, Bernard, and I pushed you away. I was the one with the commitment issues and the trust issues and all that other drama. I didn't believe in us or in you. For that, I'm sorry."

He rose and picked up his suitcase. "This is a nice speech and all, London, but just tell me straight out what it is you want from me. What are you trying to say?"

She took a deep breath. "I'm telling you that I don't want to do this anymore."

"Do what?"

"Hurt you . . . hurt me. I can't make you happy, B, not as your wife."

"I take it that you want to proceed with the divorce then."

"I have to face the facts. You're miserable, and it's because of me. I'm a terrible wife and what's worse is that I've been a horrible friend. And I love you too much—I love our friendship too much—to let things go on like this."

He chuckled and shook his head. "In other words, you love me so much that you can't wait to sign your name on the dotted line to kick me out of your life for good."

"I know that it's what you want, too. You don't have to pretend anymore."

He shook his head. "So you think that you know what I want, huh?" He grabbed her hand to pull her up, too. "Then you should know that I want a woman who gets me, who knows my mood without me even telling her because she knows me so well. And who knows that I can't stand for a female to pass gas in front of me or to wear bedroom shoes in public and who knows that I'm allergic to chamomile and that I cried when I saw *Finding Nemo*." London smiled in spite of herself. He lifted her chin; their eyes met. "I want a woman who's my soul mate, my rib. That's you, London! I want you. It's always been you."

"What about Rayne?"

He sighed. "Rayne's a great girl and a good friend, but I don't belong with her. I belong with you."

"What about China? I thought that was the reason you were here packing up your stuff."

"We saw each other a little while ago, and I told her that I couldn't go with her. She was disappointed, but she understood. With that, we hugged and wished each other the best."

"And it's over, just like that?" she asked in disbelief.

"It never really started. I admit that I got caught up for a second there, but even then, I knew my heart was with you."

"And did you . . ." asked London, bracing for his response.

"I never slept with her, London, I promise. Yeah, I was tempted, but I hope that you can forgive me for that."

"I'm in no position to judge you. I was just as bad with Creighton."

"To be honest with you, the whole time I was with her, I was dying inside to be with you." At hearing that, London broke into tears. "Hey, what's all this? Why are you crying?"

"I thought I had lost you."

"Babe, you couldn't do that if you tried. You're my wife, London, and I'm your husband. I think it's about time we started acting like it, don't you?"

"We've wasted so much time," she said, sobbing.

"Then let's not waste anymore. I love you, London. You're the one."

She threw her arms around his neck. "I love you, too. I want our life back. I want you to come home."

"London, wait." He broke away from her. "I don't think that's such a good idea."

London was dumbfounded. "What?"

"Moving back in here with you." He walked away from her. "I can't do it. I'm sorry."

She panicked. "But you said . . . I thought—"

"You thought I was just going to drop everything I have going on and go running back to your place? It's too late for that."

London could feel the tears rising to her eyes. Bernard broke into a smile and drew her to him. "We'll live in my house. It's much bigger and already has room for a baby and for your grandmother, too, if she wants it."

She punched him in the chest and pulled him into a kiss. "Don't ever scare me like that again!"

"That was no scarier than you are first thing in the morning." She rolled her eyes, and he locked his arms around her waist. "But I missed that—the flannel night gown, the fuzzy bedroom shoes, the curling irons all over the bathroom sink—all of it."

London smiled. "I guess ol' Rayne's rollers didn't do it for you, huh?"

"Nah . . . Rayne's hair is naturally curly." He laughed as London playfully tried to break free from him. "She still wasn't half as beautiful as you, though." He sealed her lips with his.

"Are we really going to do this?" asked London.

"Babe, not only are we going to do this, but I'm thinking that we should do the whole wedding ceremony again, too, in front of God and our friends and family to truly make it official. At the very least, it'll be a wedding that we actually remember."

She laughed. "I like the sound of that."

"Now, the wedding ceremony is just a formality. We're

already man and wife, so none of that saving it for the wedding night, all right?"

"You've waited this long. What's another month or two?" she joked.

He looked down at his watch. "I wonder if I still have time to make that flight to China . . ." he thought aloud, taunting her.

"The closest you're going to get to China is when you're loading up the good dishes in the dishwasher," she warned him.

He swept her up in his arms. "Who needs China when I have London?" He kissed her again. "Well, go get your stuff, woman. You're coming home with me."

Her jaw dropped. "You want me to pack right now?"

"Sure. On second thought, leave your clothes here. They're just going to end up on the floor anyway."

London smiled and looked up at her husband. "Come on," she said, grabbing his hand. "Let's go home."

Readers Group Guide Questions

1. In the novel, neither London nor Bernard has what can be constituted as a sexual affair with anyone, but they are both emotionally drawn to other people. Is having an emotional affair just as bad (or worse) than having a physical affair? Why or why not?

2. London and Bernard rush into their marriage without having any type of pre-marital counseling. Do you believe that pre-marital counseling is necessary before heading down the aisle?

3. London's grandmother, Essie, is often the voice of wisdom for the couple, but she is also a bit meddlesome. How much interference is too much when it comes to in-laws and outsiders?

4. Throughout the book, London maintains her friendship with Creighton, and Bernard has his friendship with Rayne, neither of which are friends with the spouses. Is there anything wrong with married couples having close friends of the opposite sex? Why or why not?

5. When London miscarries, the tragedy pulls the couple apart rather than drawing them together. Why do you believe that the death of a child often destroys so many couples?

6. Bernard and London were best friends before getting married, but end up losing both the friendship and the marriage during the course of the book. Would it be

harder for you to end a lifelong friendship or a long-term relationship?

7. Is pursuing a relationship with a friend worth the risk of losing the friendship? Why or why not?

8. Do you believe that Creighton ever loved London or was she just a conquest to him? Do you think that Bernard loved Rayne?

9. How did losing her parents at such a young age affect London's inability to maintain a successful relationship?

10. In the end, both London and Bernard give up on the marriage because they love each other and don't want to hurt each other anymore. Does truly loving someone mean holding on to that person and trying to work things out or letting go?

Author Biography

Shana Johnson Burton, a native of Macon, GA, began her writing career at the age of nine. In addition to writing, she teaches high school English and Journalism at her alma mater and continues to reside in Macon with her husband and two children. In addition to *First Comes Love*, she is also the author of *Suddenly Single*.

Urban Christian His Glory Book Club!

Established January 2007, *UC His Glory Book Club* is another way by which to introduce to the literary world, Urban Book's much-anticipated new imprint, **Urban Christian** and its authors. We are an online book club supporting Urban Christian authors by purchasing, reading and providing written reviews of the authors' books that are read. *UC His Glory* welcomes both men and women of the literary world who have a passion for reading Christian based fiction.

UC His Glory is the brainchild of Joylynn Jossel, Author and Executive Editor of Urban Christian and Kendra Norman-Bellamy, Copy Editor for Urban Christian. The book club will provide support, positive feedback, encouragement and a forum whereby members can openly discuss and review the literary works of Urban Christian authors. In the future, we anticipate broadening our spectrum of services to include: online author chats, author spotlights, interviews with your favorite Urban Christian author(s), special online groups for *UC Book Club* members, ability to post reviews on the website and amazon.com, membership ID cards, *UC His Glory* Yahoo Group and much more.

Even though there will be no membership fees attached to becoming a member of *UC His Glory Book Club*, we do expect our members to be active, committed and to follow the guidelines of the Book Club.

UC His Glory **members pledge to:**
- Follow the guidelines of *UC His Glory Book Club.*
- Provide input, opinions, and reviews that build up, rather than tear down.
- Commit to purchasing, reading and discussing featured book(s) of the month.
- Agree not to miss more than three consecutive online monthly meetings.
- Respect the Christian beliefs of *UC His Glory Book Club.*
- Believe that Jesus is the Christ, Son of the Living God

We look forward to the online fellowship.

Many Blessings to You!

Shelia E Lipsey
President
UC His Glory Book Club

**Visit the official Urban Christian Book Club website at *www.uchisglorybookclub.net*